PRAISE FOR

"The Hotel Egypt is a fever dream of America under Trump, of what we talk about when we talk about love, of the lies we tell ourselves, and the dreams that kick us out. The narrator Ty is a Rorschach test: see what you want in him and maybe some of them (or none of them) will be true. We are trapped in his perspective, so limited yet with imagined omniscience, in the way of Americans, of American men, of all of us during the death spiral of late capitalism and the planet."

— C. Kubasta, author of *Abjectification*

"This isn't a mere meditation on late-stage capitalism, late-stage American Judaism, and parenthood, but a ruthless dissection that gutsily gets into every dark corner of the minds of Ty and Ellory, the charmingly reprehensible protagonists of this epic novel. The rollicking, riotous, and absurd qualities of the prose call to mind Stanley Elkin, its shrewdness and sophistication Robert Coover, but the book, as a whole, is Rossian. A one-of-a-kind literary jolt."

— Avner Landes, author of *Meiselman: The Lean Years*

"Stuart Ross is in top form with *The Hotel Egypt*. Wise-cracking funny and gut-punching poignant, this novel will keep you wondering "what happens next?"

with every turned page. Ross's energy crackles through each scene, electrifying Ty's voice and engrossing us from start to finish."

— Alex Poppe, author of *Duende*

"The Hotel Egypt is full of so much—inventiveness, references, language. The characters may never be delivered from the contemporary wasteland they wander in a kind of ongoing dream, but Ross plumbs the depths of the unconscious and surfaces with keen reflections on selfhood and parenthood. Funnily disturbing and disturbingly funny.

— Deborah Shapiro, author of *Consolation*

"Stuart Ross is the outer-borough pop culture love child of Jane Austen, Fran Lebowitz, and Whit Stillman, crafting literary—and literate, comedy of manners for modern consumption. What makes Ross's work a must read, outside of the brilliant dialogue mind you, is the comedy so clearly emerges from a place of isolation and anger and the manners are so wholly lacking. To which I'd add—what could be more timely or contemporary than that? Not much."

— Ben Tanzer, author of *The Missing*

"If you like your books dirty, your dad rock lyrics horny, and need subtitles for your prestige TV, you'll want to check in to *The Hotel Egypt*. Ross's characters refuse to be your friend, and embody late-capitalist American culture so sincerely, I couldn't decide if I wanted to hug them or punch them in the face."

— Jeremy T. Wilson, author of *The Quail Who Wears the Shirt*

PRAISE FOR STUART M. ROSS'S *JENNY IN CORONA*

"A beautiful, moving, and utterly strange novel."
— Centered on Books

"*Jenny in Corona* is a must read for those looking for something a little more peculiar than the typical recommendation. This is a career you'll want to follow."
— Debutiful

"A vivid representation of the diffuse, ambiguous, turbulent nature of youth."
— Eclectica Magazine

"*Jenny in Corona* is a remarkable New York City novel, a book as funny as it is moving."
— Largehearted Boy

"*Jenny in Corona* grabs your attention with its narrative voice."
— New City Lit

"It's a pleasure to dive into the warped mind of *Jenny in Corona*'s protagonist, and see Queens through his eyes."
— Writer's Bone

"There's something wonderful about the way Stuart Ross sees the world and the way he translates that over into this book filled with confused people in confusing times. *Jenny in Corona* takes the mundane and twists it into something that is funny, bittersweet, and undeniably brilliant. He's given us the modern bildungsroman that we need as much as we deserve."
— Jason Diamond

"Stuart Ross is a natural, as very few novelists are: *Jenny in Corona* comes trippingly off the page, with a lightness of touch and wicked charm to spare. You can't not love his every deluded character—because he loves them so well himself. Alive inside forgotten time or some fugitive place, this is a tender farewell to the wreck of the 20th century. "
— Miles Klee

"*Jenny in Corona* is by turns hilarious and devastating and profound. Stuart Ross has one of the strangest minds I've ever encountered; I say this not as a warning but as an enthusiastic endorsement."
— Rebecca Makkai

"If you've ever doubted whether our contemporary discourse (much less predicament) could inspire truly stirring music, then Stuart Ross has a filibuster for you.

Throughout *Jenny in Corona*, his prose evokes a dizzying assortment of past American masters of the sublimely vulgar, from Stanley Elkin to Joy Williams to Bret Easton Ellis to Ishmael Reed, all while carrying its own unmistakable tune with disarmingly perfect pitch. Call it the comic novel of now that we don't deserve—but with whose satiric insights we've been graced nevertheless."

— Joe Milazzo

"This saga about Ty, a beyond-alienated business consultant and artisanal builder of doomed relationships, feels written by Joshua Ferris's even more mischievous brother. Each and every sentence is wonderful, full of hairpin turns, city fresh details, and insight. 'Never forget that Americans invented cheerleading,' Ty warns us. I'll not forget this book. Irreverent, scathingly funny, and emotionally piercing, *Jenny in Corona* is a resplendent debut."

— Andy Mozina

"*Jenny in Corona* is a runaway ride on the R train, fueled by sentences like triple shots of espresso. This novel is an extra-long Tom Waits song, a day at the Stadium, a 3 A.M. breakfast in a diner. Stuart Ross knows outer-borough New York in all its glory: its hustlers, poets, Wall Street wannabes, sweet strivers. I'm homesick and smitten."

— Valerie Sayers

The Hotel Egypt

Stuart M. Ross

SPUYTEN DUYVIL

New York City

PART ONE

In some ultimate sense, every place is Egypt.
—Michael Walzer, *Exodus and Revolution*

1.

The independent bookstore is another cherished one, a holdout in this trendy neighborhood of juice bars and salad joints. We walk to the front of the stage. I scan the assembling crowd. The first few rows are the usual people who show up to book events, college professors and their students, high school English teachers with their hopeful eyes. But there are also rows and rows of normal people, who don't necessarily read, or even listen to books, but do watch TV based on critically acclaimed novels. If you draw those types to your events, like Jenny Marks has on this tour, you're a star, the literary equivalent of the Rolling Stones, or at least the National. Many of these fans hold copies of Jenny's book, *Twice Shy*. I see more stacked near the cash register, which still goes cha-ching, and more stacked on the table behind the stage, where Jenny will grin, and sign copies, after she betrays me, and our life story, in her gorgeous prose.

"I'll sit in the back," I say.

"No," Jenny says, her tone pleading yet defensive, the tone of our last year. "Stay closer."

"No, I'll sit in the back. If anyone storms in here with a gun, I'll take the bullet."

Jenny eyes me up and down, like I'm the guy most likely to shoot up this place.

I can't disagree.

When we first met, back in the schoolyard, Jenny had red hair, then it was blonde, purple, or blue, now it's a restoration project, Getty Images brown. She has amaretto eyes. I like to look into them when I come. They have maraschino whites. By that I mean she drinks a lot, she's not even trying to quit smoking or blogging about it like most of the female writers we know. She's got a pimply forehead. But the pimples are kind of sexy. She's taller than me, taller than most women, a straight shooter who's never kissed another female, even on a dare, and although she was born and raised in New York City, Jenny Marks doesn't see race in her work, only on her timeline, and identifies as Jewish-Catholic, if at all, only in private, and only at family dinners. She knows if you want to succeed as a third-generation Jewish-Catholic writer from New York you should forget about those exacting terms and just be a humble white girl from the City. They love her as a white girl from the City. She's got a sad smile. She used to wear this bohemian uniform like something out of *Pollock*, one of our favorite pre-9/11 films: black jeans, a black t-shirt, scrubbed white hi-tops, a black Mets cap. I'm not suggesting Jackson Pollock wore a Mets cap, he died before National League baseball left and returned to New York, but it's not that big of a stretch. Now, for the book tour, on the recommendation of her publicist, Jenny's hair is down, turned up, styled at the blow bar, just like it is in her press photos, and chunky bangs conceal her adult acne. I don't really know how to describe her hair, although I love when male writers use four verbs in one sentence to describe a woman's hair, but trust me, Jenny's hair is just like that. Her clothes, too, are fancier, still simple, but expensive simple. I think she's wearing a black pencil skirt. I don't know what that means.

I take my seat in the back row, very close to yet another display of Jenny's book.

I wish I could waste trees the way my girl can.

I wish I could step into the carbon footprint of her ballerina flats.

Jenny takes the stage. Pats the top of her head, because she still forgets she's hit the big time, and she's not wearing her Mets cap anymore. There's a whoop, a yell, and after most people have put their hands back in their laps, a few must clap a bit more.

I notice a beautiful woman in my back aisle, wearing a bright red beret.

Jenny says she's going to read the title essay from *Twice Shy*.

***

We've been drifting apart for at least fifteen years. But this year, after she made it, Jenny started spending even more time with the downtown types I can't stand, and they can't stand me, and she was talking more and more about wanting to move down there with them. We had long arguments when she got home late, and I'd stayed up waiting for her, because I can't fall asleep without her beside me. In the dark, I asked her how much the cab was, I made a wordless remark, trying to keep control of her with my credit card, but she was changing, and she answered, Well, we should move closer to downtown. I told her I didn't want to live downtown, which I define as below 61st Street, and if that's where she wanted to go, she could go out on her own, without me. And then I would giggle because I wasn't serious.

She said she didn't want to break up. I told her she *also* needed therapy. She told me her therapy was her *work*. And things were changing with her career. The book advance was real money. Not as much as a man would've gotten, but enough to cover more than splurges. Then there was the TV adaptation interest. Sickening, against our climatic principles, but you don't win an Emmy for turning down an original series. Jenny was also thinking of guest lecturing. She went back to our alma mater and got this reception they never gave me, so at least I had a good excuse for making a scene. But I was happy for her. That this had finally happened for her. I was so happy it was happening to her, in fact, it was *almost* like fame had found me, and no matter what,

I wouldn't move downtown. I created a false image of downtown like all the false images I create in my life, and yearned for a beforetime I didn't even take part in, never realizing that if those times were contemporary with my times, I would've scorned them just as much. I liked to think the cafeterias hadn't been replaced by food trucks. I liked to think anyone actually *read* the books instead of taking pictures of them, that anyone still studied what I couldn't unlearn. It was dirty downtown. It was suddenly too clean. I'd grown tired of being around that much joy.

Jenny told me my ideas about the Lower East Side were old.

I reminded her that we were old, too.

During a drinking binge, I pissed myself and a public sculpture, bellowing I was a failed artist, out of aces, and that I was an orphan, half true, my mom died when I was young but my Dad held off until recently. An orphan *whom* nobody loved, I said, pissing on Brer Rabbit, or was it an orphan *who* nobody loved.

My dumb jokes didn't save me. Jenny demanded I get myself to therapy or we were through.

She even treated me, using a kill fee, to the first co-pay.

In therapy, which the people in my class of family history didn't do, I learned my father had forgiven me. And that mom's death was not my own. The therapist—

"please call me by my first name, Scarlett"—concurred that maybe I was, technically, an *orphan*, which I'll admit I call myself only when plastered, because I mistrust that Hallmark branding. *Orphan* suggests there will be twists in my next installment, that my emotional circumstances will untangle, that the backend of my story will offer the reader hope, that I am, as ever, a still small voice murmuring at the protest, a supporting role that looks good on young guys, but has passed me by.

Scarlett didn't buy it. She suggested I was a better man than that. I learned that therapists, like the people I work with, think, and write, and talk, in PowerPoint. There are only three ideas, they show a process, they have two or three bullets below them that describe the process of those three ideas. That's promotion. The upper limit of human intelligence. And the delicate flower called the human personality is made up of *parts*, Scarlett told me, like textbook flowers from back in the day, stamen and pistil. The parts don't always align to allow the shower of life to spray along. According to what we worked out across our fifty-five-minute sessions, my personality had two parts, the 1) hippie part, and 2) the husband part. Scarlett and I agreed the husband part had long ago trampled the hippie.

I told Scarlett, "I would prefer not to be the husband."

She said, "Now we're getting somewhere."

That's the lesson of therapy: you must change your

life.

But I knew I was the natural born husband, the modern man of our apartment, a dark and stony studio uptown, on York Avenue, which I bought for us (in only my name) after my father died and I sold the family relics in Queens, so that the next generation could arrive, get the money, and play out the immigrant song that skipped over me. At home I overwatered the succulents, did the laundry—we have this efficient, in-unit combo. I changed the bedsheets, purchased the pillowcases, laid down the bug traps and dismissed the bohemian from our living space. I washed Jenny's period-stained whites in cold water, and I never thought about telling the internet. I told the takeout app we didn't need the utensils, and recycled them when they arrived anyway. The takeout app listens to me even less than America. I emptied the plastic container with the hoisin sauce, washed it out. I saved the napkins for when we had guests, which we rarely did. When we did, Jenny got too drunk and/or too stoned and scared them away, unless they liked to see her lose control, which made them stalkers, or party reporters, but eventually scared them away, too. Nobody but me can handle Jenny's energy long-term. On top of all that, I rode the local mule down to Wall Street and wrote business news nobody read, while Jenny stayed uptown writing essays everybody talked about.

Most of the time, though, she didn't even write. *She* was the hippie, with no wife part budding in. I knew it wasn't easy. Being the hippie. I knew she had power over me, and that made me want to support her, because if I just did everything she wanted, neither of us would ever run away again. It was hard, I certainly knew, to write the story of your life, like Jenny did, instead of making up fictional characters to hide your true self, which is what I had always done, when I was writing and having all those fun days, forever giving birth but failing to finish the life and place my body in the ground. It was hard to be true. It was hard to be gentle, hard to be an original, hard to concur, or at least describe, with precision, the sentiments of the simmering mob. It was hard to be important to fifty downtown people who all knew each other, and did the hard work of setting the tastes for us uptown millions. It was hard to pretend you were annoyed by meditation app reminders, all people need a few inward minutes of nonjudgmental reflection, regardless of their socioeconomic status. It was hard to pretend you were bad at *career*, the classic careerist move. It was hard to pretend, like Jenny did across social media, that writing isn't a competition, that we shouldn't compete with each other, that your art production is the same as my art production, that there's no hierarchy in literature, even when, like Jenny Marks, you had the most sought-after press agents in the business, more social media followers than the population of an up-and-coming small town, TV intellectuals adapting your prose, and a husband like me paying your mortgage.

We aren't officially married, by the way. Even though we often tell people we are. I could never admit that to Scarlett. In my dreams, I was married—but to a different woman. I hadn't fallen in love for years, hadn't cheated on Jenny this year, in fact, I can no longer imagine being intimate with anyone else, although I sometimes weep, find myself all shook up, by the beauty of another human being.

I am still young enough to meet this woman.

My dream girl, maybe this woman in the bright red beret.

And maybe, this would be good, she'll work in publishing. She's an editorial assistant who wants no career path outside of editorial. She spends her office days posting thousands of rejection letters, and with this postgrad, at the sea or in the mountains, I share the sorrow of my romantic life. She rejects my unmarkable story on the page, but publishes me in her heart.

She's absolutely lovely. Absolutely lonely. I hum Ornette Coleman's 'Lonely Woman,' I even hear this energizing ballad, from a graphic novel saxophone, drowning out Jenny's centerstage complaint. She's a leftist Jewish woman in a trench coat standing at the Hudson River, wondering how another summer passed us by. There's her bosky birthright hair, and soon it's down, and now it's up, in a cream puff, a loose profiterole, word up. She sleeps on my shoulder on the midnight train. She wraps herself in my scarf. A tangled scent lingers. Part skunk, part vetiver.

Or, this could be better, my future wife, my age, will still be a writer, but one who writes with a straighter pen. Steamy plantation sagas with magical narrators, maroon lipstick romances over war-torn Berlin, the granddaughter finds the diary the grandmother wrote. Literature like mine will just be *weird* to her, but I'm another achievement. My hot dad bod on the sidelines of our kid's soccer games. She'll cheat on me with media studies professors, but always return home. She quit smoking. She never vaped. She sets her manuscript pages on the floor with Post-it notes, crafting her stories wood strong, as Jesus built his trestles. My mistake with Jenny was marrying, without actually marrying, a writer who can't stick to her outline.

Or, best, my dream girl isn't a writer at all. She's a suburban confidence woman, a little older than me, a non-practicing attorney who loves the arts without working in them. A woman with, and from, a considerable inheritance.

I leave Jenny. I meet this twice-divorced woman. We marry. We appreciate art instead of creating it. She reads her books, I share mine, we die a little every night. We sit with chilled wine. John Coltrane's *A Love Supreme* one Sunday morning. We subscribe to the Philharmonic. They're doing Mahler's Fourth again. They're doing Beethoven's Seventh again. They're doing Holst's *The Planets* again—I love Mars. They're doing the Bryce Dessner *Violin Concerto.* We hear one genius bounce ideas off another at the 92nd Street Y. We pass through the museum walls where *The Dance* meets *The Red Room.* We also subscribe to the intimate series at Alice Tully Hall. A Georgian woman plays the Franz Liszt Piano Sonata in B Minor. A reticent Frenchmen pounds out Prokofiev. She wants a baby. She wants to keep her figure. She carries, through a surrogate, our Kardashians to term. And my high-bouncing lover is a little botoxed, perhaps, a little racist, for sure, but only in private, just to have something to talk about. When there's nothing good on TV.

"Why do you think it is, Ty," Scarlett asked me, "that you can only define yourself through a woman?"

"Because my mom died when I was 12? Because my piano teacher molested me? Because my college professor molested me and forced me to read Wallace Stevens's 'The Emperor of Ice Cream' off the poetry seminar whiteboard? We've talked through all of this. Maybe it's Michelle Obama's fault? Ivanka's? Big SUVs piss me off. You ever seen a Noah Baumbach movie? He's my favorite film director. Oh, Scarlett, you've got to see one. I'll lend you my DVDs. Am I becoming Ben Stiller, but without Ben Stiller's corduroy wit?"

"You're doing it again, Ty. You're obscuring your emotions with humor. That's easy for you. I want you to try harder."

"Jenny calls it my Woody Allen disease. My former favorite film director."

"About that, Jenny is right. Why do you find it easier to hold on to the imaginary women in your life, as opposed to the one you actually care for? You care for Jenny, don't you."

"What kind of question is that?"

"If you listened to yourself, you'd think you hated her."

"We're just having arguments, Scarlett. This is how Jenny and I make love. We're artists. Metaphorical schizophrenics. Things will get better."

"Is that what you want? For things to get better?"

"I want romance, Scarlett. I have ancient desires."

"It's unlikely you'll find romance with Jenny. We've talked about how Jenny abuses you."

"She doesn't mean to."

"She tells you you have no feelings."

"She knows how much I love her."

"She tells you there's no emotion in your work."

"When I was writing."

"Maybe you're the one with the emotions, Ty, and

Jenny's the one incapable of love. Maybe *she* needs therapy."

"Her therapy is her work."

"No, her work is something else."

"You don't know Jenny."

"I want you to think about the process we talked about…"

"You don't know her!"

Most of the time, Jenny didn't write about me. She didn't even write about *us*. Maybe she slapped my name on the dedication, or tagged my support in a social media share. But *Twice Shy*, Jenny's viral sensation, is very much about our intimate lives, and the miscarriage we suffered.

I responded by getting seventh-grade drunk and pissing on a public sculpture.

Jenny responded with the breakthrough piece she's reading to the crowd.

And some of it's true. The miscarriage part, that's true. What isn't true—and this is the 'creative' part of Jenny's creative non-fiction—is that we immediately got pregnant again, but Jenny decided to have an abortion, without telling me, because she feared she'd have another miscarriage. During the miscarriage, Jenny wrote, she sensed a rebirth. During the fictional abortion, she was reborn. She knew now that she would never be a mother, the way Princess Diana knew she'd never be queen. She knew now that *her* definition of motherhood would never include children. A child is the longest run-on sentence in the world.

"Maybe I did have an abortion without telling you!" She screamed at me. "Maybe it isn't creative, maybe it isn't a lie. And how would you even know? You love to say I never have to tell you anything, my body is my body, because you're such a good 90s liberal kid with your Shea Stadium tears and your memories of Eddie Vedder writing *prochoice* across his forearm. Stick that forearm up your ass, Ty. Eddie Vedder is a jock, and I don't have to tell you anything, no matter what you ask, no matter how you respond. What's mine is mine."

"I thought this was happening to *us*," I replied.

"I don't have to tell you anything about anything."

Like all of Jenny's work, *Twice Shy* divided its audience. Even the guardians had to admit the story was powerful, but nevertheless the none-too-shocking sob story, they said—the male prudes said this, too—of a privileged white girl getting an abortion so she can have experiences to write about. From there began a forgettable, misremembered, online-only controversy about cisgendered white girls taking their taxpayer-funded abortions lightly. Jenny's "humble white girl from the city" image had been threatened. White women are always taking *something* lightly, they say, no matter how heavy their flow gets.

The essay changed Jenny's career. It garnered a brief mention in a *New York Times* midweek round-up of indie incursions into mainstream conversation without ever mentioning the online morality patrols, but rather taking the more subtle sperm and egg position of whether we have experiences so we can write about them or whether we publish because we have experiences. Jenny landed the literary agent whose starred clients don't see writing as a competition. She was courted by a devious publicist believed by the industry to be *undeniably sexy.* Jenny did all the book-adjacent press, turning down almost nothing. She sat with Men's Magazines in the lobbies of perfumed hotels. She told Food Magazines she didn't know how to fry an egg, and that she used her oven (my oven) for book storage. She told *Vice* she tore books down the spine if they bored her. *Vice* loved that. She told *New York* magazine what brand of Japanese stationery she couldn't live without, which made me extremely jealous: telling *New York* about my pencils had been a lifelong dream. And at the end of every interview, Jenny recommended the book her publicist told her to. Her sellout was complete.

Glowing reviews of *Twice Shy*, rushed to publication, were everywhere, positive even when negative. The reviews were now published on legendary URLs, but they contained the same words that followed Jenny

Marks her whole career.

Which drove her nuts.

"It must be nice," I said, "to be able to complain about what the *Times* says about you."

Jenny Marks was *raw*, often *brave*, not yet *poised*, sometimes a *mess*. A man would never be called a *mess*. Men could be *weird* but no longer disheveled. Men understood structure, especially when they were collapsing it. A man could always give up on art—indeed, that was often the runny moment a man found his true voice. But a woman couldn't give up on art.

Women are responsible for birth, not rebirth.

This stuff made Jenny want to kill herself.

"Kill yourself," I said. I was drunk and in-between highs on a variety of drugs, lighting a Parliament Light with the recessed filter ripped off. "Critics never get blamed for suicides. And there are battalions of raw, brave, messy women right behind you, poised to take your place."

I was deeply hurt. It wasn't getting better. Jenny had written down the words we lived, which were sad enough, but she'd also written down more than a few lies, and her lies seemed truer than the truth.

She accused me of not understanding the difference between a miscarriage, an abortion, and a birth.

She accused me of *smiling* while we were having the miscarriage.

"Maybe my husband was punishing me," she reads to the crowd, "for miscarrying, the way Trump suggested I be punished for having an abortion. Men love watching women suffer. And if there's no woman around to watch suffer, men will devise a suffering woman for themselves. Men call this *creation*. Men call this *revision*. It's the only thing that keeps men going. Female suffering is male speed."

"What do you mean," I said during our arguments, "that watching you suffer means I don't have to wake up? *I'm* the one who wakes up and goes downtown to work every day. You're the one who sits here throwing books out the window. You're the one who gets to process your feelings just because you publish something. If you aren't publishing, you aren't processing."

"You could've done the same. You could've written about our experiences, too. You could've processed."

"I can't stand process. You have a process. Scarlett has a process. You're all a bunch of PowerPoints."

"I understand, Ty, if you're upset about some of my approach to the material. That's fair."

"Our lives aren't material."

"Are you listening to yourself? What are our lives if not material?"

"Trump is material. Or Napoleon. Adolf Hitler. Not our petty bullshit in my dark apartment."

"You're wrong, Ty. Hitler never happened for girls.

Women have always had to make it up."

***

I walk out of the cherished indie bookstore during Jenny's abortion. It's one of the strangest things I've ever done. I still can't believe I'm not going back. I'm walking forward. It almost feels like a march. There are the juice bars, there are the salad joints. I'm free. I left her. But then I hear, in my soul, Alma's theme from Mahler's Sixth. When I hear Alma's theme, it becomes Jenny's theme. I remember, almost like the hush of an orgasm, how much I love Jenny, how I can't imagine life without her. No matter what she says about me to strangers.

The air outside is cooler than the bookstore air conditioning, the declining light still hard. I'm in Chicago for the first time in a non-work-trip sense. The windy city. So named for its bloviating politicians, I read in the guidebook, if not its weather. But all cities are the same, methinks, hipster airports I will never leave.

I walk past multilevel parking garages that make me furious, for the way society privileges the automobile over the pedestrian. I walk past restaurant chains Italian and Asian, a European waxing center, an ax throwing steakhouse where white men are busy at their latest recreation. Darts, snooker, killing birds: that used to be enough for the white man. Their latest fix is ax throwing indoors.

In the city everything is like that. Jokes are porridge. Wit is mush. What is tax free takes too long and compound interests are doomed. There is too much, and no intention. Fright persists in the distance between thought and action. It's a little early for the near future, a little late for the recent past.

Tonight is the Fourth of July.

Actually, that's tomorrow.

Funny, it always feels like the Fourth of July now.

I hear water, and soon find the Chicago River. The one that runs backwards. A watery metaphor for this undesired outcome I call life. On the bridge, I hear people screaming slogans into bullhorns. I look up and see we're all standing around the Trump International Hotel. Not this shit. Not today. I've already been thinking about him all day, I dreamt about him on the plane, and now I've got to see his name in lights above me.

I walk right by the protest. I'd like to raise my fist. I'd like to join them. I want to march. I start crying, and then laughing, at their bravery, my cowardice, their pure beliefs. I feel so shackled. I want to be free. I would join them. But, but, but.

I steal to the middle of the bridge to muffle the protest and then walk even further so that the signal weakens for good. Now I hear more of the city's less political hotels, the pinching whistles of bellhops, the heavy footsteps of lumpy tourists across the wooden planks, and the bridge itself rumbles when the cars, slowed and grouped by the traffic light, are given the green to turn on to the curving drive.

Should I jump in the water? Shoot up this place? Should I make myself the story of the day?

I keep close to the waist-high railing, pocked with rust, and stop beside a tree rooted in the riverwalk below. I lean over, think about jumping, lean over a little more. I think about Christopher Reeve in *Somewhere in Time* driving up Lake Shore Drive to check into the Grand Hotel and have a dream about love. That is exactly what I want to do. I need romance. Three power chords proven to move me. What did I call it that day at Scarlett's? Ancient desire. Like a housecat searching for the high place, never remembering the reason why.

In the darkening water, kayaks and geese hug the river's edge. In the distance, water taxis and tourist boats sail toward me. In my old books this river had commerce on it, helped America create. Now, as far as I can tell, there's only recreation, little else.

I face the Trump International Hotel. It's tiered, like a wedding cake, but instead of an edible bride and groom for a payoff there's a lone spire, painted white. Other than the president's bolded name, set above the parking levels and below the suites, the building has no ornaments, only its functional ugliness, beautiful in its own glassy way, silent as a buried body in concrete.

I hear the tour guide's voice of *Chicago's 1st Lady*, one of the boat tours on the river below. The guide says we're coming to one of the most photographed buildings in the city, but they aren't talking about Adrian Smith's Trump Tower, finished in 2009, they're talking about Bertrand Goldberg's Marina City, on the other side of the bridge, finished in 1967. Although modernistic in design, Marina City's round, cast-concrete forms were a clear reaction against the glass and steel towers of Mies van Der Rohe, whose style ruled Chicago at the time, and whose One IBM Plaza, finished in 1973, stands between Marina City and Trump. When the guide says *most photographed* for the second time, the tourists on deck salute with their cameras.

This is exactly where I want to be. If Chicago exists for a New Yorker, it exists only here, a young, arrogant, starchy bridge to the West, fighting modernism with more modernism. I want to pass out in those towers. On a skylit floor. I want to book a room at the Trump Hotel, and make Jenny come with me. At least it will be a decision I make for myself.

I don't want to sleep at our planned destination, the spare bedroom of Jenny's downtown New York writer friend, Rhonda Rhodes.

Like Jenny, Rhonda gained followers for her ruthless platitudes at New York parties. Her brand was that of another 'shock the bourgeoisie' white female writer who meant it, and said it in a prep-school French. Unlike us, Rhonda was originally from the southwest, had that cold cactus way about her. She had recently, and reluctantly, left the Lower East Side for Chicago, to teach experimental prose at a creative writing program that's quite mainstream about its tuition costs. She lives in a neighborhood Google describes as up-and-coming, but not yet safe enough for white men throwing axes at wi-fi connected walls.

No matter what happens with Jenny, I will not spend the night at Rhonda's. I know they gossip about why Jenny keeps me around. I'm certain Rhonda doesn't grasp the underside of our money. I'm certain that if Jenny *did* have the abortion, Rhonda's stockbroker boyfriend, who undertips the golf cart girl, paid for Jenny's cabs, earning Delta Sky Miles from the Uber account linked to his Amex Gold…

A man taps me on the shoulder.

"Can you take a picture? My wife and I?"

"Of course," I smile. This is the first productive thing I'll do in months.

When I raise the camera I see the UMP in TRUMP polluting the frame.

"Do you want to move a little," I say. "To the right, maybe? That'll get it all out. Or if you move to the left, that'll get it all in. It depends on what you want.

24

This other building," I point behind us, "is the most photographed building in Chicago."

"I think this is good," the husband says.

"No, get it all in," the wife says.

"Get it all in," the husband smiles. "The little lady's always right, right?"

"I know what you mean. Let me get it all in. This won't hurt a bit."

I have no suitcase for this one-night trip. A Men's Magazine once suggested such daring, and I've been waiting for just the right overnight journey to try out such a gentlemanly gamble. But now I realize I have no toothbrush, no underwear, no razor, no comb. It's so obvious to me that I'm drunk. From the night before, from the plane this afternoon, I've been drunk since Memorial Day, drunk since the day I pissed on poor Alice, drunk at my Scarlett sessions, drunk at work. I smell of that liquor life. That endurance. But it isn't clear what I smell like in the external world. The evening's warm, steady wind keeps reminding me of my spiritual reek, keeps blowing me further away from the bookstore, from Jenny, from my source.

At the traffic light, I cross to the other side of the bridge. The graffiti says *Suspect*, the graffiti says *Demon*. There's a statue of George Washington flanked by the Briton and the Jew who financed the Revolutionary War.

25

The first legal Americans were Brits, I suddenly realize, the way the first illegal Christians were Jews. Once the Law arrives, you never know who gets to count as a person.

A trumpet calls me back to the bridge. I approach the player, a gray-haired, light-skinned black American, fudging the licks of Pachelbel's Canon. He sits under a lamp with two lights, one over the walkway, one over the car bridge. The lamp pole bisects the president's name so that one man's eye would see TR, the other eye UMP. At the busker's side, doggie bag noodles stick together in an aluminum tray.

I open my wallet and feather a fifty into his plunger mute. He removes his lips from his mouthpiece. "Man, I must be dreaming. Did you mean this one?"

"Yeah, man," I say, "I carry fifties to impress my wife, but you can have one. Happy Independence Day."

"God bless America."

"She's not actually my wife."

"Alright."

"Let me ask you a question, man. What color is this river?"

"Only Capone knows the color of the Chicago River, man." He moves the fifty from his mute to his shirt pocket. "Most days, I think it's blue."

"I agree. The river is Capone blue. Play something else. Play *anything* else. Canons are for weddings. You know Ornette Coleman's 'Lonely Women'?"

"You get beat up for playing that, man," the busker says.

I look out over the real estate I will never own. This really is a lovely place. Even the Trump building fits in. From this side of the bridge, I see overphotographed Marina City, spiraling towers that resemble lint brushes. The skyward floors appear on the cover of Wilco's *Yankee Hotel Foxtrot*, an album that seemed to predict 9/11 with lyrics like, "skyscrapers are scraping together." This, no doubt, is the white indie rock side of the bridge, whereas the Trump side, the glass and steel side, is black metal music, *the steel of our resolve*, as George W. Bush put it, and like twenty years later we're still living in those *steely years* Don DeLillo promised were in store for us.

As for the music on the bridge itself, that's whatever the busker plays.

The tour boat passing in this direction, *The Emerald Lady*, tells its passengers that van Der Rohe was once asked why he painted all his buildings black, and the starchitect gave the most pragmatic answer. But I don't hear this pragmatic answer because the boat sails under the bridge. On the riverwalk below, tourists waddle. The vendors hawk handheld American flags, neon pinwheels, hot dogs, selfie sticks. Evening light stretches and folds over the Capone blue surf. This is not *that* part of Chicago that Trump calls an "infested war zone." I take out my phone and google: *think piece by a black Marxist about what 'Chicago is dangerous' really means.*

"You got a lot to say in there," the busker says.

"I'm just talking to the computer."

"Cough drop blue," he replies. "That's the river's color."

"Menthol blue."

"Ice *cool* menthol blue. Triple-action."

"Hey, let me ask you one more question, man. If I bought you a night up in Trump, you'd take it, right? My wife wouldn't stay up there. She'd rather sleep on someone's twin bed, you know, with all the hip books on the night table, instead of enjoying the thread count on those hotel sheets."

"Man, I don't know. Good thing you never married her."

"And she has an expense account. Why do *you* live in Chicago? Other than strange men offering to buy you hotel rooms."

The busker considers this question, as if he's not going to say the first few reasons out loud. Then he says, "The rabbits, man."

"What are those?"

"The bunnies, friend. The bunny rabbits in the park."

My right side vibrates, but my phone's back in my left pocket. I take it out and see a text from Jenny with nothing but two question marks.

"You alright? You don't look too good." The busker offers me a napkin, from his tray of takeout noodles. I wait a moment, then use it to wipe my eye.

I share my location with Jenny, write back and say I'm okay, I just wasn't feeling well. I want to add, Thanks for asking, babe. But I can't. *Thanks for asking* is never an easy thing for me to say.

***

The night we lost the baby, I had to keep telling myself it wasn't our fault.

It wasn't happening because of the Adderall, the Xanax, or the American Spirit blues.

It wasn't happening because of the two-day hangover—that lost weekend happened before we knew.

Jenny did chase Advil with aspirin during the two-day hangover.

That had to be the reason.

During the first ultrasound, which billed at $78.60, we heard the fetal heartbeat, we saw the splash of light, we took the printout home. We called the embryo many names, mostly *it*, but also *baby, thing, light, fetus, fella, dame, boy, girl*, and *prefer not to say*. We called it *messiah*, but that was too soon. We called it *Ella, Billie, Springsteen, Yorke, Gershwin, Hetfield, Axl, Tweedy, Dylan, Sphere, Jagger, Joni, Thurston, Rollins*, and *Miles*.

We called it *the woman from Portishead*. We called it *no traffic on the FDR drive* and *what an inventive new bistro in Gowanus*. We stuck the landing on *Aurora*, which means dawn. We sounded ridiculous saying *Aurora* in what was left of our Queens accents, and we loved this. Maybe we would move back to Queens to raise her. We discussed when we would have the "Queens talk" with our baby girl. "People will never come see you in your home," we would have to tell her. "You will have to go to Manhattan or Brooklyn to see them." We found it impossible to pronounce *give Aurora some water*, though we kept on trying. *Aurora Marks* sounds like a private dancer, right, and *Aurora Rossberg* a lawyer you don't want to double cross. Then, Jenny had some weird cramps one day, it was probably nothing, and during the second ultrasound, down a darker corridor of the medical center, where the exact same imaging billed at $156.72, Aurora Marks Rossberg wasn't there anymore. We heard nothing, saw only Jenny's skin, there was nothing left to print out—no *their* there. Our Aurora would never bend a rosy finger. Our dawn was the brown blood you rarely read about in epics.

Jenny started gushing days later. Both of us couldn't believe how much *it* there was, how much anxiety and pain. Nobody ever talks about this shit! The doctor on-call, like some clever Jane Austen narrator, told Jenny that a miscarriage at eight-to-ten weeks is "unfairly common." Only when Jenny thought *it* was all out did the loss actually begin. New cramping that gained confidence from all the cramping past, the pain passing, the pain returning, the cramping bad, the spotting worse, the dizziness again. The new doctor-on-call, an indie narrator, slipped out: "I fucking hate miscarriages."

I had only one job. Get thee to the drugstore to buy what I was calling the *heaviest tampons with wings on the side*. I almost got hit crossing the avenue against the waving horns of uptown taxis. At the drugstore, the clerk told me, "You don't mean tampons, honey, you mean pads. Follow me." I thought I was devastated, but I still had enough sense to think to myself, it's not like my blunder makes her a genius. She's not Lucille Clifton, she's just this lady who works at Duane Reade. I still had enough sense to remove myself from her inner life, and type in my rewards numbers at the register.

Back in our apartment, Jenny was still losing *it*. When did she see me smile? I wasn't smiling. We did have, what seemed to me, a very typical argument in this exceptional situation, where I said, "I wish I could do it for you, I wish it were happening to *me*." And Jenny cried back, "What do you mean, Ty, it is happening to *you*. It's happening to *us*."

We put on a DVD of *Clueless*.

Even though it's available on streaming.

I watched Jenny sweating, moaning, and cramping

on all fours, the same position she was in during conception. I wasn't smiling. Not even at the *Clueless* quips. But then I remembered another lost weekend, just before we knew, when we'd gotten drunk and stoned, ripped off the recessed filters, ate a second pizza we swore we never ordered, and on a river bench at dawn, snorted cocaine I'd found in my vintage Members Only jacket, one that I had only worn—I was sure of this, I was so high I was seeing vultures and cormorants and twisted eagles—to whack Tony Soprano. *That* had to be the moment Jenny looked over at me, and that had to be the moment I smiled.

I had made the perfect *Sopranos* reference.

Tomorrow I would make the perfect *Simpsons* reference and our baby would still be gone.

In the morning, Jenny told Rhonda what happened. Rhonda sent a Lucille Clifton poem.

I have gathered my losses
into a spray of pain.

And to that bouquet, Clifton adds an unborn child.

Little love, little
Flower
Who walked unannounced
into my life
And almost blossomed there.

After opening Rhonda's email, Jenny read the poem to herself. Then she tried to read it aloud. But she couldn't do it. She didn't have the strength to make it through without breaking down. She asked if I could do it. I wasn't sure I could. But when I tried, a strength arrived I hadn't felt in a long time. The poem reminded me that I had made it through times even tougher than this one.

Over the next few weeks, I read "Bouquet" to Jenny every morning. Soon enough she regained her strength, and we read it together.

"You see what I mean, Ty," Jenny said. "It did happen to us."

***

I keep googling *dangerous Chicago* on my phone. But then I fall down a rabbit hole of Chicago River bridge facts. They raise to allow tall boats to pass through. The word is *bascule*, French for seesaw. There are triangles, leaves, *spans* that aren't prefixed by *life* or *wing*, counterweights and axles. There are trusses, trunnions, friends of the bascule bridges, there are trustees, they have foundations. There are *tender houses*, similar to lighthouses, where operators once lived, moving the seesaw up and down. I want a job as a tender house operator. Jenny can co-tender, we will keep a tender home.

I locate this structure, thronged with protestors, and then the sky above it, the spaces between the shooting

33

steel. It's not the steel but the sky I blame, the sky where I will never be, the sky where my father never is. I ask the sky why this is happening to us, why this is happening to America. I get no response.

I sense Jenny walking toward me, holding a bouquet. She raises her flowered fist to the protesters, screams a slogan of sympathy back into their rounds. When she reaches me, I see she holds just two flowers, knocked-about daisies, and around her shoulder a new tote bag from the bookstore. Jenny does have a carry-on with her, because tomorrow she's flying to Denver, and then the West Coast stops that round out her tour. Every time I see her again, her wardrobe makeover continues to surprise. Her cheeks glow, from all the attention she received during her performance.

"Flowers are so heavy," she says. "I never know if I'm supposed to hold them up, down, or across my chest like a first communion girl."

The busker places his mute over his bell, puts his mouth to his mouthpiece, but he doesn't sound another note.

"For you," Jenny says, offering him one.

"Flowers don't really suit you," I say to Jenny, wishing I could take it back.

"Maybe that's why you never bought them for me." She sticks the other daisy in the tote bag. "That bookseller was too, too much. She said she could've *listened to me*

34

read forever. Her breath was horrible."

"Don't they always say that?"

"She handed me two daisies, for both fetuses, or whatever, that I lost."

"Did you tell her it's a lie?"

"*She* seemed lost."

"I always feel pity for those booksellers," I say. "I picture them writing all that small print on those recommendation cards. It gets to me."

"Where did *you* get lost?"

"I just went for a walk."

"You didn't have any questions for Jenny Marks?"

"No, I live it. At least the real parts."

"How do you know what's real, Ty?"

"I mean this is my problem. I don't."

"I'm sorry therapy isn't working…"

"…no, no…"

"If only you could write again…"

"…please don't'…"

"…it's fucked up you left. You realize that? We're both in a strange place."

"This place looks pretty simple to me," I say. "Ax throwing, tall buildings, bascule bridges."

Jenny looks down into the water. "It is really beautiful." Then she looks at the Trump sign and says, "But ugly, too."

"I think I might move here, actually."

"You've been to the airport and the bookstore."

"I've seen the sky. I've been to this bridge. All cities are the same, hipster airports…"

"…yeah I know, Ty, blah blah blah, hipster airports you can never leave."

I blush. Then, my redness quickly turns to anger. "You should move here too, shack up with Rhonda. And I'll live as far away from the both of you as possible."

"I'd never. It's too clean."

"I googled contrary takes," I whisper. "You know, on how beautiful it is here. The horrible parts of Chicago Trump's always talking about? Only a few miles away. That's why black intellectuals don't like this central area. They think it's only for white people. If there's one thing black intellectuals don't like, it's common areas."

"Maybe that's because they couldn't use the same public bathrooms as us until like five minutes ago."

"But there's *nature* here, Jenny. "Rabbits, right man?"

"Rabbits, friend," the busker says. "Little bunnies."

"Real animals. Not like in New York where nature is the skyline. In Chicago, if you leave your house after midnight, you interrupt a rabbit orgy…"

"…a rabbi orgy, Ty?"

"No, babe, a *rabbit* orgy. Fat Midwestern rabbits. Hairy leporine BBWs."

"Enough, you know, with the puns? Your Woody Allen disease is flaring up again. Shit is different now."

36

"Oh yeah, shit has *never* been like this before. All my shit-has-never-been-like-this-before ended around the battle for Fallujah. I just booked us a room."

"What?"

"Up there."

"That's disgusting. We have a place to stay."

"I can't stay there. I bet you Rhonda has a mouse, and she's probably written an essay about her mouse, and how she's struggled with what it means to put her white voice in the voice of her gray mouse. I bet you she's never killed an ant."

"Don't the rabbits eat the mice?"

"Rabbits are vegetarians."

"Aren't the mice part of the 'real animals,' too, like the rabbits?"

"No, mice aren't real animals, they're pests."

"You *should* move out here, Ty. So you can meet one of those Midwestern girls you like to cheat on me with. They'd love staying in that shithole."

"That was a long time ago."

"If you go sleep up there, our 'long time ago' starts now."

"What do you think the protestors are going to do? *Shoot* at us? They're not the ones with the guns."

Jenny eyes the busker. "Give *him* the room, if he wants it. Although I'm sure you don't want to sleep up there, right sir?"

"There's that liberal bullshit right there," I say. "Why wouldn't he want the room? He's homeless."

"How do you know he's homeless?"

During this conversation the busker has stood up, cased his trumpet, and slung it over his shoulder. He takes his noodles with him, but offers me the rest of the napkins. With Jenny's flower behind his ear, he walks toward the protestors, who are thinning out along with the daytime police. Those cops have been leaning on their bicycles, twirling their mustaches, scrolling their phones. But now the nightshift cops are arriving. They're wearing armor. Wielding truncheons. They're ready to spill blood.

"On the Fourth of July," Jenny seethes. "Why am I not surprised?"

"Look, I'm sorry..."

"...I don't care..."

"....please forgive me. But I can't understand why you want to sleep in Rhonda's up-and-coming neighborhood, which is like an hour away, instead of a nice bed, right up there."

"Rhonda's our friend."

"She's your friend. Like all our friends. She hates me."

"No she doesn't, Ty. You hate *her*. She's never done anything but root for us."

"Ha, that's funny..."

"...and before I forgive you, let me put it in terms

that will appeal to you. Terms you will understand. If the pyramids were built on the backs of the storybook slaves, then why would we go back, voluntarily, into those pyramids now? Why would we go back to Egypt? That sign doesn't only say TRUMP, Ty. It says EGYPT. It says SLAVERY. And sure, a lot of people do want those chains. But why do *you* want them? Everything you do is aimed to help you fit in where you don't belong. This is like when your dad died and you bought all those right-wing polo shirts. Those first editions of Rush Limbaugh's books."

"Trump's from Queens, you know. He's one of us."

"Right. He's every single one of us we're trying to stop being. He's every truth about us we're running away from."

"The hardest thing to do is pray for the hated."

"The world has no lack of monsters to choose from. Why choose him? Just because you want to get back at me?"

"For what?"

"You know."

"No, I don't."

"For *it*. Aurora."

"It's not that, Jenny. My god, I'm not mad at you for that. I'm mad at you for the made-up abortion! If it said HILTON, it would still be EGYPT."

"I'm not going up there."

"Will you marry me?"

"Ty."

"I think I'll just stay here. I'm not going back to the city. Why do I have to leave? All cities are the same."

"All of our friends are in New York."

"Your friends."

"Suit yourself," Jenny says, taking out her phone. "If you leave New York, you leave me. And you'll be living with, you'll be married to someone else, I know it, like within a month. One night without me and you'll become the normie you know you are. You'll get down on your knees for some..."

"...please don't say Midwestern slut..."

"...you'll be within striking distance of all those corporate sluts from Ohio you're always gawking at in New York, only there's got to be even more of them in Chicago than there are in Murray Hill. You'll leave New York, which is a self-defeating look on someone like you, to poison a new city with your bitchy observations, all the energy you expend on hate because you don't have the courage, you lack the vision, to mount a defense for love, and you'll walk into one of the worst bars in the city, with more TVs than patrons, only you'll think you like it, because you've always had that boring fantasy of a good girl with porn eyelashes in varsity underwear, and you'll marry the first one, the first boring rich girl from the *Home Alone* suburbs. She will think racist jokes are funny, too. She will also diss black intellectuals. She will think, Say what you will about our president, but he does entertain. Another false prophet, like you, who can't find a way out of her narcissism. You'll think she's brilliant because she once read two hundred pages of *The Idiot*. Because you love those women who think they're suffering because of their beauty. She'll laugh at your woman-hating jokes. She'll come when you call her *chick*. Oh, don't mind my hubby, for him, misogyny is just table stakes—he hasn't even placed his real bets yet. And you'll think, she's just like Jenny, in a sense. Because you think all women are the same once they get to you. All your dream girls. You're going to hate her more than you hate me, but at least you'll have the courage to hit her. Her daddy always said a man doesn't truly grow up until he starts raising his hand. After her daddy gives you the cash for your down payment."

"Thanks so much for writing your next book. Sounds like a classic return to form. I can't wait for your tour de force to never leave my shopping cart."

"Sorry you can't write it yourself. Sorry you're past a prime you never had. Sorry the culture has moved on. Sorry you think just because you read a year of women writers, women writers are going to read a week of you. Sorry you never figured out you don't get to be the writer you want to be. Sorry I don't owe you shit. Sorry you don't know what you think. Sorry not sorry."

"Okay, so you're leaving. At least let me give you money for this cab."

"I don't need your money. I never have. I only take your money because it makes you feel good."

"Fuck, wow. Oh yeah, right, wow—you've got your expense account now."

"I worked my ass off for it."

"Because you're so brilliant at promoting yourself and pretending you don't care about promoting. But where would you be without me supporting your daydreams all these years? I spend every day in Egypt, waiting to get outsourced to Babylon, and I do it to make money that protects us. No matter what I do, I'm in Egypt. No matter what I do, I'm screwed. This isn't the Chicago River, it's the Nile. You know that book I'm thinking of, right? I think about that one line constantly. 'In some ultimate sense, every place is Egypt.'"

"You always forget the *end* of that book, Ty, because you never follow through. Sure, okay, we're probably in Egypt, no matter where we are, no matter where we go. Humanity is screwed. But there's always a better place. A promised land. And the way through to that land is not through culture. The way to that land is through the wilderness. And there's no way to get through the wilderness except by joining together and marching."

"I don't think I can do that."

"I know you can't. Even though there's never been

an easier time to realize it. Nobody cares what we think when the thinking is being done for us—by *them*." Jenny points across the bridge at the night cops, who have started beating the protestors. "Fuck! And that's why I don't love you anymore."

"This is how we're breaking up. At a fucking Trump protest."

"How else did you think it would happen?"

"Who am I, Jenny, Forrest Gump?"

"If only."

"I'm sorry."

"But we *are* worried about you, Ty, oh my God, we're all so worried about *you*. Maybe I did a horrible thing by not going to your dad's funeral with you. And you know what? For that, I really am sorry. That should've been a day that *was* all about you, but I couldn't handle it. Maybe because I handle so well all the days that should be about anything else."

"Do you remember *why* you didn't come with me to my dad's? Because you were *working through a problem in your draft*."

"I couldn't be around anyone else."

"You left me to stand alone at my father's grave because you were too busy revising your *fucking essay*. And, somehow, I forgave you for that."

"How? How could you forgive me for that?"

"I just love you, Jenny, what can I say? Nothing you

could ever do to me would make me hate you."

"Your love sounds like a threat. It's always 'forgive' with you, and then nobody knows where they stand. Nobody knows when you're really hurt, you've got such a boner for forgiveness. If only you could forgive *yourself*."

"I know, I'm sorry."

"Stop apologizing like a little bitch."

"I'm sorry I don't know what to think."

I start crying, and wipe my tears with the busker's napkins. I remember his music, his wedding canon, and feel better. But I'm also terrified that I might smile at Jenny, involuntarily, and that if I smile at her, she might strike me.

"It's okay, Ty. It's *so* okay. I only hope, for your sake, that you're nearing the end of your reckless actions, and that this isn't the beginning."

"Then come with me."

"Don't go up there."

"Come with me."

Jenny walks to the other side of the bridge. I follow her. It's strangely quiet on this side, just a normal city. She spots a cab. Puts her hand up. The cab stops.

I will not apologize again. I feel like a bellhop, stuffing her luggage in the trunk and telling the cars behind us to shut up. I feel strong, yelling into the wind, the tears resting on my eyes. But then I remember the horrible night I went to buy the heaviest tampons with wings on the side, and how I crossed against the stoplight, and almost got run over, and how I wished I would've been the first white guy on the Upper East Side to get arrested for jaywalking. I hate myself for thinking that getting arrested, and leaving Jenny to bleed out in our apartment that night, was all I truly wanted.

There are sirens now, and bullhorns telling us the bridge will be raised to kettle the protestors. I can either run across the bridge into the hotel, or jump in the cab with Jenny. I tap the back window for her to lower it.

"I'm sorry. No, I'm not sorry. I'll come with you to Rhonda's."

Jenny takes the other daisy out of her tote bag and offers it to me. I know, somehow, that this means we're not going to make it.

"When I saw you walking down the bridge," I say, accepting the flower, "I thought you held a bouquet. But it was only two. You were the most beautiful thing I'd seen since the last time I saw you."

"Little flower," Jenny responds.

"Who walked unannounced into my life," I say.

"And," we say together, "almost blossomed there."

Jenny tells the driver to go. My eyes follow their turn. I sense a tender house operator arriving. To raise the bridge as the protest excites to riot. To protect Trump property. I want to hang off the bridge when it raises, like in my old nightmares, and instead of drowning in the makeshift cataract and startling the geese I'll perform a swan dive up into the steely heavens. As a child I dreamt like that, believed in the miracle of crossings, from evil to good, from hell to heaven, and I even wanted, for a whole summer, to grow up to be the toll booth captain of the George Washington Bridge. I would see so many happy riders paying the toll, answering the riddle with clinking gold, their coins swallowed, the green light flashing: *accepted.* I want the acceptance only exact change can bring. But the sirens are blaring. The protestors bleeding. The cars traversing their final chance. I start running. And I don't understand what I'm feeling. For all I profess, I am still an amateur when it comes to love.

2.

I check in. And fall hard asleep. The next thing I know it's not even midnight. A sanitized TV remote pokes my sagging thigh. I raise the device, press power, and hear the clarion flourish of a news alert.

And now for more on the story nobody's talking about.

I listen. And don't mind the news. With the right news, man is less alone. On the bedside table I see a half-eaten club sandwich peeling off a gold-lined plate, the stems of strawberries floating in a champagne flute. I don't remember ordering anything, but now I *do* remember that Jenny left me, and I'm wakehumming 'Lonely Woman,' only I don't know why.

I try and remember my dream. I know it involved the bookstore woman in the bright red beret, but she's disappearing by the second.

I swallow the last of the flat champagne, nibble the last of the club. The bacon is cold, the lettuce grossly warm. I finger the turning avocado mayo. I google: *how to get laid (for free or low cost) in downtown Chicago (not dangerous Chicago) by women my age who take care of themselves.*

I learn the bars near the expressway stay open until 3AM, the bars *under* the expressway, in neighborhoods where it isn't yet safe for white men to mow their lawns, stay open, it seems, all night.

On the news, a retired general is making fun of civilians. I try changing the channels but they're all the same. Only then do I remember the raising bridge, and how I saved myself by running into the hotel, and how the cops celebrated on the backs of the protestors like Ewoks on stormtrooper helmets. I swallow some warm lettuce. Life feels so hopeless. There's Caesar. Unlimited refills of Caesar. There's nothing else.

I splash water on my face, dim the lights to conserve electricity, and ride the elevator down. In the hotel lobby, partisans are gathering for the Fourth of July. Women in candy-striped dresses and pink-flesh-colored heels, men in boat shoes with side laces, pressed tan suits. These patriots are buzzed, buzzcut, and bussed-in from the suburbs, flown in from plain states with small populations that enjoy disproportional representation in federal government. They wave flags the next size up from swizzle sticks, and many of them raise children-of-color along for the ride with their white inheritors. An oboe choir hums a smooth jazz version of 'Strike Up the Band,' a trucker-hatted DJ spins parental advisory hip-hop. Behind the music, on a housepainter's ladder, a pierced biracial paints a mural of the Trump family on a portable white wall.

A model emerges wearing a red, white, and blue evening gown. It's Ivanka Trump, the First Princess. She hushes the oboe choir, neck chops the hip-hop, and says to the clinking audience, "I am so pleased to be with you all here, on my family's visit to Chicagoland, within our American interior, to celebrate this, our Day of Independence. I never was a child, but ever since I was a beautiful young girl I've loved how the Fourth of July makes me feel. For Frederick Douglass, it was brass-fronted impudence, but for William Shakespeare, it was the captain jewel in a wondrous necklace."

The oboe choir sounds a vivid chord.

"Sylvia Plath," the First Princess resumes, holding up her phone, "a 20th century Boston poet..."

"...fuck Boston," a ketchup pouring man yells from the bar.

"'November Graveyard' by Sylvia Plath."

I can't believe it. One of Jenny's favorite poems.

The choir sounds an autumnal chord.

"*At the essential landscape stare, stare, till your eyes foist a vision dazzling on the wind...*"

I stare at the Princess, and because of her rock star skills, I'm certain she's found only me in the crowd, and she stares right back.

When she's done, and the patriots start dancing, I push through to the front.

"I just wanted to tell you that that was so, so good. That's one of the poems my college professor had on the whiteboard when he molested me. I could have listened to you read it forever. Can I buy you a drink?"

"Oh, I'm flattered," the First Princess says, "but I'm taken."

"Right. To a Jew who loves Egypt more than Joseph."

"Sorry?"

"Nothing," I say. "I'm sorry, too."

***

I leave the hotel. Out in the street, the bridge is low again, the protestors and cops gone, the curfew called.

It's like nothing happened at all.

I walk to the middle of the bridge, and look at the letters T R U M P.

They seem to turn to E G Y P T.

Am I still dreaming? Am I a slave in Egypt, or a free man in Trump, and, for me, what's the difference?

The letters keep changing. Like shutters on *Wheel of Fortune*. I try to remember what the rabbis always say about Egypt.

A rabbi appears.

"Remind me what you always say about Egypt?"

"We say a lot of things about Egypt?"

"Start from the place I'm thinking?"

"Why are we talking like podcasters and making things questions that aren't questions?"

"Because we're Jews?"

"Egypt," the rabbi says, "is the pinching of a 34 waist

50

when you should be wearing a 36."

"I know that feeling."

"A fitted cap, size 7, when you need 7 ¼."

"Yeah that makes sense, and it was on final sale."

"Egypt the squeeze, the pressure, Egypt the narrows."

"The narrows. Does that have anything to do with the strategic importance of the strait of Hormuz?"

"Egypt, the emotional straitjackets."

"But the linens in the hotel are so nice."

"We don't doubt the niceness of the enemy's sheets. But it's more complicated than that."

"I hate it when you guys say *it's more complicated than that*."

I run away from the rabbi, over the bridge.

When I turn around, the rabbi is a donkey.

***

The next spot is too big for a bar, too small for a club, and tonight it's hosting an Indie Sleaze Dance Party, which is so dope. I see her. And want her. She tells me her heart skipped a beat the moment I walked through that door. I believe that. And lob open-ended questions that require more than one-word answers. But then I slip up with a crucial, yes-or-no question: "Are you alone?"

"Freeze!" she replies, and we hold up each other's hands to find no rings, no tan lines, even though I think there might be a tan line on her wedding ring finger, it's hard to tell under the strobe light. Every other finger, including her thumbs, do have some kind of ring. Around her neck she wears a gold star of David. Her hair is long and black, her eyes a reaching blue. I can't concentrate on any one part of her, though, her entire being turns me on.

She asks if I prefer Tyrone or Ty, and I say Ty, mostly. She prefers Ellory over El, never Ellé or we're fighting, but I can call her El as much as I like, it means God.

"It does," I say. "A rational name for you."

"Heaven ain't close in a place like this," she sings back to me.

We dance in the back room, drink in the front. Both of us agree we aren't normally in tourist neighborhoods like this one, with all of these Schaumburgians, and I say, "Yeah, all these Schaumburgians," without knowing what that means, I assume a Chicago synonym for the south shore of Long Island. I take out my phone to see if Jenny's sent a message, but Ellory taps it away. She just wanted something rowdy tonight, she says, something close to home. No fireworks over the lake, no barbeques in the suburbs. We agree the Fourth of July is one of our favorite holidays. I ask if she thinks Trump ruined it, and she answers, "Let's not talk about silly stuff like that." We dance to The Killers, The Strokes, we dance to The Thrills, Kanye's 'All Falls Down,' that one Interpol song I can never remember the name of, and during Girl Talk's 'Smash Your Head' we raise our hands in the air and shout, "It was all a dream!"

"To be honest," Ellory says, "I like this cornball place. And all its married men." She takes my wrist. "Nice Roley. So classy. And this jacket is nice."

I wear a dark blazer with black jeans, a black silk button-down, chocolate brown monk straps. My typical uniform. Ellory wears a sleeveless black dress with a silver-linked belt, a light denim jacket, black ankle boots. She slinks out of the jacket, presses into me. I run my fingers around her sculpted shoulders. She pushes my blazer off, pretending that's more difficult than it is, and brushes the silk beneath, which I pretend not to notice, which is what a man's supposed to do.

A guy pushes into us, sweaty but smooth, white teeth and gold wrists. He forces his smile into Ellory's space, says to us, what a *night night night*.

"Let's go get a drink," I say.

"We can do whatever we want," she says in the front room, downing shots.

"You, for sure, can do anything you want."

"The thing about feminists is that they've never met an actual woman."

"Excuse me?"

She leans forward for a kiss. It's neat, but then it's sloppy. We're kissing right next to another couple, the *night night night* guy and whatever girl just said yes to him, who are also kissing, it's obvious, for the first time.

"Should *we* just kiss?" Ellory says to the guy. "Or *us*?" she asks the girl.

The guy lunges for Ellory.

"No!"

"Excuse me?" Ellory says.

"No, wait," I say. "I'm sorry."

"Don't apologize to me."

"I meant, don't leave." I blush and say, "You're my dream girl."

The *night night night* guy laughs. "If this is your dream girl, man, then you've got problems."

We leave the front room and return to the dance floor. They're playing 'Hotel Yorba' by the White Stripes. We raise our hands in the air and shout, "Let's get married!"

"I can't believe," Ellory says, "that these songs are *oldies* now."

"Thank you for taking me back. I'm progressive, not possessive. I just want you to myself tonight."

"I think that's what Oprah means, child, when she says *possessive*."

"I want to be hungover with you in the morning," I say. "And I got this nice hotel room. But it's in…"

"…every married man in here has a nice hotel room."

I hold up my hands. "No tan lines!"

"I want you, too," Ellory says.

"I wanted you the moment I saw you."

"Never heard that one before."

"I wanted you *more* when we started talking. Talk to me, more. Tell me everything."

"Everything."

"Yes, everything."

We find two barstools in the corner of the front room bar. We order whiskeys, and I steady myself when I announce to the bartender, "Also two waters." We sip the whiskeys. We don't touch the water.

"Where are you from?" Ellory asks. "You're not from here. But you're not from Schaumburg, either."

"New York." I stir my whiskey. "New York. But I'm thinking of moving here."

"Then I doubt you're from New York."

"It doesn't mean as much to me as it used to."

"Like New York City."

"Nothing but."

"People around here love to say they're *from Chicago* when they're from Schaumburg."

"People born in Manhattan wouldn't say I'm from New York City, they'd say the name of their Manhattan neighborhood. But that's a different story. And not a very interesting one."

"I had this roommate in New York," Ellory says. "In Manhattan, where I lived for like only a month after college, pretending I was interested in the fashion industry, pretending *everything*, really. I hated New York. I hated the West Village the most. I was so stupid, thinking I would move there and *make it*. Like some even bigger-nosed Carrie Bradshaw."

"The West Village confuses a lot of people."

"Everyone has such a ballroom sense of themselves."

"They have to. Their apartments are so small."

"But also there are all these normal people around. You just feel like you're participating in one of those oral history documentaries all the time."

"Totally. Like some oral history of the last punk scene that the new punk scene *respects*. Not going to lie, though, I eat that shit up."

"You have to pretend artistic history exists in New York. But the only history in New York is legal history."

"The formal disclosure one signs before participating in the oral history."

"And I still, to this day, can't remember my roommate's name. Do you remember my name?"

"Ellory Allen. I love the way you said both names. You remember my name, right?"

"Tyrone Rossberg. You prefer Ty over Tyrone. I remember everyone else's name. The man who fixed the plumbing after three days. Then the plumbing was fine. But every night he knocked on our door, just to make sure."

"That can be gross, right."

"Yeah the toilet was so gross. Even when it worked. Everything was gross in that apartment. And I remember the name of my landlord. At the carpet store where I dropped off the rent. This lovely Persian guy. You know they always have such beautiful skin, different kinds of clothes. He would always count the $100s I had to get from the bank. Lick his finger over each $100. One day he told me he loved going down on Israeli girls with rich daddies and big stinky bushes. I told him I wasn't Israeli. I'm from Winnetka, which is just north of here. But my father lives in Highland Park now. Although Daddy still pretends he's Augie March from Humboldt Park, because he owns half of it."

"You've read that book. *Augie March*?"

"It's beautiful."

"Yes, of course it is."

"I have a memory of crying over the bird parts. In high school in the park. It was sunny out, so lovely. I don't remember anything else, just the sunny day and the book. He never believed I wasn't Israeli. My landlord. Iran doesn't recognize Israel's right to exist, but it recognizes Israeli girls. He gave me a free rug at Christmas. I still have it, you'll see."

"I want to see."

"But tonight let's go to your *nice* hotel room. There's too much going on at my place right now. She was this drippy girl I spent hundreds of hours with. My roommate. We slept so close to each other in this gross 'junior one-bedroom,' which is a real estate name for a studio with a dry wall."

"Those were sleazy times. I loved them."

"Everybody was always out. Not like now. One night we pretended girl-on-girl-in-a-porno. For this stockbroker with great blow. Just cracking up before things got sexual. And this broker, whose name I *do* remember, Jonathan, kept asking us to do 'ass-to-ass,' which is from a movie, we'd never seen it, he made a point of telling us about it, and why do I remember Jonathan's name, Ty, but not her name, and why do I have a better memory of inhaling her butt than looking in her eyes, which I did so much, because we spent so much time in that apartment just smoking Parliaments and doing crap."

"Licking each other's butts?"

"No, just looking at each other. Sitting on the windowsill and smoking. Like those lovelies in *Frances Ha*."

"You love that movie? I love that movie, too."

"I think we love the same things."

"I think we do, too."

"We click. Sometimes I think she was this Southern sorority girl. Sometimes I think she was this stuffy journalist from Boston. Maybe I see her name in the paper, and I don't make the connection it's her. You know what I'm dying to see right now? *Clueless.*"

"I own the DVD."

"Do you have it with you?"

"It's in my apartment. Back in New York, I mean." And then, for the first time since Ellory and I sat down, I think about Jenny. The *Clueless* DVD was probably still in our DVD player, from the night we lost Aurora.

"You rent or own in New York?"

"I own in the city."

"With your wife?"

"It's my *Clueless* DVD. An anniversary release. The 'As If!' edition."

"I want to do it all with you."

"I think we can."

"We'll cuddle on my stinky rug and listen to adagios."

"I know we can sit on windowsills, hungover, and not say anything to each other."

"Like in a Noah Baumbach movie."

"Yes, the books on the bookshelf rumpled just so."

"Papered in red velvet. We'll only ask each other two questions. One: Do you want to walk to the lake? Two: Do you want to walk to the river? The river. The lake. The lake. The river. Those are the only two things we'll ever have to do."

"I almost jumped in the Chicago River tonight. But that was before I met you."

"Most men jump in the river after they meet me."

"Did you read *Moby-Dick* in high school? I think that's why I didn't jump. This line from it saved me. 'Water and meditation are wedded forever.'"

"That sounds like *Starry Night* toilet paper."

"Tell me more about New York."

"So this one Saturday night, something actually happened. It was raining, of course, and we were getting ready to go out, and my cousin Marcus was in town, and he got us tickets to The Strokes, I don't know how, but he can always do it, and Marcus hates New York too, by the way, he called it one big hipster shithole before that word was even cool, but he was in there for one of Daddy's deals and he wanted to see me, and when we were getting ready to go out I danced around my side of the bedroom singing 'Barely Legal' into my hairbrush, and my roommate danced around her side of the bedroom singing 'The Modern Age' into hers, and then we met each other in the common room, which was still our junior bedroom, to sing 'Last Night' together, just like we had the night before..."

"...just like thousands of other people were doing in their gross apartments all over the city..."

"...and we were snorting rails, and drinking freezer vodka, and soon enough we were ready to go out, and I wore my new trench coat, and so did my roommate, but my trench was nicer, underneath a short dress, just like this one, but for sure shorter, and a belt, just like this one, but redder. Maybe her name was Rebecca. I didn't want to live with a non-Jew, or at the very least someone presenting as a white Jew."

"What do you mean?"

"I didn't want to live with someone who wasn't white."

"No. I mean I get that."

"This was the first and last time in my life I had a roommate. Maybe her name was Naomi. We were pretty hopped up, but also laid back, you know, in a way that fit that after 9/11 moment. But it wasn't *post*-9/11 just yet, this was the *pre-post*-9/11 period, right. You know what I mean. So like an hour later we got arrested, totally insane, we got cuffed, if you can believe it, for snorting a little key coke outside the club, which, like, every single person waiting to get into the club was doing. I think the cops did it just because of me, you know."

"What do you mean?"

"They wanted to talk to me. The way you wanted to talk to me. And I like cops, in general. I mean they've always protected me. At the police station they threw my cousin Marcus and my roommate in the cell and they made me sit on top of this radiator. I felt like one of those prostitutes you always see in a TV show police station. The lights were so bright. So different than under the club marquee. And this dark-skinned black cop stepped to me and sniffed, 'You know what they say about Israeli girls.' And I was like, 'I'm not Israeli, I'm

Palestinian—what sexuality do Palestinian girls have?' I so *clearly* remember saying that. And then the Iowa cop came over, and said he wanted to see the tanning salon bunny sticker on my hip bone. This was right after 9/11, so I showed it to him. And then I was like, can you let my cousin and my roommate out of the cell?"

"So fucked up," I say.

"Cops have been doing this stuff to me since I was like 12. Probably earlier. And anyway, I like cops. I just hate the dumb ones. And Italian and Brazilian cops are much better at torture, believe me, than any torture the dumbest American cop can come up with."

"No, yeah. During, before, or after 9/11, right."

"So then, I heard my roommate screaming, and Marcus cursing, and then I start screaming because of what I'm smelling. The actual criminal in the cell shit himself. Just pulled down his pants and started smearing his shit all over the walls. And the cops took their sweet time opening the cell, and then they started beating the shit, you know, the outer shit, out of the homeless guy, but some of his inner shit got on my roommate's trench—Ty, I need to tell you that I just *hate* shit, when it's in me I need to get it out as quickly as possible— and my roommate screamed louder than anyone I'd ever heard scream before."

"It's like every Southern sorority girl's greatest fear of *exactly* what will happen to them when they move to

New York City to participate in an oral history."

"I can't remember her name. But I always think I'm seeing her, you know, crossing the street, in the salon, she's always right *here,* I even feel like she's *here right now.* The cops got tired of beating the homeless guy. But I felt like it was only them getting tired of the beginning of beating him. First, they let us all go. And told us to one, keep quiet, and two, stop snorting cocaine in public. Marcus was like, 'I can't believe we missed The Strokes for this *Law & Order* episode, maybe Interpol's playing somewhere.' But we were too spent to reconfront the night, so we went back to our place, and Marcus stayed that night, and—I actually think this is why I remember this story—my roommate moved out in the morning. Because she wanted Marcus all to herself. And that's not something I'll ever allow."

"What do you mean?"

"I guess I mean that after my roommate moved out, I knew I had to get out of New York, too. I couldn't even spend one night alone in that apartment."

I want to clarify my question. What did she mean about her cousin? But instead, I lean in to kiss her again. I've never stuck my tongue deeper into a woman's mouth before, with the hopes that it'd either give her the energy to continue talking, or stop her from ever speaking again.

"I love it," she says, "when your tongue holds my

tongue and we smile. I don't even care if you're taken."

"It's not like that," I say.

"No, it is."

"What if *you're* taken, Ellory?"

"We know I'm not."

"Why did you tell the *night night night* guy you wanted to kiss him."

"That black guy? I wouldn't have done it."

"You told the girl the same thing. I mean, it's okay."

"I never know what to do for love. It's the thing I've done the most for in my life, and I still don't know what it is."

I take her hand, and say, "I have to confess something. My nice room. It's a nice *suite*, actually. But it's at the Trump hotel. And I'm happy to discuss that. But I would *much* prefer we discuss it in the actual room. Are you okay with that? Or I mean, we could forget the room and go to your place."

"I love the linens at Trump," she says. "So much nicer than at the Peninsula."

***

We leave the club and head back to the Tower.

I spot the First Princess mopping the floor.

"Don't look so surprised," Ellory says. "She'd do anything for the organization."

I look back, wishing we could take the First Princess with us, but she's transformed into the same donkey the rabbi did. When the elevator doors close, Ellory opens her denim jacket, hikes up her dress. I slip two fingers in, raise them to my mouth and laugh, *stinky bush*. She kisses my chest, unbuttons my fly. It feels like we start having sex even before I have time to open the door to the suite. The suite I never would've gotten if I'd listened to Jenny, if I'd done the right thing.

Speaking of doing the right thing, I should pull out. I want to hold back, and present her that final strawberry floating in my champagne flute. But she won't let go.

"Deeper, baby. I don't wanna miss a thing."

"Are you on birth control?"

"No, I need my period to think. Don't you want a baby? Don't you feel like every woman who never gave you a baby took something away from you? Wait, do you have kids."

I don't exactly answer the question, just turn my heavy head onto her shoulder. For a moment, we're quiet. There's no noise from other rooms, the cooling systems. The digital clock doesn't give off light and the nightlight in the bathroom doesn't enter the main room. This is the first quiet light I remember since the plane ride from New York. I should appreciate it, but it makes me anxious, so I start talking. I want her to learn something about me.

"When I got out of college, just after 9/11, I worked down by the World Trade Center ruins."

"During the *pre*-post."

"I had this dream we would honor Ground Zero by doing nothing. Just let it grow wild. There's this artist from the 80s who tended a wheatfield down there. That's what I wanted then—wheat instead of a Freedom Tower. Etymologically, hope *is* wheat. Everyone thought it might finally end, this horrible civilization. People were excited World War III might happen. Then, we could fight World War IV with wheat."

"But I love our civilization. And you do, too, baby. Look how beautiful you talk about it. Hope is wheat. That makes me cry. And I'm gluten free."

"I mean you too, babe. You're an amazing talker. And we didn't even have any blow."

"I have some. You want a bump? I didn't mean to keep it from you."

"No, I'm good. You know the writer Jenny Marks, right?"

"Is *she* your wife?"

"No, we're not married. I thought I saw you, tonight, though, at her reading. And then when I first saw you at the club. I thought for sure you were this woman from the reading, wearing this bright red beret."

"*Mais non.*"

"But you'd gone home and changed your book event

clothes into what you're wearing now."

"I'm not wearing anything now."

"Jenny's friend, Rhonda. I hate her."

"Rhonda's your wife."

"Stop. Rhonda had this mouse. I thought her mouse was my father. I feel like I'm dreaming. There was this guy. On the bridge. Talking about rabbits."

"You'd think rabbits would eat mice, right. But they're vegetarians, like me." She opens her snakeskin purse, on the bedside table, and takes out a pack of Marlboro Lights.

"I thought you smoked Parliaments."

"I outgrew them. You always go back to what you smoked first."

"You can't smoke in here, El."

"It's fine."

"Yeah the fine will be like $5,000 or something."

"It's okay."

"But…"

"…what?"

"Nothing, it's cool. Can I have one?"

"Do you smoke, Ty?"

"Not anymore."

"Then don't smoke."

"I want to, though."

"No, you only think you do. To fit it in with all the other bad things you're doing tonight, like cheating on your wife."

"Enough. Really."

After she exhales, Ellory says, "Maybe rabbits eat Beyond Mice."

"I want to be vegetarian, too, like you."

"You want to hear about the men who have hurt me, don't you baby, and how I've come out the other side even stronger. I must begin with my first cousin, Marcus."

"He's your *first* cousin?"

"It wasn't anyone's fault. We were only children. I still see the walkway of Grandpa Irving's house. The peony bushes."

"Please let me have a drag."

"No. In the springtime, Marcus and I play, and Grandpa tends the wild onions that bloom under our dogwood tree. Then, suddenly, it's summer. You know how that happens. And we never want summer to end, but summers end, that's what they do, and when they do, I understand what poetry is, how you can teach yourself to say a little less than you feel, and forget a little more than you know. That's poetry, and that's Marcus. Now he uses words like *landowner* but who cares who cares who cares. In late August, Ty, I swear it's on the thirty-second day of August, I swear I would've done anything that year to stop the September from septembering, She-Ra dies, and we bury her under our dogwood tree. Grandpa and Marcus are sad, but I'm happy when She-Ra dies, and I don't know why, it scares me, it's the first time I hate myself because of how I feel. That night I go into Marcus's room, and wake him up, and I ask him, Why am I happy that She-Ra died? He doesn't answer, he just kisses me, and I kiss him back, and we fall in love.

"The next thing I remember we have a new princess, Leia, pawing at She-Ra's grave. This is later, after we bury Grandpa Irving. My father and uncle are downstairs, carefully reading the will, and Marcus has been bothering me all day, trying to kiss me, touching my butt, touching my breasts, and pulling my hair. He's asking how many fingers I've had in me, so I tell him he knows the number, because he's really good at math, and because they were his three fingers.

"'Only three?' Marcus says. 'That's *nothing*, El.' When I think of it now, I want to tell him, What are you, twelve? But he knows we're twelve, because, back then, we were. 'What about four fingers, or five?' When he runs out of fists, I say, I don't want to have sex with you. That day, he honors my wishes. We wait. I never know if I should say *we* wait or *he* waits. And we leave the city over Christmas, for the islands, as a family like we do every year, to get away from the cold, to get away from Christmas and the Christian New Year. And on the Virgin Islands I'm arranging subpopulations of vacationers so that Marcus and I never have to be alone, but eventually, we are alone, in my uncle's suite. It just happens naturally on a winter beach vacation, you can't stick to the schedule. This isn't our Noah Baumbach movie, Ty. This is that guy who did the ass-to-ass movie."

"Darren Aronofsky, I think."

"Why do you say you *think*, when you *know*? Marcus keeps saying, Marry me, then sex, marry me, then sex, I wanna sex you up, tick-tock you don't stop. He tries to give me a ring. I realize it's my step aunt's. We were always doing mean things to her. I don't know her anymore. My uncle got another wife. And I push the ring away, even though I should take it, it's a beautiful ring, and I long for marriage, Ty, when I'm a young girl, I long to leap. His swim trunks say *don't have a cow*. When I hear about the *Simpsons*, I remember them."

"Did you tell him," I ask, "that you didn't consent?"

"I didn't know the word *consent* when we were twelve, Ty, the way girls do now. I told him he was hurting me. He said, No, you're hurting me. That's what Marcus the landowner thinks now. Every time he evicts his tenants."

"I'm really sorry."

"When we get back to the states I don't feel so good. Of course, I'm not going to tell my father I'm having his nephew's child, so my uncle drives me to a private doctor, all the way up on the Wisconsin border. My uncle asks me who did it. Even though he knows who did it, he knows it could have been any man, he knows that *he* did it, he knows that when you look at a twelve-year-old girl lustfully you have already aborted her baby in your heart. So I don't answer him. We're listening to *Tapestry* on the ride up, and I keep rewinding to 'Beautiful' so I can keep the promise to myself that I will get up every morning with a smile on my face and show the world all the love in my heart. And I want to help pay for my first. It's my Bat Mitzvah soon and I want to advance my uncle some of my gifts. He doesn't listen. And refuses to look at me no matter what I say. My abortionist, though, she does look at me, she's a presenting white Jew too, I see, so this is where all the Jewish women have gone now that they're no longer married to my father and my uncle and all their business associates. The procedure room has one of those small, high windows, for a bird's eye view of Lake Michigan, how it gets even more oceanic when you're up near Wisconsin, and when I see Lake Michigan now, walking on the beach in the moonlight, I remember that day, and I think about this line from *The Idiot*."

"You've read *The Idiot*? Sorry, I'll stop asking you that question."

"It's a little condescending. The book is half and half."

"You mean you've read the first two hundred pages."

"I love the first two hundred pages."

"What's the quote?" I ask, deflated.

"To kill, quote, for killing, is an immeasurably greater punishment than the crime itself. Endquote.

On the morning of my Bat Mitzvah, Marcus pushes me to the ground outside the synagogue. My tummy hurts so much, and I badly scrape my knee. My brain hurts, too, with all the Hebrew sloshing around. For all my pain, I've never been more intellectually excited than I was that day. You know how this celebration of my youth and intelligence goes. Everyone at temple who has come into contact with me agrees. I am exceptionally bright *and* a hard-worker *and*, it must be said, a very beautiful young woman. I am a serious young lady who has read half of Dostoevsky's *The Idiot*, and I identify with Nastasya Filippovna, its heroine, because she too had been abused out of the cradle, and I will search the great literatures of the world for women just like me, and I will come to find that I am out there.

"In my speech, I offer my flock parallels between the text and society. The Torah says you shall not murder, and that is still true today. Don't murder. There are murders all over the world and they need to be stopped. Murder is wrong, against God, my lord, there are so many victims. How do we even live, moment to moment, knowing there's such horrible violence in the world, how do we not scream, all day, every day, since we see what's going on. We do see, we are all sweet, smart, sweet, sweet people. But so often we choose what's wrong. There are victims all around us and we choose not to see, they are screaming, and we choose not to hear, and if we do hear, we don't truly listen. We are all blessèd with abundant means. You hear that I am pronouncing blessèd with the accent on the final 'e,' which is something I really liked to do when I was twelve, it warmed, it still warms, the cockles of my heart. We are all blessèd with eyes that see, so why do we pretend to be blind? You know what's going on, don't you? And I know what's going on, too. I will not murder. I am a vegetarian because I do not believe in murder."

"I know what you mean, babe. When I was young, I dreamt of a human creature unable to shed blood."

"I know you do, Ty. You're in a knot, like me."

"I still dream about that. What if violence weren't possible? What if it just didn't work."

"Hope is wheat, like you said. And I have wheat for mankind. And abortion does not murder because you cannot kill the nameless. Some people think in order for a baby to be alive, a man must scream with pleasure, but in order for a baby to be alive, a woman must scream in pain. Thou shalt not commit adultery. Adultery's wrong because you cannot initially involve everyone in adultery who will eventually be involved in adultery, like I will be implicated in my father's adultery when he leaves my stepmother, the Christian woman he'd met while committing adultery against my Jewish mother during her final cancer, for an even younger Christian woman from outside of Boston. I've forgiven my father almost everything. I've even forgiven his self-congratulatory gaze that says because my hand doesn't reach for you, daughter, I have honor, I am not a sick man like my brother, or his evil son, like all the men who go right through you. But I never forgive my father for laughing the day Timothy McVeigh is executed by Bill Clinton's government. I'm in college, then, and still quoting *The Idiot's* Prince Myshkin to my father. To kill for killing, I tell him, is an immeasurably greater punishment than the crime itself. But like most men my father believes in death more than life. Me, I weep when McVeigh is murdered, I mourn. And it pisses my father off. The day of the execution, I tell him, is the real tragedy, the real injustice. Why does the state have this monopoly on violence? What *is* the state? I ask him. *We* are the state, he answers. And he reminds me there was a daycare center on the first floor of the building McVeigh blew up. I reply, To kill for killing is an immeasurably greater punishment than the crime itself.

"My father says he's ashamed to have raised a daughter who cares more about the life of a domestic terrorist than avenging, through the law, the innocent deaths of his victims. My father craves death, feeds it to himself, craves the death of more Iraqis, more Iraqis more, during the Second Iraq War. But I cry when the U.S. army destroys Babylon. My father wonders, What kind of Jew cries for Babylon? And I cry when the treasures of

74

the Baghdad Museum are plundered. My father says, You care more about sand…do you say the *n-word*?"

"No," I say.

"Like you don't say it, say it," Ellory asks, "or you don't think it in your head?"

"Both. Every time I've heard it used by a white man, violence has quickly followed. Those aren't good memories."

"You seem like someone who listens to rap. Do you say it then? Like when you rap along."

"I change it to *brother*. Or I say nothing."

"My father loves to say it. He says it all the time. My father says, you care more about sand *n-word* knick-knacks than the freedom of the Iraqi people."

"It must be really hard," I say, trying to lighten the conversation, "to be gluten-free and vegetarian. Like, what do you eat?"

"I believe that you mean it, Ty," Ellory responds, "when you say you love me."

"I do love you."

"That gives me hope. Because a lot's happening in my life right now. Things are so confusing, so *dense*. There are all these commitments, these stupid little commitments that I need to untangle. And I need you to promise me that you'll be there for me during the untangling. I need you to stand by me as I untie this horrible knot I've made for myself. These days, I feel like more than a woman who reads books. I feel like I'm a woman *in* books, and a terrible, heartless author is pulling my strings. This horrible author is telling the reader there's no hope for my life. That I deserve what's coming to me. That I am out of wheat. That in my book, the door of hope is closed."

"I know what you mean," I say. "We will save ourselves from this terrible author. We must protect each other."

"We need to leave town."

"I will take you anywhere if you tell me more."

"My freshman year bio teacher killed himself. Because he got me pregnant."

"Who drove you to the clinic? Your uncle?"

"Yes. Mr. Lim is the first man I sleep with who doesn't smell like Marcus. Because I cannot fully return his love, Mr. Lim jumps off the bridge right below us, actually, back when this was the *Sun-Times* building, not a hotel. The thing was, he wanted me to *have* the baby. That was why, he said, he wanted to come inside of me."

"Why did you let him?"

"I was fourteen. We didn't understand internal cumshots like girls do today."

"No, you're right, we didn't. We grew up in such a more innocent time, you know. When you look at the porn of our youth it looks like a *Father Knows Best* episode."

"And Mr. Lim was such a sweet, gentle man. He gave

me *Lolita*. He had so much useless, trivial knowledge, like Nabokov. He wanted us to run away and pleaded with me to promise that I would love him forever. I did promise him, but he kept saying he knew I was lying. They said afterwards that he had a lot of other problems, but I never believed them when they said that. I knew Mr. Lim's only problem was me.

"People at school blamed me for his death. I was always being talked about. Look at that slut. I had to go into therapy. The trauma counselor suggested I volunteer at a suicide hotline. I was just another suburban Jewish girl with great hair working the phones at the suicide hotline, like I'm Andrea Zuckerman. She was at the suicide hotline right around the same time I was. I can tell you that suicide hasn't changed much since *90210*. That show was very realistic about a lot of things in our formative years. I really loved holding the heavy phones. I miss them so much. When I was really little Grandpa Irving had this chair, next to the phone, you had to sit in the chair, and hold the phone, you know what I mean, right? Back in those days you had to *place* your calls. I didn't do well, fielding calls at the suicide hotline. Mine is not a personality that follows scripts. But even worse, I was certain, coming off the events of Mr. Lim's catastrophe, which I blamed myself for, which everyone else blamed me for, that if I picked up the phone a man would die just hearing my voice. And the kinds of people who go through with killing themselves, it's sad, you know, but going through with it will always be the final idea they ever had. And, if they're successful, they'll never know if they made the right decision or not. So yeah, I had even less interest in saving other people's lives than Brenda Walsh. It's just easier to give money. I asked my father to help, so we sold a few shares of the GE stock I inherited from Grandpa Irving, and we paid to rename the bio lab in Mr. Lim's memory. When they say, during the pledge drive, *most people are giving $250,000 right now*, they're talking about me. I thought about Mr. Lim yesterday, because I ran into *another* one of my teachers, Mrs. Prowler. I believe in epiphanies, Ty. I can't stop thinking that this is the reason I met you. I can't stop thinking that because I met you, I must change my life."

"This is it, baby."

"Yes. Our life is changing as we speak."

"As you speak. Keep talking."

"I ran into Mrs. Prowler at the Art Institute. It's one of the only places I can think. I especially like to go there on my first day of heavy flow. I sit in the gardens and read. Sometimes I go in. Often I do. I walk the hallways of the Buddha, and down into Islam, the Levant. They keep Islam in the basement. At least down in Islam, if nowhere else in the world, I control my own abstraction. What I mean is, visitors don't come to the Art Institute for Islam. They come for Impressionism. Barely legal French girls holding flowers.

"When I get bored with Islam, I go to Greece. So many useful objects—forks, spoons, knives that aren't only weapons, I like the headless men best, the bowls, the barrels, the jars, atomizers, the vessels and spritzers, the amphorae and cups. But then I tire of Greece, and I leave it, and the banners tempt me with the featured attraction. But I always avoid the big attraction. No matter what, it's always Paul Gauguin, and Paul Gauguin makes me want to poke my eyes out. I'd rather be stuck in an elevator with Hillary Clinton than look at another Paul Gauguin. He just reminds me of getting hurt. Most artworks at the Art Institute remind me of the man I was with the first time I saw it. Cy Twombly paints the masterpieces Daddy's friends can ignore while molesting a child. A Jasper Johns target hits an orgasm. A Richard Prince is a dusty cowboy I just can't quit. An Edward Hopper is a middle manager who reads to his children after a busy afternoon of fucking me. A Charles Demuth is a laborer who beats his wife after a day of asking me to smile. My poor Jeff Wall boy. He thought I cared about the ironic beauty of capitalist abundance. Gerhard Richter took me to see *Fifty Shades of Gray*. My Yoshitomo Nara hairstylist who just *adores* Yoshitomo Nara, and never liked the smell of stinky bushes until he met me. But mostly it's Gauguin, Rodin, Gauguin,

Rodin, and on your anniversary—Claude Monet. Next year it's Gauguin from the perspective of the colonized, like Gauguin buying a dildo to mix things up a bit. But it's still Rodin."

"So I make my way to New Contemporary. That's where I belong. I stand in front of Damien Hirst's *Still*. Do you know it? It's this medicine cabinet, this mirrored curiosity spanning the whole wall. Feel my goosebumps, on the back of my neck, just thinking of *Still*, Ty, just saying the word. For something curious, weirdly, it's very matter of fact, one of those pieces removed from the time of death, and placed in the time of life, which is what makes it art. It's just this, you know, medical cabinet, that doesn't look like it belongs in a museum. Its shelves are filled with hospital stuff. It's as if Hirst is telling us that death not only makes you *still*, but also, no matter how hard we try to forget it, death is *still* here. The jars, bowls, and atomizers of the ancient Greeks are transformed into the nickel, steel, and rubber of the modern sick. I adore *Still*, Ty. It moves me.

"I like to sit down in front of it. A guard always comes by and asks if I need help, and I tell them I'm just going to take out a notebook and sketch, but actually, I don't have a notebook, I'm no good at art, I just want to sit on the floor and look at myself in this mirror of death. Men always ask me if I need help standing up. Men always ask me if *I'm the work of art*. I commend those guys, they're on to something. Where is my caption, the concise description of who I am, this woman who disrupts man's aesthetic contemplation? I would've saved myself, and them, a great deal of trouble all these years if I just wore, like an enslaved cow, a placard around my neck: 1977, Humboldt Park/Winnetka/Highland Park, 5 foot 7, oval face, shocking blue eyes, perfect teeth, that ass, those tits, tan lines, those lips, big Israeli hair, and water.

"I try to leave *Still* behind. But I have to turn around. Because this curio of death starts talking to me. *You think you know yourself*, it says. *But you know nothing until I know you, until my knives know you, you ungrateful hateful bitch. You selfish, heartbreaking, heartbroken wench, you white culture bitch who has caused so many people of color you've never met so much pain. You will know my black clamps, you will know my cold knives, you will know my scalpels, saws and hammers, my fasteners, spreaders, and probes, my scrub-blue saucers will overflow with your pre-code blood. You think you're lonely now, but your loneliness will be extended. Your loneliness is the disease, not the cure.* And I get so scared, Ty, I get so scared by *Still* it makes me rattle and shake. I had only wanted to be death's maiden! And so I run away from New Contemporary. I need a glass of wine from Caffè Moderno.

"I always sit at the tables that overlook the main attraction below. I guess every person's passport, their marital status, their level of aesthetic fatigue. I order another Pinot, then another, then another, keeping my empties next to me, which I always make bartenders do, because I'm a drunk, and I like to gaze at my empties as I climb in and out of my holes, and the drunker I get, the more I judge the crowd. What percentage of these patrons know how to change a tire? Swim a mile? How many will find a wallet and return it without stealing some of the cash? I think I see my old New York roommate, like a million times, Ty, a million times. What's her name? And then I see a woman scowling at me after my fourth glass. Is that my roommate? In retaliation, I down my fifth in one gulp, and stand up too quickly to order another.

"The woman rushes over to help me steady myself.

"'Ellory,' she says. 'Ellory Allen.'

"At first I don't recognize her, a fine old woman dressed for the contemplation of the museum, a woman who'd likely left her phone with her checked bag and coat. She carries a leather notebook, a small but heavy looking pen, a creased museum map in one hand, although I sense she knows the galleries like the back of her hand. Like any good teacher, Mrs. Prowler trained you to believe she was way smarter than she actually is. Mrs. Prowler was one of my first radical teachers, Ty, the first woman, other than my abortionist, other than my mother when she was dying, that I thought fearless. I will never forget how Mrs. Prowler set me on the deeper path to knowledge. When she taught us, this is weird—she was younger than we are now. I will never forget her, and I will never *forgive* her, either, for setting me on these paths, for revealing the problems of the world, and I will never forgive her for instilling in me that I'm a part of the problem. She was the first person to inspire me to be vegetarian. She told us Indians think Americans stink of meat nitrates. She told us men kill animals for the same reasons they kill women. She said, back in the early 90s, that giving birth to babies can be a prison for women, and there's no reason women need children, or need to want children, it's not even their *nature*. They said of Giotto that there was nothing in nature he could not paint, and if he couldn't paint it then it was the fault of nature, not Giotto. That's how I sometimes feel about having kids."

"I thought you said you wanted to give us a kid?"

"I also feel that way, too," Ellory says. "It's complicated."

"It's so complicated, it's rabbinical. I love that about us."

"A woman could simply choose rebirth, Mrs. Prowler told us, instead of birth. The way men had done for centuries. *Abraham begot Isaac.*"

"I remember a teacher like that," I say. "Who told the girls they didn't need to have kids. I remember thinking it was weird. What else were girls supposed to do? I remember a boy in the class whispering, Yeah, what dude would want to have sex with *you*?"

"Were you that boy, Ty?"

"I was. I sometimes think that's how I found out about sex. By learning a woman didn't want to have it."

"Where are we?"

"We're under the sheets. We're under the covers. We're safe."

"Don't you love these linens?"

"It's just you and me."

"It's so dark in here."

"I'll turn on the light."

"No leave it off. She says hello to me, Mrs. Prowler. And I'm like, who are you? She says maybe I didn't need another glass of wine, and I laugh and say she's right, even though the only thing I could taste on my tongue at that moment was the liquor the wine was prepping me for. It's like when you hear the word *cocaine*, you know, and you taste blood in your lungs. Mrs. Prowler asked if I was still friends with any of my classmates. I think I was already crying by then, for different reasons than what I told her, but I said, No, I'm not. I'm not friends with anyone, really. Why not? she asked. There were so many wonderful children in your class, you were all so lucky to grow up where you did. I said, I think I'm about to make a terrible mistake. Mrs. Prowler said, with all of her wise innocence, *Oh dear.* I cried, then, all the way into my backache. She sat on the stool next to me and held me so close.

"'Do you remember,' she asked, handing me a Kleenex, 'the day of the sick fox?'

"'No I don't,' I sniffled, 'I don't remember the sick fox. Tell me.'

"Mrs. Prowler told me the story. It had been a very humid day near the end of the school year when the class went on a field trip to the forest preserve. In the adopted animal area, there was a skulking fox. He was an arctic fox, the sign said, so what was it doing in Illinois? He looked tired, sick, deathly ill, lots of fur missing from the abuses he'd suffered as a pup. He was barely recognizable as what we would think of as a fox, his fox-ness foxed right out of him. The sign said that one of the trustees of the forest preserve had rescued the animal and brought him to this place, where he would live out the rest of his subarctic life peacefully, in a prairieland habitat. And we all said hello to the fox. Then, the rest of the class moved on, to the other rescued animals nature had left behind: the alligator who wouldn't snap at a fly, the squirrel who no longer had a taste for acorns, the owl who forgot how to hoot. But you, Ellory, stayed behind with the fox, putting pressure on yourself. I came back to check on you because I was always worried about all my children, but I was worried about children like you most of all. I worried that you were too sensitive to become a person in this world, that you would never be strong enough to fight for the justice you strained to understand. I worried that you had the knowledge, but you didn't have the wherewithal, to fight for what you believed in.'

"'Oh, I have the wherewithal,' I said to her. 'I just don't have the *guts*,' I cried, 'to fight for what I believe in. And I don't fight for it constantly.'

"'You were always concerned, dear,' she said, 'with the worst. With one eye in the slaughterhouse, one eye in the solitary confinements. You cared about genocide. But you were never looking at what was in front of you. Because you took 'love thy neighbor' too abstractly, too hard. You never understood that loving your neighbor should be the easiest thing a person can do. You never understood that it was none of your business, saving that fox.'

"'Why not?' I asked.

"'Because the sick fox,' Mrs. Prowler said, 'had already been saved.'

"I told her I understood, even though I didn't, and asked if she wanted to have an aperitif with me. But she said she didn't drink, and I shouldn't either, at least for the rest of the day. Then I asked if she wanted to stroll around New Contemporary with me. My spirits always brighten when I see Joan Snyder's *Summer*. Do you know it, Ty? But Mrs. Prowler said she was headed into Gauguin."

"I'm gonna put the light on for a sec," I say.

"You're done with me. You want me to leave."

"No, of course I don't," I say.

"You sound like you're trying to convince yourself. I know we're not supposed to mention your wife anymore."

"No, we're not," I say. But she's right. I am thinking about Jenny. And if she's going to text me in the morning—and it's almost morning—with an apology. I still have a flight back to New York. Jenny has a flight on to Denver for her next reading.

"Beware, Ty," Ellory says. "You will, *really*, *really*, need to take care of me. Take care of me *and* our baby."

"This is all I really wanna do," I say. "I want to take care of you. And our child."

"You will need to take care of me first, even after I have your baby. I will always be more important than our child."

"And I will always reward you for that honesty."

"I want our baby. But I'm not going to breastfeed."

"Maybe you don't want a baby. I can give you a ride to the clinic if we're pregnant

right now, and we need to abort. Although I guess you have your period."

"There's Plan B now. It's not like it was when we were kids."

"Maybe motherhood isn't your nature. Maybe if you got pregnant, babe, Giotto couldn't paint you."

"No, he could. And I do want a child. I don't have a lot of time left, and, really, it's the only thing I think about."

"Come on. When strong women like you tell me that, I feel like I'm being lied to. I'm not lying to you about being married, so don't you lie to me."

"Well, I don't want to end up some old maid like Mrs. Prowler. Who keeps returning to Gauguin. I want to give you a child, I just don't want to breastfeed. I'm not into matriarchy or invisible female labor. I won't perform visible or invisible female labor."

"God, babe, I hate visible and invisible female labor, too. I have read all about this, believe me. When a flight attendant smiles at me, I tell her to take it back."

"I can't wait to share my articles with you."

"And if I can help it, I will perform all the seen and unseen female labor. If I can't help it, I will cheer you on."

"You will have to put your elbow in the milk to make sure it isn't too warm. I'm never going to do that."

"Your elbow will never see the inside of a saucepan."

"We will need a lot of help, Ty. A *lot* of resources."

"Where should we go? To make it official. City Hall?"

"Take me to Rome."

"Yes, Rome."

"Are we crazy?"

"Not at all," I say. "Plots are wasted on the young."

***

I pick up my phone. But before I can look for tickets, my eye catches a cascade of messages from Jenny.

Hello.

Hello!

Oh, hi.

Hi!

Sorry.

Sorry.

So sorry I freaked out tonight.

It was dumb.

I am dumb.

The Drumpf hotel is probably nice. Obviously, it's nice. I could have closed my eyes in the elevator. Or puked a little bit in my mouth. And inside the room it'd be just like any other hotel. You were right, I was wrong, if you want it in writing, there it is.

When I hadn't responded to that string, Jenny said it all reminded her of an old college story. One time, we'd stayed at a motel upstate, near SUNY Albany, where we were visiting friends who were lucky enough to go away to college. And this motel room had a ginormous coffee maker, bigger than the machine Doc Brown dreamt up

89

to make a single ice cube in *Back to the Future III*. And Jenny was angry that weekend. She was always angry about something she was writing back then, something that imitated, something not real. But she was more pissed off by this single serving coffee machine the size of Montana. And you took charge, Ty, she writes me. I loved you so much that day. You said we could just *move* the coffee maker out of the room. I thought we couldn't do that. You said we paid for the room with cash and could do anything we wanted with it. So, we hid it in the bushes, and then, before it was time to check-out, we moved it back. This coffee maker was so heavy, we both had to carry it. It was like you always said, Ty, what you longed for—the book of friendship too heavy for one man to carry. The human creature unable to shed blood. Is the human creature unable to shed blood just going to end up being the robots? Is that the best humanity can do? Or are we going to put blood in the robots so they can bleed out when they kill each other? Remember when you used to say crazy, beautiful things? Remember how much we loved *Crazy/Beautiful*? And *Boxing Helena*? Remember when I would sit on the top step and you would stand at the bottom step and you would tell me things about your dreams for humanity that would make us cry? Remember when you had dreams? Remember when Tony Soprano said remember when is the lowest form of conversation? You know I will be the one you're thinking about when you're sitting in your fainting chair drinking pink rabbits. What I'm trying to say is that if there'd been anything in the room that said the word Drumpf on it, we could've just removed it, even if, after removing all the things that said his name, there wasn't anything left in the room. I'm sorry I didn't come up. I know you were trying to take charge, to be romantic. When I get back to NYC you're going to be uptown, right? Because I can't live uptown anymore, Ty … IF IT'S NOT WITH YOU. Come and meet me at Rhonda's. You will love this neighborhood. It's everything we always wanted in Brooklyn when you were too defiant to go to Brooklyn and you lost all the friends that meant so much to you. Come to Rhonda's. I WILL PAY FOR YOUR CAB. Or I will even come to Drumpf and meet you outside. You're probably right that, historically, Zachary Taylor was a worse president than Drumpf and killed a lot more people to do it.

I want to write Jenny back.

But not about any of that shit.

I want to tell her about my new girl, who will replace her once and for all. I need Jenny Marks to know that Ellory Allen isn't one of these girls from Ohio that she hates so much, no, Ellory is a blue-eyed mock Israeli from the Chicago suburbs, educated at an elite institution. What institution? It doesn't matter. One that bounces off any response from City College kids like us. We didn't critique there, and Ellory knows that without critiquing us. Hundreds of men failed to snag her. But I did. My woman needs her period to think, I start to write Jenny. Remind me why you need yours.

"What are you seeing?" Ellory asks.

"I'm looking for flights to Rome, babe."

"Economy Plus. At least."

"Okay, sure. I'm on Expedia."

"No, get off that. Go to the United app. Forget it, I'll call my guy."

"Yes, call your guy. Ah, Rome. I've only been there in the movies. You will be my *bella dia*, and I your *vero romano*."

I erase Jenny's messages, and then I even erase her number, even though I know it by heart because it's the number we use at the drug store, where I bought the tampons with wings on the side, and I still have it written down on a small card in my wallet, along with the numbers of so many of my other friends I no longer know.

"Thank you so much, Shel," Ellory says, hanging up with her guy. "Okay, let's get a move on!"

We stand up and get dressed. I tap my pockets to make sure I have everything. I have no idea what 'everything' is, but I appear to have it.

I open my wallet and drop a $20 on the bedside table.

"What's that for?"

"A tip. For the maid."

"Why would you tip a maid?"

"No, you're right. Wait," I say, looking at the nightstand. "Where is my powerhouse?"

"Your what?"

"My club sandwich. It's gone."

I also don't see my champagne flute.

I do see the daisy Jenny gave me on the bridge.

"Where is my powerhouse!"

"I don't know, baby," Ellory says. "What *is* your powerhouse?"

"Get out!"

I push Ellory into the hallway and slam the door.

How long will she wait for me? Five minutes? Three? I don't think a woman like her sticks around on the wrong side of the door, but then again, I've never really met a woman like her before.

A soft knock. I put my ear to the door.

"I know you're scared, Ty." I imagine her biting her lower lip. "I wasn't planning on falling in love tonight, either."

"I know, baby."

"Ty, please. I need you."

I open the door. I pull her back in.

3.

The vintage Mercedes is a pushy reddish orange, a high school graduation present from Grandpa Irving. The top's down, even in the garage, and Ellory drives us out of the city and toward O'Hare.

She's allowed to leave *me*, of course, anytime she pleases, but I will never let her go, even after I've fallen out of love with her, because I know she's too fragile for that kind of rejection. She is a ruined subject, like me, a childless, unenduring self. Sex ruined her eyes, sun ruined her flesh, sunbeds ruined her scent, tobacco ruined her lungs, cocaine ruined her nose, alcohol ruined her face, narcotics ruined her sleep, weed ruined her memory, incest made her a fragment, novels tricked her heart, life delays her burial but everything's going to be great, the scrim will lift after the clarity of a long haul and a sadistic shower from a busted water heater in a vintage Roman charm. Too bad Ellory knows little about me. Too bad we never got around to *my* downtown remorse, *my* unmarketable suffering, but there's still plenty of time for me to tell her Guatemala ruined my undershirts, girls ruined my women, the breakup of the Soviet Union coarsened my porn, and if my body is a temple, it's after destruction.

"God, there's so much news in the news these days, right? It makes me feel less alone."

"I don't believe any of it," Ellory says, tuning the cassette deck radio to Chicago's #1 Hip-Hop and R&B. "Find me a cigarette, will you, sugar?" Even though the top's down, and she blows smoke out the corner of her mouth, some of it comes back into my face. She looks so coughingly old when she says, "I learned in college that white people love critiquing consumerism unless black people are rapping about it. I don't need some basic black bitch to say *pussy* for mine to get wet."

"No no," I say in shock. "Of course you don't. These rappers don't see their whole race in bondage, they just pick up the microphone and feed it garbage."

"What do you do for work, babe?"

"I'm in management consulting."

"Do you like that?"

"No, nobody does."

"You can quit that job and manage some of our properties. Daddy has been having issues with these professors from UC-Berkeley who want a new microwave. Daddy doesn't want to buy them one, and now they're threatening to buy their own and take it with them when they break the lease."

"Sounds like they're forgetting what Marx says about leaving-with-the-microwave at the close of *Capital Volume II.*"

"Oh, honey I'm going to ask a DJ in Roma to play 'Big

Pimpin' for us. And we will dance the night away, to the end of love."

***

"Look at this *light*," we say, as we walk the walled-in Vatican, and history agrees the pooling of light at the Vatican is rich, magnificent, just superb. We walk for hours among the priceless masterpieces, until we're finally in the Sistine Chapel.

"Wait a second," I say. "This isn't the Sistine Chapel. There's no white finger."

We keep walking, and promise each other we'll keep this secret forever, that we thought we were in the Sistine Chapel before we actually got there. The next Vatican room and then the rest of them are all crazy packed, getting more and more packed, and this one *has* to be the Sistine Chapel, oh God, I'm so tired of looking at priceless art, no photos allowed, no photos! I snap a photo of the guard anyway, who points at me—Silenzio!

Silence.

Silenzio!

No Photo.

No Photos!

No Photo!

Silenzio.

No Photos!

Silence!

No Photos!!

"Do you want to talk about how, like, everyone in the Sistine Chapel is white? On the walls I mean, on the ceiling. Well, and most of the not Asian tourists in the room, too."

"No, not really," Ellory says. "Unless you do. I didn't even notice it until you said that."

"Do we need to say anything else about the Sistine Chapel?"

"No, it all looks like Gauguin."

Back at the hotel we share a champagne toast, have great sex. Ellory sleeps off her jetlag well into the chiaroscuro afternoon. I leave the room in search of an engagement ring for my Illinoisan signorina.

Through the use of four maps, I locate Via Condotti, and then an intimate shop just off this Egyptian drag. Over the diamonds stands a stunning Italian woman, probably the most beautiful woman I've ever seen, a volcanic goddess spurning all dormancies, erupting from the molten pages of a Paganini concerto, and she repairs cutely to my English, which I have trouble getting out of my mouth, but she listens with a switchboard operator's patience, as if she's accustomed to directionless American males who stumble into her intimate shop off Via Condotti, struggling, once they see her, with the fluency of their God-given English even more than with the nothingness of their Italian. She is perhaps a woman from a very tiny village where grapes and women like her are the only exports. She knows that if you speak two or more languages, you are European, and if you speak one language, you are American.

I tell this *bella dia* the entire story of my love affair with Ellory Allen. She suggests, how do you say in English, maybe wait, yes, maybe think it through before you marry this crazy American bitch?

"Pas du tout," I say, and then apologize for using movie French.

"Pas du tout," the jeweler responds, in perfect French.

"Will you just squeeze my chubby Americano cheeks," I conclude, "and sell me the largest diamond you think I can afford?"

***

Ellory is only just rousing when I return to the suite. I kneel beside the somewhat small, somewhat hard bed— not so comfortable like we have in America—and gaze into my lover's shocking blue eyes. On the bedside table I see the remnants of our champagne toast, and in my nose I smell, so clearly, the bacon from my powerhouse.

"Are you leaving me for an Italian countess?"

"There are no other women," I say, thinking about Jenny Marks, the woman in the bright red beret, the

First Princess, the Via Condotti jeweler, Elizabeth Shue in *The Karate Kid*, *Adventures in Babysitting*, and *Cocktail*; Ellen Reed from *Family Ties*, Jennifer Connelly in *Career Opportunities*, Samantha Mathis in *Pump Up the Volume*, Ally Sheedy in *War Games*, and the photo of baby Nas on the cover of *Illmatic*. "All of my life's fantasy is right here, right now, with you."

"I had a strange dream," Ellory says. "Apollo was trying to kill me."

"Did you, babe. Because I still feel like we're living in one."

"I actually don't want you to propose in Rome, honey. We must go to Greece."

Clutching the Via Condotti diamond behind my back, I say, "Greece, yes. Home of the bowls, the atomizers, the headless men and the spritzers. You will be my Narcissus, and I will be your Echo."

Ellory calls her guy. A few hours later, after an airport pasta repast—the most al dente short pasta either of us ever chewed—we fly first-class to Athens. And as the plane goes down, the sun rises, and we wander the old city, seeking pools of morning light, for here in Athens pools of light pool even more than pools of light pool in Rome.

"There's one. That's a pool of light."

"You're right. That is a pool of light."

At the Pax Americana Hotel, I read in a trilingual

guidebook that Greek prostitutes are the meanest sex workers in the world, and that the Parthenon served as a sort of central bank for the ancient Greeks, a discovery that surprises me, while also seeming quite obvious: the Parthenon looks like a Central American Bank.

"I know where we should make it official," I say.

We ride a free bus that cost 15 euros and stand on the ancient land around the Parthenon, thinking to ourselves, *This is ancient land.*

"Isn't all of the land on earth ancient?" Ellory says.

"Well, you know, there are those volcanos that form new islands. There's another one."

"Another island?"

"Another pool of light. No, no it's gone. No, now it's over there."

"Listen, Ty, I need to tell you something."

"What is it, baby?" my chest tightens, and that's become a familiar feeling.

"I love you, baby."

"I love you too," I say, staring at the central American bank. I summon a delightful, olive-skinned Greek boy I call the *garçon*. This *garçon* speaks better English than most Americans, and I let him know a magical moment of proposal will soon occur, and I want him to capture it on film.

"Do whatever it takes, man. Don't be afraid to use all 36 exposures in this disposable camera. You see it here, this camera? This is a *cam-er-a*, not a phone. I bought this camera especially for this event, at the airport in Roma…"

"…give me $20," the garçon interrupts. "20, American."

"Here are some coins from your European Union."

"I need none of this. 20, American."

"Isn't it enough to be in the presence of love? I'm going to propose. She's going to leap…"

"50…"

"…she's been waiting her whole life to leap…"

"…American."

I give the garçon the $20 that I repocketed from the bedside table back in Chicago.

"I will do now," he says, camping behind one of the Parthenon's ATMs.

I get down on one knee and present the Via Condotti diamond, but Ellory says nothing betrothed, nothing betrayed. "I'm flustered," she finally says.

"You're never flustered," I say, with a confidence that surprises me given I've only known this woman for about 24 hours of non-cruising-altitude time.

"Please rise," she laughs nervously.

"What's wrong?"

Ellory begins to cry, and I sniffle along with her, until I see, over my fiancé's perfect shoulder, the *garçon* snapping pictures. I attempt a cut-it-out gesture and I feel like the First Princess back at the hotel, cancelling the hip-hop.

"I love you," Ellory says. "I really do. I love you for bringing me to Rome, and bringing me to Greece, and even suggesting Jerusalem. I know you would take me anywhere, to Babylon, to Memphis. I told you everything. I have no secrets left. You know exactly who I am, and still, you love me. But I just need more time to think. I still haven't gotten my period."

"I thought you had your period now?"

"I was wrong. My cycle's all messed up."

"Well, that's good. It's only been a day. Maybe you're pregnant."

"Even when I don't have my period, even when I don't have any decisions to make, I will need time to be alone, by myself, I will need time to think."

"I will always give you time to think," I say, still making a cut-it-out gesture at the *garçon*. "I do have to say, though, that I thought you would leap. I thought this was our time."

"You must know I will never leap again, Ty. I already leapt once. With another man. My God I wish I hadn't. Why didn't I know you then?"

"Where'd you leap, babe?"

"On the steps of Montmartre."

"You can leap again."

"No, babe. There are no second leaps for an American woman."

"When did that happen?"

"Before."

"It doesn't matter. Take as much time as you need."

"You're sure?" she brightens.

"Of course. I would do anything for you, El. When we met all other women scattered, like droids in the presence of the force."

"You giving me this time makes me love you even more. And I didn't think that was possible, Ty, because I love you so, so much."

"BRB."

I narrow my gaze in the direction of the pompous *garçon*, put my fists up like Little Orphan Annie. This hairless child is still snapping photos, writhing his microbody like a scummy fashion photographer. If ever developed, these snaps of me reasoning away my disappointment with the non-leaping Ellory would look more like the surveillance grind of a social media concern than the greatest moment of anyone's life. At first I walk toward the young brute. When I begin a light jog, the *garçon* drops the camera, scrams. I pick it up and tap the wallet in my pocket. It is now $20 lighter than it was before. I'm more upset to lose the $20 to that running boy than anything else I've spent, so far, on my future bride.

That evening under the arbors we treat ourselves to a little gondola ride. We have dinner at a restaurant that reminds Ellory of any-old-Greek-restaurant-back-in-Greektown, Chicago, only it's even pricier and doesn't offer complimentary valet parking, nor does it have autographed photos of Chicago's #1 Storm Team on the walls behind the cashier, but there are photos of World Trade Center light beams, and sprays of fireworks over the Statue of Liberty.

"More of this delicious local wine? It's the sangria of the Greeks."

"Yes, more wine," Ellory says. "And yes, Ty, I will marry you. You gave me time to think today, and time to think is the only thing I've ever wanted."

"There's something I want, too," I say, slipping the Via Condotti diamond on my bride's finger.

"Oh, Ty, it's so beautiful."

"Are you speechless?"

"No, I can still talk."

"Good. Because I want your last name. I want yours, instead of you taking mine. I want to be Tyrone Allen. I don't want to be Tyrone Rossberg anymore. I never did."

"Yes. Everything I have is yours, my darling. But Daddy will have some papers he'll want you to sign."

***

104

We fly first-class from Athens to Chicago. The windy city feels still. Neither of us have slept, so we're hyped-up and speeding down the expressway in Ellory's high school graduation present. We park in the garage, leave the top down, and ride the elevator up to the 40th floor.

Finally, I get to see it.

Her condo.

In the elevator she lunges for me, pushes me against the wall and says, "Oh Ty, I do love you, I really do. You aren't tired of me, are you, baby?"

"Never."

"And you love me, don't you?"

"More than anything."

"We just never grow up, do we? We keep making the same mistakes. I love that about us."

Ellory opens her unlocked door. Sunlight smashes through the high, curtainless windows, drowning the open concept in cold pools of light. The room feels cold, too, never lived-in, empty except for a king-size bed in the center, sheeted in masculine pink. Along the walls are framed covers of *Crain's Chicago Business*, bookended by snarling African masks. My feet are on her Persian rug, and against the long windowless wall, a boutique style closest, with a wedding gown hanging in the center. There's a reproduction—or maybe it's the real thing—of Munch's *Death and the Maiden*. There's also a deathly man, a human being, I realize, half-dressed in a tuxedo. His pants are white, and a white tie, undone, hangs around his wrinkled, red neck.

He is Sheldon Fink, I realize, because he's the same man who won all the business awards on the wall.

"God bless America, bitch."

"Shelly," my bride-to-be says. "I'm sorry."

"Who the fuck is this?" Shelly asks, pointing at me.

"I got swept up. In other things. And I didn't know how to communicate."

"You were able to communicate the flights you needed."

"Thank you for those flights, Shelly, really, I mean it. You have a way with first-class standby that would amaze any woman."

"What the fuck's in Athens? Isn't Athens bankrupt?"

"If it isn't obvious, Shelly, it's over."

"I left my wife for you, cunt. I left my soldiers for you, I left my *daughters*. My children are never going to speak to me again."

Ellory walks over to her gown, pinches the intricate beading at its breast. "Men like you usually leave their wives *for* their daughters, don't they Shel? That's how my father's always done it. Shelly Fink, Tyrone Rossberg, Tyrone Allen, Shelly Fink."

"Ty is fine, Shelly," I say. "People rarely call me Tyrone anymore…"

"…we're getting married tonight, baby." There are

tears in Fink's eyes. He seems unusually humbled, for a man like him. I want to lunge at him, for insulting my fiancé, but I also want to hug the old man, maybe he smells like my Dad. I want to shield him from whatever swipes Ellory takes next. And it's exciting me, watching her in action. This is exactly where I want to be. The only thing I enjoy more than loving a woman is hating a man.

"I'm sorry you're upset, Shel. I am able to acknowledge that you're upset, as the politicians say. But it's been over between us for a long time."

"We've only been screwing for a week!"

"I'm going to marry Tyrone."

"Just Ty," I say.

"Just Ty, Shelly. Not you, too. Really I'm sorry."

"You kissed me," Shelly shudders, "in the pouring rain. And told me you would love me forever."

"Oh god, what did you think was going to happen? Did you think I would stand in the rain for the rest of my life and scream your name? I stand in the rain for me."

"You want to know something? Nobody loves you." Fink sniffs up his sniffling, points at me, and says, "certainly not this Cabrini Greenberg. He's just a boy."

"I'm 40. Actually, I'm 40½."

"He can't keep up with you. Look at his suit."

"This is a new suit," I say. "We bought it on the Via Condotti at one of Italy's finest fast fashion stores that has yet to open a stateside flagship…"

"…Shelly, I am sorry, but you should leave, we have to get ready."

"This is *my* apartment, you festering gape. All of it."

"Not my gown, not my rug."

"Even the shower rings."

"Be my guest."

"You're *my* guest, bitch."

Ellory takes a ginormous engagement ring off a European pillow and throws it in his face. Shelly ducks, then bends down behind him to pick up the ring. When he bends down I can see the outline of his white underwear beneath the white tuxedo pants. I say a little prayer that the pants don't rip because soon enough they will belong on my butt.

Ellory says, "Material things aren't important to me."

"HA HA HA! What do you want from her, kid? You want to tame her? You won't. You want to save her? You can't. She's gone. She doesn't want to escape. That's why she keeps running."

"She's my dream girl," I say.

"If this is your dream girl, kid, you're having a nightmare."

Shelly and I are fighting. Rolling around on the floor. The older man is much stronger. "Please, I give up! Not my face, please. I'm sorry, Daddy! I'm sorry!"

"You wimp."

"Daddy, no!"

"Sicko. I'm not your father."

Shelly punches me in the stomach, raises me off the floor and onto the masculine pink, and, gripping me by the shoulders, smacks me across the face. He cocks his fist. "No. You're not worth it. You're even less worth it than she is. You two deserve each other."

"Wait," I say. "Will you come back, Shelly? Will you come back and kiss me? Put your wet lips on my neck. Kiss me like you would kiss your sons."

"What a pervert this pervert is."

"What are these?" I ask. "They scraped the back of my neck."

"Those are my toenails," Shelly says.

"Why are your toenails on your fingers? Are you one of those tubby Jewish men who sit at your inground pool and never cut your toenails?"

"What are you, an alien?"

"But aren't you emotional at all, Shel?" Ellory says. "Won't you cry for *me*? Or was I just another notch for you, just another property?"

"I've had two heart attacks, bitch. I don't need to show my emotions. That's the thing about my emotions. Like my property my emotions belong to *me*. And I'm going to survive you too, you pretentious cunt. What do you think Marcus will say about this?"

"Oh, please Shel, don't pretend this is some kind of

inheritance plot and I'm the dowry. All I need from you right now is a little time to think."

"I'm going downstairs to call Marcus…"

"…you're such a good Jewish man, Shel, thank you…"

"…who will probably want a face-to-face when I tell him you're marrying this faggot."

"Ty," Ellory says, "how do you feel about the *f-word*?"

"Maybe you should leave," I say to Shelly.

"And when I return," Shelly responds, "I don't want anything of yours in this apartment. Because nothing in this apartment belongs to you."

"What about my Persian rug?"

"Why don't you get on it and fly away?"

Fink pulls down his white pants, and then he seems to have an idea. He pulls down his tighty-whities, too, and stands naked. In sympathy with him I pull down my own pants but leave my boxer briefs up. Fink suddenly seems ashamed and holds himself in his hands. Through his fingers, his whiteish pubic hair seems permed. It is difficult, perhaps would be difficult even without the sunlight pooling in, to locate the penis this perm protects.

I imagine it covered by Ellory's mouth. I wonder in how many planet Earth locations her swallowing of Fink's sperm occurred—on an island in the Maldives, an abandoned castle in Liechtenstein, in a club lounge at the Barcelona airport. Shelly stands naked for a long time. Then he pulls his underwear back up, takes off the white pants for good, and gets back into the cool brown suit hanging off the bed. He leaves the apartment, saying, "Even the shower rings, bitch. At least now I don't have to eat your vegan turds."

I go to the window, stand in Shelly's place, and look out on a brawl of buildings I will never own. The towers look shy from this height, in submission, in pools of river light.

"What a nice day," I say, staring down at the tux, "for a white wedding."

"Turn around, Ty. Look at me."

"I don't even understand what I just participated in."

"Oh, baby, you're such a joiner. I love that about you."

"So this is why you got so drunk at the museum with your teacher. Which one are you, Ellé, death, or the maiden?"

"I don't think of Shelly anymore, babe. I don't think about any other man. I only think about you."

"This is the big mistake you were about to make." I move over to the *Crain's Chicago Business* awards. "You were going to marry, like, the fourth richest guy in Chicago instead of me? Do you think Mrs. Prowler would be happy to hear this? She thought you were mourning the sick fox, but you were just marrying Shelly Fink."

"Mrs. Prowler will always love me no matter what. I can make it up to you, Ty. If you can forgive me."

"I forgive you."

"I know you do."

"Tell me everything,"

"There's not much, really," Ellory says, kicking off her heels and sitting in a leather chair shaped like a rabbit. "Shelly's proposal just took me by surprise, in a way that made me want to accept. I couldn't get over how much he was willing to give up to be with me. We met at Trump, you know, so that's why we were going to get married there. But now *we* are."

"I know."

"He took me to Paris."

"I might have thought it were Barcelona."

"Oh god, no, not that gaudy frat house. It was just Paris." She rises and moves over to her gown. "I leapt. Like I told you in Athens. I leapt on the ice slick steps of Montmartre. It was Christmastime, there was so much Jesus everywhere, so I rose."

"I thought he said you've only known him for a week."

"All I know is that I'd been wanting to leap my whole life. That's why I couldn't leap with you. Leaping in Paris was my last fairy tale dream. Before this one."

"What is this one?"

"This is the *one*, Ty. This is the carnival you can see but can't hear. This is the dream I've been having since I was a little girl. The one where, on my wedding night, I leave the man who is right for me, the man I don't really love, for the man I do truly love, the man I'm forbidden. And that's *you*."

"Why am I forbidden?"

"You know. You're a little different. You're from Queens and you listen to jazz. But that's why I love you. The night we met, you know, I was going to leave Shelly anyway, I really was going to leave him."

"I don't know if I believe that. You claim you're so alone, but I don't think you can be alone for one second."

"Believe me. I was going to leave him. But then *we* met, and *we* danced, and the best things happen while you're dancing, and everything changed again. For the last time, I swear Ty, everything begins. You get to be Tyrone Allen, and I'm never going to be Ellory Fink. Believe in me. And if you can't believe in me right now, believe in fate."

"Fate is our style."

"I know, baby."

"I just want things to settle down, for like, a day."

"I know. And they will. But right now, I need to get ready! Pull up your pants. We don't have much time."

***

Our wedding guests gather in the Trump Paradise Room. All-you-can-eat vegan caviar, champagne, powerhouse clubs subbed with tofurkey and shiitake bacon, and pailfuls of large, juicy strawberries. A 12-piece band hams up bossa nova versions of I'm-only-culturally-Jewish classics, including 'Gimme the Loot (Peaceful Protestor Remix).'

"Let me show you a few things about love," Abraham Allen swoons. He pulls me, his new son-in-law, to the side. Abe has a full head of thinning hair and reminds me of my leaders at work, like Nathan Wilde, who is the only man at my wedding I know. Almost all the men look like they would be my boss, or my boss's boss, jovial scumbags with trim waists.

"It isn't easy to love my daughter," Abe says. "Just ask my brother's son. Ellory's a smarter, even bitchier, better-looking version of her late mother."

"Your late wife had a Megan Fox thing going on? Like black hair and blue eyes?"

"My late wife had a lot of things going on. Many charities. I've got to say, my Ellory getting married to someone she only met last week…"

"We actually met this week, sir."

"Had you met Shelly?"

"Briefly. A strong man."

"Well, that's a Marcus conversation. This kind of switcheroo is very on brand, as the 14-to-56 crowd says, for my daughter. Trash like this writes itself. Now, what do you do?"

"I'm a management consultant, sir," I say, and shyly

name my firm. "I noticed our central region leader, here, Nathan Wilde, do you know him?"

"Well, she'll always have enough from me. I just can't say no to her." Abe tells me some moves his team will execute so we can set ourselves up in the city. First things first, Abe will buy our starter townhouse in cash.

"I can't thank you enough, sir. Ellory happened to mention some problems with tenured professors in Oakland who expect the property to have its own slow cooker."

"The microwave, you mean. That's gotten a little out of hand."

"There was something about the wattage every tenant deserves? Online petitions? Every popcorn kernel matters? I'm so sorry that's on your plate."

"And I'm sorry your …. father? …. can't be here today."

"Oh, he never would have made it anyway. I'll think of you, now, as my father."

"You have more than my properties," Abe says. "You have my blessing."

I taste rich people whiskey on my tongue and hear a deconstructed waltz, a secondary theme in a Mahler symphony I can't quite place, something that suggests the village idiot getting plastered in the brasses, and the oboes making fun of him for it.

It's time to start drinking.

In the middle hours of this contest, I escape to the bathrooms. On the way back to the Paradise Room, I run into the First Princess.

"You're still in the American interior!"

"We're returning to New York tomorrow," she smiles.

"You got these floors really clean."

"I'm sorry?"

"Did you manage to get your father drunk, by the way? I picture you as one of Lot's daughters. You're like looking down on the ruins of Sodom and there's nothing left to do but go back to your dad's tent and spread your legs."

"Well, that's not how I picture myself."

"Right. Of course. Sorry, wrong allusion. I meant I took you more for a 'Daddy' girl, from a Sylvia Plath perspective. But thank you for choosing 'November Graveyard' the other night. What a sense of context."

Nathan Wilde, my central region leader, saunters over. He is tall, with financially eccentric blonde hair. He's gained some weight since the last time I saw him, but he can still rock a black, two-button Hugo Boss.

"Now here's a *the one*," Nathan says, spreading his arms.

The Princess flies away.

"Well that's too bad," Wilde continues. "After everything I've seen and everything I've learned and everything I know and everything I've been truly appalled by, I want to say—on the record—that I'd still happily munch that poon."

"Noice."

"So listen, I spoke to Tweed yesterday, and he asked you to call or text. He might have a project for you in the East Region."

"I mean, where is the East Region? It could be Virginia, it could be Maine."

"I think it's East Midtown."

"I'm not going back to the rotten apple, no way. I've had enough of that place. Unless you guys really need me to. Then of course I will."

"Let's sleep on it. Don't think about work on your wedding night. At least not *that* kind of work."

"Noice."

"My congratulations to you and your storybook bride." And Nathan hands me an envelope filled with fifty $100s, American.

***

For our wedding song, Ellory and I chose 'All By Myself' by Eric Carmen. She shares a feature dance with her cousin Marcus, 'Didn't We Almost Have It All' by Whitney Houston. Marcus returns with Ellory to our table in a bespoke suit he'd wear any day of the week.

"You are the luckiest man," he tells me.

117

"Thank you so much, Marcus."

"But not so fast. Look around. There are other luckiest men in the world. Plenty of the luckiest men in the world right here in this room. In fact, the only luckiest man in the world I don't see right now is Shelly Fink. But he might be waiting for you outside."

Marcus lights up a Dunhill full flavor, tells Ellory he wants to show her some of the new *Star Wars* action figures he's got in his suite. They're the same ones he had as a kid, but now they cost him thousands of dollars to rebuy.

"There's no smoking inside, please," a waiter says. Marcus exhales out the corner of his mouth into their face.

"Marcus Zanzinger," I say, "killed poor Hattie Carroll."

"I'll be right back, honey," Ellory says to me.

"No. No! Please, don't go with him."

"It's okay, honey. Refresh my drink?"

I watch my bride walk out of the Paradise Room with her first lover. I still have a few exposures left in my Athenian camera, and I snap a photo of them walking away. I know I must now destroy this camera, I know such pictures can't develop.

I refresh my drink and I refresh hers.

After Ellory returns, more and more drinks are refreshed. Everyone gets drunk at our wedding, that's good luck. A lot of people hook up, that's a good omen. But Ellory ends up too drunk, the drunkest person at her own wedding, which is horrible luck for a bride, and I must carry her up to our suite. She holds her weight like a dead baby, and for a moment I fear my bride has expired, and if she dies, I wonder, will I still get to manage my new father's Oakland property?

"I hate myself," Ellory slurs.

"I know, baby, me too. That's why we're such a great match."

My finger reaches for the emergency button on the elevator, but the government won't solve this problem.

Not that there are problems.

Everything's going to be fine.

I carry the spoiled child across the threshold. I stand her up, remove her gown, and gently lay her on the bed. She smells like a wet dog in a Walmart. I'm doing the best I can, but I can't keep it all out of her dress. Some of it is streaking down her leg and onto the bed linens. Only now do I see what it is, even though it's the most familiar thing a human being can see. I wish I had a computer to help me with this shit. I need a pooper scooper. But what I find are paper coasters that say Trump in gold lettering. Gripping the coasters to halves, I tweeze poop off my bride and the linens.

I do this for what seems like a long time. It's painstaking work, meth head spring cleaning. This whole time, Ellory hasn't moved. I shift my queen around on the king-sized bed, she's much lighter now, and I remove the bed linens, pile them on top of her gown. Ellory snores. I take the gown, the linens, the Athenian camera, the cigarettes, the lighter, and a crisp copy of the *Wall Street Journal* with me out into the hallway.

Everything's going to be great, I laugh, then I cough like a cancer patient. It's only then I realize how drunk I am—this is going to be so good.

In the stairwell, I lick some of my wife's shit off my finger.

It tastes like being online.

The *Atlantic Monthly* runs a cover story about how fewer young people are getting married, but those who do are shitting themselves on their wedding night. I puke into my mouth just a little bit, ball up the real estate pages of the *Journal* lifestyle section, how to redesign the quaint but outdated kitchen in your ski-in, ski-out, and why it can be so stressful.

I remember how Ellory told me, You are going to have to do *everything*.

We still haven't gotten around to *my* suffering and there's so much my girl needs to know. I used to shit my sweatpants, babe ... tomorrow I will tell her ... babe, it's okay, I shit myself too—we talked about so much about your crap, we never got to mine, and everything's going to be fine, I'm excited to team with Nathan, all these anarchist political headwinds are good for business. The sensible tax cut means consulting budgets will increase. Firms will have more money for nice-to-have projects, a consultant's bread 'n butter. Abe Allen doesn't use consultants because he runs a lean family business and owns, with his silent Saudi partners, nearly all of the parking garages in Chicago. But big companies, owned loudly by China, still need men like me, Tyrone Allen. I need new suits. I need new ideas. I will even send Wilde a few buckets of ideas in the morning—it's almost morning—sketching out new offerings, and Nathan will reply, What are you doing working on your honeymoon, boss?

Everything's going to be great.

I set fire to the *Wall Street Journal*. Destroying nature to build your dream house, and why it can be so stressful to add nature back to it.

The gown and linens flare up.

I wait for the sprinklers to ablute my actions, but the sprinklers don't go off, and the fire alarms don't go off, someone must've loosened the regulations.

I need more *Journal* kindling. How to profit off the capture of my bride's agricultural waste, and why it can be so stressful on the sow.

I should set myself on fire, too. In sympathetic celebration. My self-immolation might be mistaken for direct political action within the walls of this politically charged stairwell. Burn yourself, not our flag, I say, throwing in the Athenian camera. Burn yourself, not our flag, I tell myself, you normcore socialist, you backward subject. I will do it. I want to do it. America wants me to do it, poetry wants me to do it, the novel wants me to do it. I will burn myself out of consumption, ash myself into simplicity, char myself 100% off, I am the ultimate Black Friday deal.

But first, I must learn more about the Oakland property.

Back in the bridal suite I catch Ellory in an up-snore, murmuring Shelly Fink's name.

I call down to room service and order us a carton of unsweetened coconut water and a very large glass.

"Do you smell anything?" I ask the server.

"Nah, I get paid not to smell shit."

"Thank you so much," I say, accurately tipping the young man.

I bring the very large glass to the stairwell and scoop up some ashes, being careful to exclude bits of charred battery from the Athenian camera.

Back in the suite I stand in front of the bathroom mirror stirring ashes into the coconut beverage. I stir, I stir, I feel so sorry for her, but everything's going to be great, at least I'm a real man, and this has got to be what Bob Dylan meant when he sang, *Empty the ashtrays on a whole other level*.

I'm thinking about how I learned the first few lines of 'Idiot Wind' from Hootie and the Blowfish, not Bob Dylan, and that must be why this is happening to me.

When Ellory awakens, she calls my name, not Shelly's.

"*Boker tov*," she says, joining me at the bathroom mirror. "Oh, my head."

"Drink some of this," I offer. "My secret hangover cure."

"Pulpy. Like we like."

"How do you know I like pulpy? We don't even know each other."

"I know everything about you. Here, have some."

"No, it's all for you. I feel okay, believe it or not. I drank a lot of water after we came up."

"I love being hungover with you, Ty. Never forget what I said the night we met."

"You said so much."

"We have it all."

PART TWO

"Leave procreants alone and shut the door."
— *Othello*

4.

The first thing we do is buy legal weed in a weed legal state where you can buy enough legal weed to kill yourself. Not that anyone has ever died from legal weed, as the dope store workers love to remind tourists, when they can remember, because they're always too stoned on dope talking too fast or too slow about legal weed in their free dope state, and how this strain of dope makes you a dope this way, and this strain of dope makes you a dope in the other. Dope was weaker in the 90s, weaker in the 70s, weaker in the 60s, dope was weaker pre-post-9/11, stronger after the Great Recession, and today dope is *stony*, so you can forget.

"I just want something that will make us happy," I announce.

"Are you guys not happy?" the Elevation 420 worker asks.

"No, we're on vacation. We're thrilled."

"But nothing," Ellory says, "that will turn us into gamers."

"This cheese is something."

"What are its observed effects?"

"Euphoria, pain relief, appetite stimulation."

"Appetite stimulation. Isn't that all weed?"

"Yeah."

127

We buy the cheese and a delivery system, a bright red chillum that enchants Ellory, the most striking piece of paraphernalia she's ever seen. As soon as we're stoned she knows that now, because she possesses this chillum, it will change her life.

"Mountain time, baby!"

"No, Washington State is Pacific Standard. I'm too stoned to drive."

We stand in the Elevation 420 parking lot for what feels like a lifetime but only ten minutes have passed. When we get back in the car, I'm still too stoned to drive. Ellory, who has always been the better stoned driver because she's a good drunk driver, and because women, she says, are much better at lying to themselves about what will and won't hurt them, says she can drive.

"I hope the car's insured. We didn't get the collusion."

"The collision."

"Whatever. I'm worried."

"The car is always insured."

"How can we know for sure, though?"

We got a blue Subaru hatchback, which we christened the Blubaru.

Not only did I get Ellory to take this, for her, slummy vacation—a tour of the Washington's Olympic Peninsula—I also convinced her to rent a car in a lower class than Mercedes. The Blubaru has an AUX port but not Sirius XM, and the USB can't learn to support the files from our phone's latest upgrades, and since we can't get the Bluetooth working, we can't listen to podcasts to understand what's happening in America, not those pleated flowcharts in the *Pod Save America* posse, nor those cantankerous loons in the *Chapo Trap House* aviary, nor repetitious Terry Gross, nor the bean-dropping episode of *Analyze Phish*, nor those *U Talkin' U2 To Me* episodes we have little interest in because of accusations brought against Bono in the Panama Papers, and because U2 sucks. And although our connectivity issue could be googled and a solution found, we will never go that far, because sometimes it's wonderful, especially on vacation, for things to be broken. The only music we have, then, other than the crinkly radio stations talking whiskey country and chicken-fried Jesus—those stations that pop up once you're so happy to be outside the city center and gulping the true mountain air—are the tracks located inside my Classic iPod, which I have with me because I *knew* this would happen with the ports in the rental car, an iPod that holds 122.30 GB of music. 15,978 tracks that would take 52.6 days to hear.

"Hendrix, first," I say, "and then Nirvana. Because we're in Seattle."

"iPooed," Ellory says.

"What? You shit yourself again?"

"No, asshole. I was just thinking of the way a Hindu genius in the Apple store says iPod. iPooed."

"Enough, you know."

"Come on, Ty, you're no phone."

"What?"

"I mean you're no fun."

"I can't believe Kurt is dead, but Dave Grohl is still alive."

"Grohl is a weird word."

"Grohl and Grohl and Grohl and Grohl, always the procreant Grohl of the world."

From my phone I read aloud that the front of the boat is the bow, the back of the boat is the stern, and John Muir deemed Puget Sound the Mediterranean of America.

"In Chicago nobody thinks about John Muir," Ellory observes. "But out here on the west coast it's always John Muir this, John Muir that."

"Noice, babe. I'll call 'John Muir this and John Muir that' the first joke of our trip. Many refer to the mountains on this peninsula as the American Alps. And this valley is warmed by a sun shadow—a sun shadow!—created due to a meteorological phenomenon ... a meteorological phenomenon ... that's hard to say ... a me-tee-or-logical phenom-ee-nom nom nom, involving the Pacific Ocean. Simply put, our weather right now, this weather right here? This weather is created by the ocean. It's coming off the Pacific!"

"Weather comes off the Pacific," Ellory says. "That's

very poetic. As if the weather is being erased from the ocean."

"Totally, babe. Scrubbed away. John Muir this and John Muir that."

***

We stay in several locations that week, inching closer and closer to the rugged Pacific. We drive the Blubaru to the next trail, lace up and hike in-and-outs with a waterfall payoff, and we try to make a baby under the waterfall, just like Tom Cruise and Elizabeth Shue in *Cocktail*. Then we climb back into the Blubaru listening to Neil Young. The roadside whiskey bars are named after natives and pioneers who slaughtered each other, the general stores are going out of business, and the luxury property brokers thank the peninsula for a wonderful six years.

When we arrive at the next VRBO we unpack the car, and the next morning we repack the car, removing sticky gum wrappers and unused napkins from cup holders and door pockets. Before a strenuous day hike, we wonder if we need anything else from the car. Often we return to the Blubaru three or four times. To get smart on our surroundings, we spend thousands of dollars at a local outfitter, and then we walk the 0.8 mile interpretive trail, headbutting senior citizens and learning the names of wildflowers and trees and geological formations we will immediately forget, peculiar to this area, like Flett's violet, never retaining, halfway understanding, even after hearing the loveliest of analogies offered by the gentle copywriters, just-so stories of shifting plates and glacial puddles and how successful mountains are failed oceans. The more lucid the interpretive trail analogies, the easier it is to appreciate the use of analogy in natural description, but that doesn't mean we move any closer to understanding the natural law the analogy serves. We just like being entertained with information, not absorbing it. On day hikes longer than 0.8 miles, we outfit ourselves with headlamps, high-SPF sunscreen and extra water, sunglasses, sun hats and visors, low-SPF lip balm and collapsible rain slickers because you never know how the weather will change above the timberline, walking through the clouds on a sunny day that might suddenly turn vicious.

We are the happiest couple when we set out on a hike. I take my dream girl's hand and swing it high, back and forth, an exaggerated schoolyard activity. We could not love each other more as we set out on our way, sinking and squishing into the soft Olympic ground. Often we smoke and/or ingest legal cheese and silent-hike, and then we return to the car and take off our hiking boots and socks and leave those in the trunk for a moment as we strap on our Chacos and wiggle sore toes, Ellory's painted pin-up pink for the summer, which looks démodé in the mountains, where unpainted toes are the proper cosmetic. I'm embarrassed by my own feet and think I need a pedicure, during which I will think, No man deserves pedicures. We brown our toes, foraging the dozens of protein bars in the disposable back seat cooler and drinking the cooled distilled emergency water. We deposit our waste in bearproof refuse containers, which seem to be human-proof, too. We drive on, even though there's not that much farther west we can go, past the desecrated logging communities where lives don't matter, past the Indian reservations set off from the highway like country club cemeteries where lives *really* don't matter, driving stoned higher into the hills, back down into the valley and beyond the snow-washed mountains toward the driftwood beaches at the end of the contiguous world.

We stand on the cool sands of Ruby Beach.

What a generative place the seashore is.

Facing the rugged Pacific, we embrace.

"Is this epoch worthy of us?" Ellory asks. "Is this ocean the third being we're searching for?"

"Are we searching for a third being? Let us remember this moment as the end of America."

"Don't you want to drive to Cape Flattery?"

"No way, I'm too stoned to drive to Cape Flattery. Weather comes from there," I point out into the surf, and on that largest ocean, Ellory, wearing my hoodie as a head scarf, also sets her gaze, and we kiss by the book, remembering we're in the mountains to have a child, and we say to each other weather comes off the Pacific, John Muir this and John Muir that—the bear-proof container is human-proof, too—and all of earth's oceans, just like the two of us, are one.

We walk the enormous sands of Ruby Beach, poke anemones, and make fun of the way I say *anemones* in what remains of my Queens accent. I turn away from my bride, and over the ocean I see Jenny Marks, levitating above the bascule bridge on the Chicago River.

It's there!

It's my tender house!

Jenny, Jenny, Jenny!

But then Jenny and our tender house disappear.

A selfie comes out perfectly, and Ellory decides not to post it now but save it for takeoff, so we will have Likes from people we've never met waiting for us when we return home.

"And when we get back near Sea-Tac, I want to stop at Hendrix's grave."

"Stop mentioning the airport at the beach," Ellory says, spreading across Ruby Beach with Joni Mitchell hands.

"Dayenu," I offer, staring out into the Jennyless Pacific.

We unpack, repack, but at this new place, the wi-fi doesn't work.

The VRBO caretaker calls herself Marilyn.

She claims to have an AOL email address.

It's time to deal with some bullshit from the American people.

I assume Marilyn has white-ethnically profiled me as a sinful Jew from Seattle, or possibly somewhere out east, a transcendentalist Jew who has had the same profession for a millennium—a spiritual consultant, like a rabbi, or a management consultant, like me, or, even worse, a lawyer who brings frivolous lawsuits, an abortionist, a titty bubbler, a labiaplasting cheapskate. And I can see Marilyn's hatred and contempt for my existence when she scans my vacation stubble, my dark sexual eyes and bumpy sexual nose, and my burnt sienna cargo shorts, the most fashionable cargo shorts imaginable, totally reinventing, as my Men's Magazines put it, the idea of the cargo short, even Donald Glover or Harrison Ford would rock these cargo shorts while dating a stunning Persian woman with a good sense of humor who is through making men smile.

To make this 'Marilyn' even angrier, I try to Jew-her-down on the retail cost of her locally made, lavender-scented body lotion, shelved and tagged in the cabin's bathroom like a handle of Evian at a Eurotrash hotel.

"$17 each," Marilyn says again. She is a lovely woman with a wise, stoic, wind-blown face, burnished from generations of living in these milky foothills beneath the stars.

"What about 2 for $28.50," I yell loud enough so that Ellory has to step out of our rustic yet updated cabin and ask, in a Dixie accent, if there's any little ol' problem here.

"This hausfrau thinks I'm selling dope. A lot of people don't know," I continue, "that the word 'jewelry' comes from the word 'Jew.'"

"You'd be surprised," Marilyn the Christian says, "what people know and don't know around here. That's why *we* won. And I know you know that, sir, because you can't shut up about it."

"Look, lady, I'm on vacation. I'm not a political creature in nature. But I see the network, I see the lock, you've even got an extender, I know it's there. I just want your main wi-fi password."

"We received your emails and your text messages," Marilyn says, the wind sweeping her rust-colored hair and the rust-covered windchimes. "And we received the emails you re-forwarded to yourself from the app and then replied in duplication back to us. If you could just show a little patience, sir, and try restarting the router."

"Fuck that. I know the wi-fi is faster in the main

136

house," I scream, pointing to the radiating carpenter's mansion up the slight hill.

"It says in the rental agreement, the rental agreement YOU E-SIGNED, that we aren't responsible for the speed of the wi-fi."

Marilyn's son appears, holding a shotgun. He walks to the front step of the cabin and fixes us in his gunsight. He wears the exact same cargo shorts as me, but they haven't reinvented the idea of the cargo short, they are the original invention.

"The city folk want their wi-fi, huh. No wi-fi, no tweets, no life!" The son pulls the shotgun, says, "Harvard swine!"

"Come on," I say. "I was educated in the New York City public schools and I will never let you forget it!"

"I dropped out of Reed," Ellory says, "and it wasn't a big deal! I still graduated, of course. Please don't hurt us."

Marilyn pats her son's butt inside, and I, somewhat out of breath but also surprisingly unmoved by being that close to death, resume my pleas. "I am a patient man, lady, I am an ally. But I swear to you, there is something wrong with the connection in here. My contacts won't load."

Marilyn places her hands on her hips and says, "Maybe nobody's trying to contact you."

We hope to consume the #1 tourist attraction in the Olympics. Hurricane Ridge is a magnificent natural site, a glacial wedding cake of frosted peaks opening into the strait of Juan de Fuca. We guide our Blubaru into the last remaining spot, which is handicapped. Ellory takes a handicapped sign out of her bag and hangs it over the mirror—a birthday present, from Abe Allen's police department contacts, when she turned 16.

The visitor's center smells of natural pine and pine oil cleaner. The floor is carpeted in a dark, torn-up brown. Guides to wildlife line the wooden bookshelves, and taxidermy eagles hang from a cantilevered, cobwebbed ceiling. The bathrooms are large, very clean, the water from the drinking fountains very cold. The main floor overflows with embattled tourists. Children scream at other children, kick their adults. Postcard consumers line up at the cash registers where CCTVs show a never-ending, never-changing, never-interesting film of the many, many Hurricane Ridge peaks miles above the parking lot. Tears fill my eyes when I see an older man, a father and a grandfather, standing in the center of the floor, holding out, to no one in particular, a creased page of his National Parks Passport Book. He is my father. I'm sure of it. None of the rangers on duty have the bandwidth to give my father his Olympic National

Park stamp. My dad looks like a refugee with the wrong papers.

Ellory and I need a plan. We corner a ranger, who tells us the parking lot up the mountain—the only way in and out of Hurricane Ridge—is at max capacity, with lines and lines of cars queued up to re-capacify it. There's likely no chance we'll make it up to Hurricane Ridge today.

"Shoot," I say, not wanting to curse in the Visitor Center. "We shouldn't have saved the #1 attraction for the Fourth."

"That's what happens when you travel around the Fourth," says a sunglasses-on-his-baseball-cap man, wearing a brown sweatshirt with a bear on it. "Everyone else does, too."

"You're so right," Ellory says.

"Thanks, sweetheart."

Another man wonders aloud if the lack of parking capacity has anything to do with the current administration's cuts to the National Parks Service. He asks a ranger if that is indeed the case. He then asks the ranger if she follows Rogue NPS on Twitter. The park ranger looks terrified, has no idea what to say.

Ellory scouts another, equally overwhelmed, a film of sweat around her lip. This ranger asks us if we have a plan B.

"What would a plan B be?"

"Oh sweetie, anything else, anything. Why not drive up Deer Park Road? First nine miles paved, last nine unpaved. It'll be empty up there because *nine unpaved miles* turns summer people off. The view isn't Hurricane Ridge—nothing is. But it's really something."

"Is that the backcountry?" I ask. I love this word. *Backcountry*.

"No," the ranger says. "It's well-marked. It's just not Hurricane Ridge."

Ellory murmurs that the Blubaru's AWD/FWD will come in handy.

"Do you know the difference between AWD and FWD?" I ask the ranger.

"I don't drive," the ranger says.

"Me neither," I say.

The ranger draws Ellory a handwritten map. While this is happening, the impertinent man shuffles over, screaming at the ranger about the daily barrage of threats to our democracy. I pat his shoulder and say, "It's alright bro, we lost. I know you know that because you can't shut up about it."

"Excuse me," the man snaps back. "I am not your *bro*, nor am I a part of your *we*."

"Okay, man, chill. I've read Ta-Nehisi Coates in *Playboy* at the sperm bank, just like you. But right now, you're ruining everyone's vacation."

Map in hand, we leave the visitor center and climb

back into our Blubaru. Enough dope has worn off for me to take the wheel. Ellory shunts off her Chacos and puts a high-arched foot up in the wedge between the window and the dash. Once we're on the road, she packs the bright red chillum. She still thinks it has magical powers, only now it's clogged.

The paved parts of the road to Deer Creek are frightening, the unpaved parts even scarier. Gaining all that elevation, the exterior temperature drops fourteen degrees.

"I don't want to forget Hendrix's grave," I say. "When we get back to the airport."

"Set a reminder for yourself."

"Of course, we shouldn't be talking about graves right now," I say, white knuckling the final swirls up the mountain, thinking to myself, these are hairpin turns. I can't see the breathtaking vistas because if I take my eyes off the hairpin turns the car will fall off the mountain and we'll die.

I've learned, in short time, to respect the mount.

"How's it looking down there?" I ask.

"*Très incroyable*," my bride says. "I'm so glad we did this instead of the *de rigueur* tourist thing."

"Yeah we are in the know, baby."

The parking summit is in the clouds.

Silence in the high alpine meadow.

Jagged, snowy peaks in the near, medium, and far

distance, peaks all over the place—holy shit. This *has* to be backcountry.

We take deep inhales and rub sunscreen on our forearms and faces. We consume a vegan, paleo, and keto-friendly energy bar apiece and drink from the gallon of ambient emergency distilled water in the Blubaru's trunk. At the trailhead we read the inspirational quotes by John Muir.

"John Muir." Ellory says. "He's to the mountains what James Baldwin is to the ghetto."

"Come on," I say.

"Oh what, Ty, can't you let me have my brain? If you go to the ghetto, you see James Baldwin quotes on the wall. If you come to the mountains, you see John Muir."

"Here's that well-marked trail sign the ranger mentioned. What are you up for? Loop? In-and-out?"

"Let's just start walking and see how far we get before we get bored."

"Shit, it's not a loop. Therefore, it's an in-and-out."

Ellory flicks at a cardstock flyer, written in bright red marker.

<u>MISSING!</u>

Male, aged 55, about 6'5"
Dark Caucasian, bald, bearded.
Last seen near Obstruction Point, wearing snow

pants and a green soccer jersey.

Unusual, memorable dude.

Kind of bizarre but overall a sweet man and very good conversationalist, if a little gloomy.

A perfectly good man.

(You get the sense he had nice hair before he went bald.)

A gentle man of rare learning.

TBH, this guy was a little nuts, but in a really calm way.

If you find him, maybe you'd be better off letting him set the terms of his own rescue.

We fear the worst.

Contact us immediately if you find our friend.

555-1212 (texting is best)

— — —

"That's a tall drink of lost hiker," Ellory whistles. "Is 'dark Caucasian' code for Jew?"

We read the sign once more before galloping on down into the subalpine ridge, which roars with unseen life. Once again we are in the mountains, and also entering the mountains, and also marveling at the mountains around us, which are also the mountains we're in. I take my wife's hand and kiss her wrist. She welcomes my touch. We can hardly bear our mutual sense of gratitude for this time, a happiness beyond description. If only this happiness, if only these first few steps, dayenu. We're so overcome with joy we walk nearly three-tenths of a mile without saying anything.

"What magnificent peaks," I resume. "We're so far from civilization. I read last night, that when pressure and air temperature drop, the air can no longer hold the moisture. What does that mean?"

"Pass me that," Ellory says. "Ow!"

A charging man has crashed into Ellory, smacking the bright red chillum out of her mouth with what appears to be a golden clarinet.

I lunge for my wife, to make sure she doesn't fall off the mountain. But there's no time to save the bright red chillum.

"Oh my God," the man says. "I am so sorry! Forgive me. Oh my God, are you okay?"

"Is that a soprano?" I ask. "I thought at first it was a clarinet."

"Yeah, dude! A soprano. Do you play?"

"Not anymore, man. I mean I never played soprano per say, but, you know, I played music, man. Enough to know that's a soprano sax you just nailed my wife with."

"What'd you play, brother?"

"Hello?" Ellory says. "Am I bleeding?"

"Sorry, let me see," the hiker says, lifting Ellory's chin. "Just a little bit. On your tooth. Or below your lip, I can't tell."

"I *feel* it on my tooth. Is it bad?"

"Let me look," I say, lifting my wife's chin, and already, I feel like I'm competing with this man. "We always say this," I say, addressing him, "but that could've been worse. You could've been carrying a tenor sax."

"I didn't hit you with my horn, thank God. That would've been much, much worse."

"Wow. I'm OK. Because your clarinet hit the chillum, not me."

"Wow, babe, you were right. That chillum had special powers. I mean, it probably saved your life." I pull a one-hitter out of my cargo shorts. "Hey, man, you want some? We still got this."

"I'm good," the hiker says. "Never had a stoned thought I cared to remember."

"Me neither," I say, taking a little hit.

"But I smoke pigs," the hiker smiles. "Is that sativa or indica?"

"We're vegans."

"Vegetarians."

"Today's pigs are tomorrow's chicharrons. Forgive me for saying that. I take that back if you keep the boys in blue in your thoughts and prayers."

"Oh please, we're cool."

"I'm a little shocked," Ellory says. "Actually, I'm really shocked. But I'm okay."

"Seriously, she's OK."

The hiker bends down, plucks a purple wildflower. "If you brush this across your cheek it will quiet the swelling."

"How do you know that?" Ellory asks defensively. "You brush me. Do it now."

"Is that Flett's violet? I was reading about that flower last night. Flett's violet. It's peculiar to this area."

"I'm so glad we found you," Ellory says to the hiker. "You've got a missing poster."

"I'm famous."

"The poster left out that soprano sax you're playing, though."

"So *that's* why they haven't found me."

"Okay, now I feel a little dizzy."

"Where's your water?" I ask the hiker.

"Gone. You got any?"

I produce my forest green Nalgene. "Here, honey. Have some of this ambient emergency water."

"No, I'm fine," Ellory says, her lip blowing up. "Let's keep walking. Walk with us..."

"Moses. Moses Murray."

"Tyrone and Ellory Allen. It's nice to be at an age where we can introduce ourselves with our full names. We're headed back, too."

"I'm so sorry, Ellory," Moses says. "Do you go by El? It means God. A reasonable name for you."

"El, yes. Not Ellé unless we're fighting."

146

"I think you guys already fought."

"Don't be sorry, Moses. I like the little moments in life that smack you across the face. You're hurt too." Ellory motions to a bandage on Moses's forehead.

"You should see the other cliff."

"So here we are in the Jewish mountains," I chuckle. "It's going to be a laugh a minute."

"Jewish laughter is a glitch in the matrix," Ellory says.

"You seem to be back to your old self, honey."

***

"This is a new composition," Moses says. "It's called 'The Bright Redness of the Bright Red Chillum.'"

The mountain prophet holds the horn near his mouth but doesn't play it. He never plays it for the whole piece. Then, at the very end, he furiously fingers the horn's keys, keeping his mouth close to the reed but never touching it. A few seconds later, we realize the piece is over.

"Wow that's dope," I say. "So conceptual."

"I can't believe you still use that word," Ellory says.

"What word, conceptual?"

"My husband is a walking Philly blunt. How'd you end up missing?" Ellory turns to Moses. "You don't seem lost."

147

The hiker tells us his story. He's from around here, Seattle, the town of Forks, actually, like Bella in *Twilight*. He's lived in the PNW his whole life, and he's got the waterlogged fingers to prove it. This year, he'd camped through late spring and into early summer up Deer Creek Road. He was alone, as he liked it, with only the park ranger for company, and the ranger wasn't up Deer Creek to do much socializing, either. Every morning Moses hiked out to the barriers of the obstruction point, but really he spent most of his time brooding in his tent, reading his favorite book, *Don Quixote*. The day before he'd gone on a hike with stoned tourists in town for the Fourth. It was nice to walk with new people, but he soon missed being alone near sundown, aggressively so, and on the way back to camp he veered off from the group and hid behind a tree—the same way Henry James once hid behind a tree, you dig, to avoid having a conversation with Edith Wharton.

"That's good," I say.

"I've known your Jamesian tree," Ellory says, "and have hidden behind it before. You had that feeling you couldn't even speak *half* a word to another human being. You had to be alone, that instant, even if it meant you'd be lost, even if it meant your own death. Yes, Moses, I know that feeling well."

Back at the trailhead, we read the language on his missing poster.

"You're a dark Caucasian."

"Yeah, interesting. Of mild interest. Not only did they forget my horn," Moses says, touching a discolored spot below his ear, "they forgot my beauty mark."

Ellory and I look at it.

This discoloration is the whitest part of Moses's face. It's not really clear to me if he's white or black or something else. Moses Murray has that kind of biracialism that fools even the most discerning human resources departments, where true whiteness emerges only in scars.

"Most white people are dead," he tells us, remixing a John Muir quote on the nature of the Indian savage. "Or civilized into useless innocence."

"See, that's something James Baldwin could've said."

"White people," I theorize, "only get to be Caucasians when they're lost."

"Are you biracial?" Ellory asks. "Or are you, actually, a dark Caucasian?"

"I don't know. I just keep getting poorer and poorer. Can you guys give me a ride?"

"Shall we?" I say, unlocking the Blubaru. Moses holds the passenger door open for Ellory and then climbs into the backseat behind me. I find it easier to ride the breaks down Deer Creek Road than I did pumping the gas on the way up. Also, I want to kill us all. With Moses in the backseat, though, I feel like I've got a psychological edge.

I know a man like myself—who serves capital, who fled New York and his one true love to marry Ellory Allen, an idle rich girl—might get struck down by God at any moment. But there's no way Moses Murray, a soprano-wielding hiker barely lost in the Jewish mountains, will tempt this earth any time soon. I know I'm fated to die, that I need to be silenced, but I'm also sure a guy like Moses Murray lives forever. And that's the kind of friend I want behind me on the hairpin turns.

"We're from *downtown* Chicago," Ellory adds, as she was born in the suburbs. "Right now, we're on a procreation vacation."

"Not our first," I add.

"Ty, watch the road."

"Maybe you could try with me," Moses says. "I could be your baby. I'm already in your backseat."

"Wonderful. Are you potty-trained?"

"Ellory isn't exactly potty-trained."

"That's hot," Moses says. "Love me a pee tape."

"You must make a choice in married life," I say. "Do you want children, or do you want to go to nice restaurants? More and more I want restaurants. And I think I might be too culturally damaged to inseminate her. We've seen footage. Read articles. Our brains are one tremendous essay about why the world doesn't need more people like us. I know all about the mysterious decline in white America's sperm counts, due to the non-mysterious use of plastics by all Americans. I've read exquisite Jewish novels about glum transpersonal professors who transform Dolores Haze into a plated octopus they want to screw more than their friend, who is a girl, but not their girlfriend."

"It's a beautiful book," Ellory says. "Hopefully in treatment."

"Sorry to hear that," Moses says.

"Haven't Jewish novels ruined my potency more than plastics? Is this really who I am, a charming ejaculating man, nutting Coenzyme-q10-fortified seed into *her* folate-fortified womb, pills I then crush into her powdered magnesium…"

"…pulpy, the way I like it…"

"…and after sex I go back to the couch and rewatch Season 1 of *Law & Order*. A baby-cheeked Cynthia Nixon is read her Miranda rights by a baby-cheeked Chris Noth. I understand all those references. Hasn't that ruined my potency? I'm obsessed with American slavery movies. I watch them every Passover, right after *The Ten Commandments*. I fast-forward to the historical white-on-black violence. I feel so guilty about this. I masturbate into no-show socks."

"Watch the road."

"It sounds like you guys need some silence."

"You seem to specialize in silence. I'm thinking of your composition back there, 'The Bright Redness of the

Bright Red Chillum.'"

"Loud or soft, you guys need a warm mental compress. That'll open up your reproductive pores. You should come to the club tonight. We're doing something a little different."

"Like what you just did? That conceptual thing of not playing?"

"We're taking that dope concept even further."

"Dope doesn't sound as awkward," Ellory says, "when he says it."

"Amazing," I say, asking Moses if he wouldn't mind putting up his backseat window because we're done now with the hairpin turns and gaining speed on the relatively flat 101.

"Yes, sir."

"I like that. When you call me *sir*."

"I'm glad, sir."

"There's just so many trucks. All the exhaust."

"Of course. And you don't want a bear jumping in the car."

"Wow, would that really happen?"

"Nah, I'm playing."

"Nice. Hey, where'd you go to college?"

"I dropped out," Moses says. "When I had like only two credits to go."

"There's no reason for a true artist to go to college," Ellory says.

I press Moses on the exact reason that he dropped out of college.

That's a question you can punish a man with for the rest of his life.

Sipping the ambient distilled emergency water, Moses says he dropped out simply because he wanted to. "Not knowing where I'm going," he says, "makes me understand where I am."

"That's why *Don Quixote* is your favorite book," Ellory announces. "A hero, a true hero like the Quixote, must always be blindfolded. Otherwise, the true hero would take no foolish actions."

"Yeah, yeah, no. For a while I forgot about that. That I was an idealist."

"All of you boys lose your way. But it sounds like you were *living* it, Moses. You were simply living your ideals."

"If living your ideals means working seven days a week at a coffee shop."

"That's what's so wonderful about capitalism," I say to this bohemian prick. "People like you, who can't afford to live in nice neighborhoods, at least get to work in them."

"You were alive," my wife says, and her glance to me makes me feel like I'm dead. "You *are* alive, Moses, because we found you. What good are the books we read if we're too cowardly to live out the lessons we learn from them? I'm like that with *The Idiot*. I know it backwards and forwards, somehow…"

"…you know the first two hundred pages of it backwards and forwards, honey…"

"…but have I learned anything?"

"You remind me of Nastasya from that book," Moses says.

"You're not the first man to say that, dude."

"But do you know why you remind me of her?"

"No, why," I ask the college dropout in my backseat.

"Because I can see, El, on your face, that you've suffered."

"I have suffered," Ellory whispers.

"I think you see that on her face," I say, "because you smacked it with your horn. Where are you a barista now?"

"Great books, yeah," Moses says. "Taught me how to etch a leaf in a cappuccino."

"But it's so hard," Ellory says, still flushed, "to quantify the true value of a liberal arts degree."

"Even harder for Moses, honey, because he never earned one."

"Wow, Ty, for someone who hates where everyone else went to college, you sure put a lot of faith in college education."

"I moved to Portland after school," Moses says. "Then I moved back here. I was voted Portland's best barista in 1994."

"Whoa," I say. "That's the coolest thing I've ever heard, right?"

"Hands on the wheel, Ty," Ellory says, because now I'm folding my arms against my chest, even though I'm still driving. Portland 1994 my ass, I think. This hipster who brushed a wildflower across my wife's cheek has spent the last twenty years making *my* coffee.

"Ty! Hands on the wheel!"

"10 and 2," Moses hollers, "stat!"

I grab the wheel, slam the brakes. The truck behind us swerves just in time, and with a thundering honk. Sheets of rainwater storm off the truck's cab, drenching the hood of the Blubaru and the highway around us in pools of light.

"I'm sorry! I don't know how to drive, I'm from New York."

"Shut up!"

"The signs say do not pass!"

"Stuff like that happens," Moses says, "all the time."

"But he was the reckless one, right?"

"You were the reckless one, dude. He passed you to save our lives."

"We don't feel safe," I say, my breath quick. "That's for sure. I have money, but I'm not proud of it. You're not proud of it, are you, honey?"

"Watch the road!"

"I think about setting myself on fire."

155

"Where's my lighter."

"I think about that too, dude," Moses says.

"Don't die," Ellory says. "You seem so happy. What's more narcissistic than wanting to kill yourself? Only trying to figure out why someone else did."

"You shouldn't think things like that," Moses says. "Don't you believe in mental illness?"

"No, I guess I don't. I more believe in suicide as a curated thing, an Etsy product, not something you just pick up on Amazon."

"Those who decide to die can seem happy," Moses says, "right up to their closing act. Y'all know the backstory of Pearl Jam's 'Corduroy,' right? It's not a bitter love song, it's about one man's relationship with money, and how money corrupts the seat of your pants. When Vedder sings, 'I would rather starve than eat your bread,' he's talking about Caesar's bread, not someone he loved."

"I always thought he was singing 'I would rather starve than eat your *breast*.'"

"Are you sure you're not hungry?" Ellory asks. "Please, take a protein bar. We have so, so many. And there are even more in the stores."

"No, I'm fine," Moses says. "Thank you."

"Maybe you would rather starve," Ellory continues, "than eat our protein bars."

"Over here. On the left."

I slow down with exaggerated, good-driver

156

movements.

"Not *this* left," Ellory says. "That left."

"Sorry. Yes, that left. That left it is."

"So have you guy's been here, yet?" Moses asks.

"Where is here?"

"My club. The Beaver Den."

"No," we say with a smile. "Not yet."

"Well, it's the best, and the only, jazz club in Beaver. First set's 9 PM."

Before getting out, Moses moves forward, saying he wants to kiss his mommy and daddy goodbye. First, he bends toward his mommy, kissing Ellory full on her swollen lip. She laughs, which hurts her jaw, and kisses him some more. Next, Moses moves toward me in the driver's seat, but with a tender, confused smile, I inch away. I do want him to kiss me. I want him to fuck me. But I'm too scared.

"Put your number in here, El," Moses says. "So I can hunt you guys down tonight."

When we're back on the road I say, "We should try to make a baby tonight."

"We should try twice."

"Anally, too."

"No, let's stay out of my ass while we're in Beaver. He's like Prince Myshkin, or something. Telling me I've got a lot of suffering on my face."

"You think you have suffering on your face?"

"I don't know. I've never seen my face."

"Where do you want to go?"

"Let's go to Forks. I want to see where he grew up."

"He kissed you. And he tried to kiss me. Kiddo was a real seer. I think he's changing our lives, but I can't tell for the better or the worse."

"Watch the road," Ellory says. "I'm hungry."

5.

Forks is a small clean American town named for the confluence of three rivers with Indigenous names. It has one road in and one road out, a clapboard diner, a railcar diner, a burger joint that serves booze, and a burger joint that packs it to-go. With traffic rerouted for Forks's Independence Day parade, it takes us like twenty minutes to find a parking spot even with Ellory's handicap sticker, the longest it has ever taken anyone to find a spot in the history of Forks.

We enter the clapboard diner. There are only two customers, opioid addicts with a plate of disco fries in front of them. One of the victims of the opioid crisis is pouring ketchup down on their fries, eyes closed. The victim she's with doesn't seem to notice because his eyes are also closed, and he's also holding a bottle of ketchup pouring down, thankfully unscrewed.

"Stop!" Ellory screams. "Sir, your ketchup!"

"Oh, shitty fuck," the reviving victim of deceptive pharmaceutical marketing says.

"Yo," I say to the sleeping man, "yo, yo, yo! Her ketchup!"

The waitress hands us menus, says, "That's just Donny and Marie on a good day."

"Thank you so much," I say. "Do you want to sit down, honey? We know they don't have Heinz, but I'm

159

sure the guidebook would say we will receive a no-frills, serviceable meal here."

Ellory walks toward the door.

"No offense," I say to the waitress.

"A little offense," Ellory starts.

"None at all…"

"…none at all taken," the waitress replies. "Happy Fourth."

***

On Main Street the people of Forks are celebrating America's independence. They wave Union, Confederate, and Blue Lives Matter flags, they light sparklers and drink original taste Coke and smoke full-flavored cigarettes steps away from their children. It's easy to get a sense why there was no disabled parking available. These people are in bad shape.

I'm thinking everyone in America is either a Jew or a hick. But I'm still uncomfortable. Certainly, someone at this parade wants to stand his ground against me. And then make a killing selling the gun he used to kill me on eBay. These bearded lumberjacks waving the flag of Southern aggression hundreds of miles west of the continental divide are racially profiling me as a dark Caucasian from the big bad city. I'm an out-of-network orthopedist who won't overprescribe sympathy for their knee pain. I'm running for political office as Forks's only Jew. Maybe, in Yiddish, comptroller means Jew. I will self-brand as the kind of carpetbagging urbanite who doesn't know how to screw in a light bulb without downloading an app, but a man with the acumen to unfollow those virus-spreading swamp rats in D.C. and shake things up for the management of Type II diabetes in America's forgotten towns. My opponents slam me on Rural Twitter: If you elect this day-tripping vegan vegetarian darkie from Seattle, he will take away our logger's axes, take away our daughter's purity.

Ellory points to a ginormous Ford truck proceeding down Main Street at 5 miles-per-hour, as if it were in neutral during a car wash. And in a sense, my stoned wife suggests, a Fourth of July parade is like a car wash, in that it washes anew the pride—here in Forks the lower-class cishet pride—of any small American town. In the bed of the Ford truck stand several brawny men wearing XXL t-shirts splattered with psychedelic bald eagles.

LOGGER LIVES MATTER!

MADE FROM 100% RECYCLED PAPER WILL NOT REPLACE US!

BURN YOURSELF, NOT OUR FLAG!

"Is this bitch looking at us?' Ellory asks.

"*Burn yourself, not our flag.* I mean I was *just* talking about that with Moses. I can't believe a man like him grew up in this town."

"I can. He's very brawny."

"She's got the right idea. Self-immolation is the only carbon neutral activity."

"Let's get out of here," Ellory says.

"Don't you want to see the demolition derby?"

"I have no idea what that means."

"Well, don't you want to find Moses's birthplace?"

"No," Ellory says, "he was born in our hearts."

We find our car in a silence, which lasts longer than a minute, and when we start talking I say, No, stop, Moses said we need silence, and we keep the silence a few seconds more, on the drive back to Beaver.

***

In the glowing evening before the stony darkness comes down from the mountain into the fertile valley we settle into our VRBO short queen bed skimming anti-slavery long reads on our phones for a minute and then picking up our books for two minutes and then putting down our books and picking up our phones again, one eye on the local TV. On this night of the Fourth *Independence Day* shows on every channel, and it's also one of the DVDs that comes with the rustic yet updated cabin, along with *Good Will Hunting*, *Miss Congeniality*, and *The American President*.

"What are you skimming and not retaining?" I ask.

"A think piece about your ex-wife's book."

"No matter what they write, the miscarriage part, you should know, that's true."

"Yes, Ty, you've told me."

"What isn't true is the abortion."

"How do you know?"

"She wasn't my wife, by the way."

"You still pay her mortgage."

"I pay *my* mortgage, it's *my* property, it's *our* investment."

"I've never forgiven you for lying to me about your relationship with her."

"And I will never forgive you, Ellé, for kissing Moses in our Blubaru."

"This piece. It's quite good. It's not about Miss Jenny Marks *only*, by the way, it's one of those roundups about Marks and writers like her, with commas between writers who have nothing in common outside of their fashionableness, and they put the names of the four books at the top of the piece, with the publisher and the page count and all that. All the page counts, let's see, are 224 pages. And this piece, oh Ty it's so good, it's by that white trans Jew who came out of nowhere."

"I'm glad it's the Jewish women who are now explaining our sexualities to us. Just moments ago they were Jewish men."

"That's transphobic."

"You're transphilic."

"They don't like it. Jenny Marks's little book. They don't like *any* of these books. They mistrust the Salingerian idea that books are supposed to make you feel like you've got a friend. Books should, rather, give you a respectable enemy."

"Has there been any investigative reporting into whether or not she had the abortion?"

"Imagine, quote, *The Catcher in the Rye* without Phoebe, or the ducks, and you would have these you've-got-a-friend books. Imagine, quote, if someone rewrote *The Great Gatsby* but they forgot to include Daisy, Gatsby, Nick, and Tom, and they published *Jordan Baker Volleys with Her Feelings*. That is the future of art fiction in this country."

"I have to stand up for Jenny's work in this case..."

"...because you're still in love with her..."

"...you yourself once told me you learned, at a young age, that poetry means saying a little bit less than you feel."

"That was before Mr. Lim killed himself. The suffering of cisgendered white ladies ... this is the article, not me... is overengineered. The writer says they don't understand heterosexual desire."

"You don't need a master's degree to understand heterosexual desire."

"Kathy Acker once said …. this is the article … that the male Jewish dead, who were alive at the time, were the bougie novelists she was running away from. She herself was running away from the middle-class, from the Upper West Side, sort of, and toward downtown forms of kinship, sort of, so of course Acker was running away from the suit and tie bards of 79th and Columbus. Because she didn't want to be Kathy Acker, her husband's name at the time, a sweet bookish boy. She wanted something darker. She wanted *Kathy Blacker*. But if Blacker were alive today she wouldn't be running away from Big Male Jews, she'd be running away from these little white lady books pitched in set piece Brooklyn, or snoozefest Berlin, internet addicted and centering a humorless Lena Dunham or Tao Lin jittery subject—Rupi Kaur without a sentimental education—who is only offering their damage *for* the likes. And these novels, you'll notice, are all 224 pages long, and many of these books, like Jenny's, have three portentous asterisks separating their micro paragraphs—as if white space predicts Black meaning. And these white ladies *love* to tout Kathy Blacker as an influence for the length of a borrowed cigarette at a party. But Blacker would've had about as much interest in their predictably daring subject matter as she would've had in building a vinyl collection from Urban Outfitters. It's similar to how humorless male writers in the 1990s couldn't figure out how to end a short story after *American Psycho* without a brutal act of violence taking place in a public bathroom. It all reminds the transthinker of a line from Blacker's 1982 novel, *Great Expectations*—there's nothing as harmless to a materialist as formalist experimentation..."

"...*you* proved this afternoon," I scream, "that you're het enough for the both of us. *You* certainly still highly rate your own cisgendered Jewish female suffering."

"Yes but I don't feel the need to write creative nonfiction about it."

"That's why I love you, babe."

"I'm so, so lost," Ellory frowns. "I try to get lost, like Moses did up Deer Creek, but the tourists keep finding me. I guess I'm not lazy enough."

"Oh, you're lazy enough."

"Do you want to talk about it?"

"Logger Lives Matter?"

"No, Moses. The mischief on the mount."

"No, I don't. Am I cuck, babe, or are we poly?"

"With a question like that, you're cuck either way."

"I just want to set myself on fire."

"Well, make sure there aren't any Confederate flags around."

***

We smoke cheese, we have sex, we smoke more

166

cheese. I place the *Independence Day* disc in the plastic tray and say, "This is going to be great!"

"I want to set Jeff Goldblum on fire," Ellory says.

"Yeah he's annoying. An almost universally cherished guy. He's often on the cover of my Men's Magazines. I browse the photos, skip the interview. Impeccable style."

"For the ancient Greeks," my stoned wife says, "persuasion was a God. I think her name was like Peitho or something."

"That's the one God you can be sure is dead. You can't persuade anyone about anything anymore, except their thirst for death."

Jeff Goldblum will save the earth from the enemy. Jeff Goldblum cared about climate change before it was cool. His good Jewish father gifts his climate-avenging son a prayer book before he shoots into space with Will Smith to defeat the enemy. Remade for today's neurotics, it would be a kooky Muslim dad gifting a deckled Koran to the Earl of Wakanda, but the story's the same, the center holds, kill the enemy and earn mock spiritual redemption through total war.

We observe many other similarities to our political climate and the political climate of *Independence Day*. You hate the enemy. Fuck the enemy. You didn't ask for the enemy, but the enemy is there. You try to speak to the enemy. *You* try speaking to the enemy. The enemy doesn't listen. Does the enemy speak in your voice,

America? The enemy doesn't care. The enemy can help with that! The enemy doesn't want to be your friend, the enemy wants to tear out your blue-eyed soul. You try enlisting the enemy, you try shooting the enemy, you try nuking the alien bastards, but come morning the enemy and the aftermath are still there. In order to keep fighting the enemy, keep reading the enemy, because the enemy keeps writing. The enemy isn't scared of riots. The enemy fears nothing. The enemy is an electronic fireplace. The enemy doesn't have infertility issues, oh, quite the contrary. The enemy knows you've never been to Coachella. The enemy has never declined a cookie, and the enemy lets you know it in the style of Cookie Monster. The enemy knows it *did* snow this early last year. The enemy is a walk in the park. The enemy is an obsolete word.

At the close of *Independence Day*, Will Smith and Jeff Goldblum save the planet not worth saving.

We try to make a baby again.

My post-sex dream begins as a sex dream.

It's the Fourth of July.

I feel like I'm back in the bookstore with Jenny, and all the pieces are assembling to create the dreamscape.

I am once again nestled safely in the white noise of Trump International.

In fact, in this dream, I'm certain I've been dreaming all along. I'm still sleeping in the Trump International.

I never did meet Ellory Allen. None of this, all of this stuff, has actually happened.

But then I hear silent music, like the sound emanating from Moses' soprano, on an even higher floor, a residential penthouse, and this time Jenny Marks swallowed her sanctimony and went up to the hotel suite with me, and we're making love on the orange, oceanic floor.

The dreamscapes shifts.

We're together again, in New York, in my apartment on the Upper East Side, doing exactly the same thing, but on a twin-sized bed, with screaming babies to diaper and soothe, telling each other false stories about how the seasons will keep on changing, and the cows flying over the moon will go on a milk strike.

Then all of that disappears.

I'm alone, again, back in Chicago.

In a church basement kitchen, arms full of mewling broccoli crowns.

I attempt to baptize the florets into a pizza box, but the pizza box has a map of Hungary instead of Italy.

I carry my cruciferous load out of the church and up the river bridge below Trump International.

A tourist dressed in beaver skins asks me to take a picture of him and his savage wife. When I raise the camera I notice the YPT in EGYPT polluting the frame.

A sail barge, heavy with post-consumer rot, rolls under the bridge.

I wave to the garbage at sea, throw down my green crowns, and the garbage yodels back, We're glad you're here!

The heavens part, and an almighty shows up.

You, God says, wagging his emoji-skinned finger, are destroying my planet. Burn yourself, not our flag. It's the only carbon-neutral activity.

That's what I'm always saying, the guard from the Sistine Chapel says.

Yeah, Mr. Silence, thanks for showing up. Is there any place in the world with a larger carbon footprint than the Sistine Chapel? Mecca? The Statue of Liberty?

Did somebody call my name? Christ says. Christ stands behind me, starts rubbing my shoulder blades, and says to God, Leave my child alone, Dad! Global warming's not a man-made activity. I'd have to understand more about so-called climate change until I can get on board with any policy decisions.

Thank you Christ! I shout, fisting the air. And then Christ gets replaced by something much worse—actual Christians, a whole gang of innocent brutes marshalled by the wi-fi password-withholding Marilyn, who wears a black Mets cap.

What you looking at? the Christians ask me.

Men have eyes, God says, so let them gaze.

I want to follow white Jesus like you, I tell the Christians. Please test the sodium content of my Cracker

Barrel Christianity.

Beware! Marilyn says to her brethren. Shield yourself from these dark Caucasian eyes. Look at his nest of curly hair, his Bob Dylan beard, his brilliant robes, his know-all-the-essays swagger—there's a Jewish pig in our pen.

On the next episode of *Yale*, rich Jews from Harvard argue with mean Jews from Princeton until the maternal Jew from Brown objects. *You* are that Brown Jew.

I am not a Brown Jew! I say proudly. I can do many things. I know how to retrack the drawers, for example. And I know how to start a fire, swish the wipers, spackle a crackle, clean any number of filters, and screw in the light bulb without dropping the old one. Brown Jews expect women to burn the bushes for them. That's not me.

Burn yourself, then, not our flag.

But I am not a Brown Jewish pig, my brethren. I am a Christian chicken sandwich made in China, a real American pig just like you. For I too have wept in a McDonald's parking lot owned by my father-in-law.

Real Americans don't cry, the brutes say. We know a Jew when we see one, upchucker of content, teller of jokes, swearer on money, carrier of plague. A rich sense of comedy, sure, but no brain for what sits on the other side of laughter, no mind for the still, small voice in the wilderness.

Yeah, um, I think you Christians appropriated the

tiny voice at the protest from *us*.

The brutes cock their legal automatic weapons, chambers warming with pig blood.

You'll be going, Marilyn says to me. Get, get.

I jump off the bridge and swan dive through a river of irregularly sized thumbnails.

There's Jeff Goldblum, the actor, the Jew who tells lies.

There's Lawrence Fink, the businessman, the Jew who tells the truth.

There's Noah Baumbach, the writer, the Jew who knows the difference between them.

Pyramidically, above these photos of Jeff, Larry, and Noah—a trinity of legal Jews—there's an historical photo of an illegal Jew, forcibly knelt before a cropped grave of freshly dead relatives, a licit firearm to his head. This rarer photo, a masterpiece of pointed cruelty—rarer because it depicts the act, not the result—preserves an otherwise routine massacre carried out by German ICE agents and their Ukrainian gig workers, circa 1941. The unknown photographer, likely one of the Texas Rangers standing on the other side of the Jew-filled ditch, wrote 'The Last Jew in Vinnitsa' on the back of the photograph.

Tall, trim, with good posture for a man about to be nonchalantly executed, the last Jew wears a slim fitting surplus trench, has thick black Jewish hair. In a previous wave of life, the last Jew earned a great sense of power, clumping that liberal head of hair in his hands. Throughout his life, culture saved him. He nailed the *Simpsons* reference, and the *Sopranos* reference, too—he implored a tearful shiksa to explain exactly how she meant the word *narcissistic*. But now, in the fertile scope of the Ukrainian's Walther, and the Nazi's Leica, every one of the last Jew's cultural locks are broken.

When I wake up, I quickly understand that Jeff Goldblum, Noah Baumbach, and Larry Fink all symbolize Moses Murray, although Larry Fink may also symbolize Shelly Fink, duh. And the Jew getting shot, and the Nazi shooting him, and the relaxed yet impatient agents massed behind the Jew-filled ditch—for whom the Holocaust will never happen—all those guys, too, are Moses Murray, and even the Nazi who saved and savored this photograph, the Nazi who gave this photo its descriptive, poetic name, he too is the prophet from the mountains we met today up Deer Creek Road.

But in the Jew who steals the photo from that Nazi and carries it through the halls of Arendtian justice; the Jew who always magically appears, bending himself to the will of the stars like a Chagall extra to make all Jewish fairy tales believable; the Jew who knows 'The Last Jew in Vinnitsa' ends up on the slate gray walls of every Holocaust museum in the overdocumented west and in the post-sex dreams of every self-persecuted smart ass, in that Jew, I see only myself.

As dreamy Ben Stiller.

***

On *her* side of the post-sex bed, with the earth rescue sequence of *Independence Day* rerunning on the TV, my wife debates whether or not to respond to a string of messages she's received from Moses Murray.

The content of his conversation delights her. She's amazed Moses can write so ardently on a flip phone. His last missive ends with the question every girl wants to hear: Does Ellory know Furtwängler's recording of Mozart's wind serenade?

My wife has received messages like these before. I've sent them to her myself. There was that drippy guy, her ex before Shelly Fink, who couldn't hear Rachmaninoff's *Paganini Variations* without wanting to push her into an early grave. Or the dude who couldn't hear *Rhapsody in Blue* without wanting to murder her in Harlem. Ellory Allen isn't some Murakami manic pixie classical music dream girl. She hates that mechanical pencil Hello Kitty twee shit. But she answers any message from a man who loves her. She encourages desperate, brilliant men.

Yes, she responds to Moses, I know it.

Then you know Furtwängler, Moses replies, transforms this gorgeous chamber serenade, gorgeous even for Mozart, beyond the composer, beyond Mozart, beyond music, so that nothing of Mozart's gorgeous genius remains. And that's exactly how you moved me today, El. As soon as you looked up from being bruised by my soprano, I knew you were the most beautiful woman I'd ever seen. For your beauty moves me beyond the genius of Mozart. I don't want to say that me hitting you with my soprano must have felt like a kiss.

Then don't, don't say that. Simply say, our kiss felt like a kiss.

Our kiss felt like a kiss. Oh, I am so glad to hear you say that! And I am not a man who will ever take you lightly. Your husband, he takes you for granted.

You don't know my husband.

Do *you*? Because I think he takes you lightly, and it's a mistake to take you lightly. Just as it's a common mistake to take Mozart lightly, a grave mistake to think Mozart wistful, merely tuneful, Mozart for dishwashing, to think Mozart's music 'as-is' with nothing to be brought to it. You are perfect, El, it's true. You are exactly my type.

What is your type?

A woman like you, with black hair, blue eyes, a mischievous yet innocent look.

Don't you think I deserve a placard at the Art Institute?

Indeed. You should be hung. You are Mozart made flesh. A late sonata in living form. But only an amateur like your husband would see you and think, This woman is a gift from God, this woman was written by a genius, so nothing needs to be done. Only a man as deaf as your husband would think, All I must do is listen while she speaks to me, ask open-ended questions, do whatever she says—all I must do is play the right notes. On the contrary. That is not how genius works. There is a tremendous amount of care and divination that must be brought to perfect things. The score never plays itself. We must persuade the beautiful out of the trendy clutches of quotidian oblivion...

...are you typing on a flip-phone, or a laptop? Do you dictate? I hope you're not operating heavy machinery right now.

No, ha ha, I'm at the Beaver Den, on my old black MacBook, warming up, waiting for you, my miracle, to walk through that door.

I love my husband, Ellory writes to Moses. But I've loved men before. A part of me wants to spend the rest of my life telling men like you that I love my husband, I'm saving all my love for Ty, I'm through being an asshole. But that's not what I'm feeling right now. Right now, I want change. I want art. I want to take you deep in my mouth. If I tell you *I love my husband* it's like I'm saying *I hate Mozart*. And who can hate Mozart for long?

I am so hard, Moses writes.

Are you, baby?

Yes. I'm thinking of a passage. From the *Quixote*.

The *Quixote*, you say.

A passage from the *Quixote* that reminds me of you. The plea of Marcela, a woman trapped in the valley: Let these mountains mark the limit of my desire.

Let these mountains, Ellory writes, mark the limit of my desire. How beautiful. The limit on desire is the invention of heterosexuality, is it not? And I don't want anything as limiting as heterosexuality coming between us.

Nor I, my sweet. Do you know the story of Marcela?

Remind me.

She was a beautiful woman, a serenade incarnate. Because of her beauty, she could find no peace.

I am like that, Moses. Because of my beauty, I can find no peace.

Marcela wanted to be left by herself...

...that is all I want...

...in the valley, so she could remain a virgin...

...well, it's a bit late for that...

...and ward off the advances of lustful men. And that is what you long for, El.

Tell me what I long for, Moses.

You long for an end to prickly desire. That is me. I am your prick. Your man in the mountains. The limit of your desire is me.

First *The Idiot*'s Nastasya, and now the *Quixote*'s

Marcela. You're seducing me.

And it's working. For I am going to steal you away. Your husband, in protest, will set himself on fire.

Oh please. Ty can't even light a match.

I'm not against anyone killing themselves. If killing ourselves is our only escape from killing others then kill yourself, I say.

I say that too. People who kill themselves have executed their only original idea.

That's right. And in their destruction they create one less mouth. Hey lover, are you an anti-natalist?

I am. Although we desperately want a child.

Right, right. Well, I'm sorry to hear that. Your husband won't kill himself, you know. He will do something much worse. He will survive. And he'll get over you. Because he lacks courage, your husband. Your husband is a happy man.

It would sadden him to hear you say so.

I like your husband. And I applaud his hard work and success. You, of course, being his central achievement. And at one point in my life, I too wanted to achieve, I too wanted to work hard like your husband. And I could have. The winds of privilege blew me along. I dreamt of living the life of the high-earning man, the man who turns into his circular drive without signaling, the man who owns a wristwatch that costs more $29.99. A man, like your husband, who has an angry 20th century man deep inside of him. But I dropped out. I'm nothing, now, I'm even less than a man, who draws leaves in coffee seven days a week…

…oh Moses we need to get you out of that, you can manage some of Daddy's properties…

…who has no airline miles, but when I look up I still see the sky. Your husband has hundreds of thousands of miles, yards and yards of sky. All he wants to do is earn points, points he will surely miss. He can't accept his happiness. For him, happiness is something you need to get rid of. When you leave your husband for me …

…who says I am leaving my husband?…

…when you leave your husband for me, he will be relieved. I could see that on his face today on the mountain. He will do nothing, absolutely nothing, to get you back. He will follow his happiness away from you because you are not where his happiness resides.

You learned all of this about us in like twenty minutes.

I learned much, much more, my passion flower, my iris, my single petal of a rose. You and your husband seemed more like debate team combatants than husband and wife. More like rappers in rival crews than high-bouncing lovers.

Oh Moses, Moses, men have killed themselves for me before. What makes you think Ty won't kill himself if I leave him for you?

I am one of those men who would die for you, El. Not

your husband. You must leave your husband. You must leave him TONIGHT. You must leave him if you don't want another man to die.

I want to leave him. I really kind of do. And I haven't felt like this for a long time. Will you take me to Tokyo tonight?

Why Tokyo?

I've never been to Japan.

I can't even afford a cup of saké, honey.

Have no fear. Ty and I will take care of the arrangements. On the flight I will have time to tell you the history of my body. I will tell you about Marcus. Mr. Lim. My horrible father. I will tell you about Grandpa Irving. With you I will remember my roommate's name. But maybe we will need more time than the flight from Seattle to Tokyo for me to tell you about all my suffering. We will need to *sail* to Tokyo, yes, an ocean liner. At sea I will have enough time to tell you the history of my body, the history of my mind, and my mind/body problems. Well, we won't sail from Seattle to Tokyo, though, we'll fly from Seattle to New York and then to Paris, and after a week in Paris take a train to Moscow, then the Trans-Siberian across Russia, the Trans-Manchurian through Mongolia and Beijing, and finally, from Hong Kong we'll fly private into the land of the rising sun. And maybe that'll be enough time to prove to you that you have guessed correctly about the suffering you see in my face, that you have been able to sum up the cost of my unlimited desire.

I love everything you just said, Moses writes. I have only one condition. You can't bring your guilt. You leave your guilt on the commute between me and your husband. You don't bring your guilt to either destination, no matter who you choose. If you come to me, you have no guilt. If you stay with him, same.

Marcela. I am Marcela. I am so lonely.

Yes, my sweet, Marcela, you are. A woman too beautiful to be left alone. Even though being left alone was all she wanted. A woman who wanted mountains, not men, to assert the borders of her map. A lonesome valley girl, surrounded by thousands of suitors.

So lonely.

Very lonely, you are. As the Italians say—*solissima*.

Solissima. That is right. Very lonely in Italian. Why, that's so often how I feel.

Very lonely, in Italian.

"*Solissima*," Ellory says aloud. "*Soliss...*"

"...who's Solissima," I ask.

"No, *solissima*, babe," she says.

"Who's that? Your gyno? Did we bring the toenail clipper with us?"

"No, we have the small clipper."

"Are you masturbating?"

"Yes."

"Let me help."

"No. You find the clipper, baby."

"We check bags," I say in a comedic Adam Sandler accent, "and we don't even bring the toenail clipper!?!"

"You can use the small clipper on your toenails, honey."

"No, you can't."

"Yes, yes, yes, you can."

"My dad always said you shouldn't do that."

I look around the cabin for the small clipper. I use it and, just as I feared, clip too close to the skin. Agony. What horrible pain! The nail reddens into the idea of blood, then appears to go gray.

"Shit. This'll ruin my life for a week."

"*Solissima*," Ellory gasps.

"Who were you texting with?"

"Moses."

"Ah, the prophet. Tell me everything."

"What do you want to know, babe?"

"Every single thing."

I admire my throbbing toe. The joke's on me, and the vipers are in the grass. In the old books, I would've learned Ellory Allen was leaving me for Moses Murray by some trick of perspective, some crafty innovation, like I'm staring through the peephole, like the letters have been crossed, so I can save my wife, my queen, my castle, my kingdom. But that's not how I learn about things today. Today every man is a dynasty. Today I am my own voiceover, smarter than even I realize, the pain in my toe telling me I need to walk out of this life, walk out on this girl, and go back to New York where people like me belong. But I can't. I have to say. I wouldn't miss this for the world.

6.

We leave the cabin and drive to downtown Beaver. There's an overflow in the parking lot, and Ellory instructs me to park on the side of the road, the right side that I'd previously thought the left. I'm hesitant, but Ellory insists that's what people do in the mountains, they improvise parking spots.

"You think there are cops, though, checking the meters?"

"There are no *parking meters* at this altitude!"

"I bet you that Rogue NPS Twitter dude, who isn't my bro, would beg to disagree with you."

"He's not here," Ellory says.

We beep the Blubaru shut and walk to the entrance, guarded by a jaunty young man on a high stool. He has a handlebar mustache, like a relief pitcher from the 1970s. He has an unlit, brown-filtered cigarette in his mouth. On his lap sits an overturned copy of Jane Austen's *Mansfield Park*.

"You're fine," he says to me. "Can I see yours real quick?"

"We're exactly the same age," I say, annoyed that men only card my wife so they can look at her for a few more seconds. "That novel," I say, "is about a bunch of young people putting on a play, isn't it?"

"You read it?"

"No. I mean nobody *reads* Jane Austen. But I saw this movie once about a guy who had also never read it, but he'd read a Lionel Trilling essay about it."

"Have you read the Lionel Trilling essay?"

"Nah."

"Okay, you guys are good. Enjoy."

***

The Den, Beaver's only jazz club, is a dark and cozy performance space. There are red lights strung up in the bar mirror, which makes the whole place look bigger than it is. The stage is near the back, slightly elevated, an upright piano, drum set with a pillow to muffle the bass drum, a double bass on its side, and three saxophones in the center. In front of the stage are small round tables, illuminated by candles in covered domes.

We choose a table against the stage left wall, under a reproduction of *A Great Day in Harlem*. We're 3,000 miles from Harlem, yet through the miracle of photography, Harlem is right behind us, just like Confederate flags, through the miracle of racism, were at the parade today in Forks.

"I'm really happy we motivated," Ellory says.

"Oh, sure. What would our marriage mean if we didn't destroy it? Excuse me, I've got to use the can."

I know I should just get out of here, but I walk down the hall, my toenail smarting, and I'm smelling French fries, so yummy, they smell like the powerhouse club that disappeared from my nightstand at Trump International. The hallway's lined with more prestige posters of Jazz Age New York: the awning of the Village Vanguard, raindrop reflections in the front window of the Blue Note, the stairway leading down to Smalls. There's an unplugged Arkanoid video game, a gumball machine for muscular dystrophy, a no-logo, high-fee ATM, and tied stacks of a newspaper, *The Stranger,* which must be Seattle's struggling alt-weekly.

In the dank bathroom, lit by red bulbs over scratched mirrors, there are cheaply framed pictures of brawny loggers, hundreds of quietly energetic men standing afront the trees they've felled. When using the stall, I notice the one next to me has no fixture but instead a recessed garden, a glowing, beetle-backed terrarium, and I want to burrow into this garden, and out of this Beaver Den, to avoid my upcoming humiliation. But I return to the table, and see Moses Murray sitting in *my* seat, a plate of disco fries in front of him, a bottle of Heinz.

"I mean, we're in Beaver. But we could be in the West Village."

"Isn't that the vibe, brother?" Moses says.

"Oh yeah, no doubt, buddy, those are the viberoonis."

"You want a fry, Fry Ty?" Moses asks, his mouth full of them.

"Beware," Ellory says. "He said they're fried in duck fat."

"Don't you wish I hadn't told you now?"

"No. I'm glad you told me."

"Come on, babe," I say, "we're on vacation. We can have some duck fat fries."

"I don't want duck fat fries."

Moses stuffs his mouth.

"You eat like a pig," Ellory says. "Wait, why blame the pigs? You eat like a human being."

"Oink, oink."

"We're vegetarians."

"Vegans."

"Right, I mean, I get it, I get it, I mean, I'm vegetarian too, bro."

"*You're*   vegetarian."

"I just don't have the energy," Moses says, "to talk about it all the time."

"Maybe you need more protein."

"Or maybe it's because your mouth's full of duck fat fries."

"What's one duck?"

"When's your first set?" I ask.

"We're only playing one. Here, finish these. Eat around the duck fat. I'm so glad you guys came."

"Us too," we smile in unison.

***

There are maybe twenty people in the club when the Moses Murray Quartet takes the stage. Most of the crowd are beatniks who look like they read books and are also *in* books, but there are a few bearded loggers too, who could've just stepped off the Logger Lives Matter float at the parade. The other musicians are dressed just like Moses in dark pants, a tuxedo shirt, chauffeur's cap, and Capone blue bowties.

Moses stands in front of his saxophones, shuffles his hips like Elvis, and asks the already quiet crowd to simmer down.

"Happy Independence Day," he begins, greeted by boos. "I hear you, my friends. Independence Day means many things to many people. It means what Freddie Douglass said it meant, brass fronted impudence, y'all. But it also means yummy white mama potato salad, you dig."

The loggers applaud, the beatniks sniff.

"All right, all right. Now we play free music here, everyone, free improvised music. But donations are always accepted, ha. Y'all know that *Onion* article, right: "Experimental Band Theoretically Good?" I swear sometimes you can't tell what's real and what's from the

Onion!"

"Oh, shut the fuck up," a heckler shouts.

"Now we play free music here," Moses begins again. "We don't call it jazz music. And we're not ashamed to not call it jazz music. What's more American than jazz music? No-abortions-even-in-the-case-of-rape-or-incest is the only thing more American than jazz, you dig. And that's why we don't play jazz. Because we fear for the health of all you motherfuckers. And we have a free composition for you here, ladies and gentlemen. Now I met a beautiful couple today. A couple from the East, from the middle of the country, from the Middle East, from an elite Middle Eastern ci-tay. And we were munching on protein bars, only we never ate one. Man, I've never talked about protein bars so much in my lifetime as I talked about protein bars today. The ways of proteins, the vanilla beans of proteins, the proteins of the haves, the proteins of the have-nots, the proteins with the rice brand flour, you dig, and those proteins full of carrageen. Y'all know those soy isolate dirges, shit, y'all know those maltodextrin blues."

"Play your horn!" a heckler shouts.

"Play 'Freddie Freeloader!'" shouts another.

"You bum!"

"And during our talk about protein bars," Moses resumes, "I felt like I was in chains. And I remembered a story Anthony Braxton once told me. How Brother

Tony was too poor to be vegetarian. He and some other musicians were looking for food in Copenhagen, or maybe Sofia, cap ci-tay of Bulgaria, if you've ever been, beautiful place. They were looking for vegetarian food because the wealthy journalist wanted some. But Braxton couldn't afford vegetarian food. He was looking for the nearest McDonalds. Because he was poor. And it's such a bore, as Brother Langston wrote, being always poor. And it was around this time, you dig, that Tony wrote his composition for one hundred tubas. Now I don't believe, and I don't know if any of you know, or my band mates know—no, they're shaking their heads, they don't know, and y'all are shaking your head, so you don't know—if that composition for one hundred tubas has ever been recorded, or even performed. I suppose we could rev up our googling engines, right right, but I'd rather leave Tony's tubas un-googled. I'd rather meditate on the audaci-tay of this silly, meat-eating man, who wrote a composition for one hundred tubas, when he couldn't even afford a TLT. That's a tempeh lettuce and tomato, you dig. I want you to imagine being so poor, and so happy, and so silly, that you too wrote a piece for one hundred tubas. Because that's what the day of our independence is all about."

Moses looks back at his quartet, turns back around to the audience, and raises his arms like he's conducting the crowd. He lids his eyes, sucks in a long pause. "This next composition is called, 'One Hundred Vegetarian Tubas.'"

He places his tenor reed to his mouth and counts the number off in 7/4 time. But just like earlier that day on the mountain, he doesn't play. The piano player doesn't play, only spreads her hands across the piano. The bass player bends his fingers, but he doesn't pluck. The drummer holds his brushes above the snare, without brushing. The Quartet doesn't play for what feels like hours, but only a few seconds pass. Finally, Moses releases the reed from his mouth, smiles, and nods his head, suggesting to the room that this piece, which had never been played before, and wasn't played for the first time just now, can now be applauded.

The crowd roars.

"Thank you very much, ladies and gentlemen. That one takes a *lot* out of us. Now I'd like to introduce the band. Carl Icahn on the bass, everyone. Carl Icahn. You know what cats used to say, Carl. When the bass player takes a solo, it's time to spark up a joint. Not that I smoke."

"You've never had a stoned thought," I heckle him, "that you care to remember!"

"That's correct, my son. Warren Buffet on percussion, ladies and gentlemen. Warren Buffet. And, last but never least, Roberta Appelbaum on the poorly tempered clavier, everybody. Roberta-berta-berta-berta Appelbaum! Bertie

Appelbaum, you gotta put me on, Bertie Appelbaum I said you gotta put me on!"

Roberta shocks her shoulders forward, spreading her hands across the piano to play the jazziest chord of all time.

Which she doesn't sound.

"One more program note, ladies and gentlemen, before we continue. I'm sorry Marco Esquandolas couldn't be with us tonight. Marco Esquandolas, ladies and gentlemen, on synthesizers, had a gig in the ci-tay. Y'all won't be hearing any synthesizers tonight, but you can imagine them."

"Play 'Freddie Freeloader!'"

"And I'm Moses Murray Jr., thank you very much. Moses-Murray-Part II-I've-had-enough-of-you! as my mama used to call me. Thank you so much."

"Play 'So What,' you bum!"

"Now you know why we don't play jazz music?" Moses continues. "Because jazz music causes pain. They threw *rocks* at Braxton in Europe, you dig. And at a dance hall in Baton Rouge back in the day, Ornette Coleman's jazz almost got him killed. His unorthodox playing stopped a dance. Just like peckerwood Marty McFly playing 'Johnny B. Goode' for those kids who weren't ready for it. Well, those cats weren't ready for Ornette, neither. Some of them guys crept up on him outside. One of them asked, How you doin'? Only it weren't no question. The other said, Where you from? These were all black guys hounding the great black experimenter. They hurled the dark word at Ornette, telling him he mustn't be from around here, with his hipster beard, and all his long hair. They said: You must be one of those Yankee kind of n-words!"

"One of those Yankee kind of n-words!" Warren Buffet calls out.

"One of those Yankee kind of n-words!" Bertie Applebaum shouts in response.

Some of the loggers in the audience shout it back to the stage, only they say the whole word.

"Now now," Moses says, "quit that. Then, all of a sudden, the black guys kicked Ornette down to the ground. And Ornette cradled his horn in his crying arms as these straight-edge fools. And I think there might be some straight-edge fools in here tonight. And I'm very happy to see they're standing up to leave right now. Have a good night, fellas. We are anti-racist here at the Beaver Den. So the black guys were beating Ornette to death. And a white cop strolled over, you know, waving his baton like an extension of his you-know-what, and this white cop said: What y'all doin' with that longhaired? And the white cop started calling Ornette the dark word, too, and the white cop said that if them other n-words didn't finish him off, he'd be happy to."

"If them other n-words didn't finish him off!" Carl

Icahn sings.

"We'd be happy to!" Buffet and Bertie respond.

"So you see, you can get beat up for playing jazz music. You can get knocked across your face with your own horn for giving jazz a go. And by your own people. That's real bleak, don't you think. And you know why jazz causes pain? Because jazz hurts. Jazz is pain, man. Jazz is *stupid*, man, as Sir Dwight Schrute once said. That's why the Moses Murray Quartet doesn't play jazz. And we don't play jazz perfectly."

Moses raises his horn to his mouth. Without playing a note, he removes it. He bows, and the audience gives him a standing ovation.

"Please, please sit down. We're all on the same level here. And thank you again, so much, for coming here tonight. You could've been at the demolition derby, but you're here. I'm Moses Murray Jr. Please have a look at our merch."

***

The hecklers walk out front to smoke tobacco and cheese. Carl Icahn and Warren Buffett, who seem to be friends with their own hecklers, follow behind them, muttering something about politics. The bartender emerges and plugs in the Arkanoid. The remaining loggers approach the machine, excited to break some bricks.

I want to smash something, too. I stare down Moses as the bandleader waltzes over to our table.

"Moses," Ellory says, "that was very interesting music."

"Just amazing," I agree. "*Such* an improvement on that usual genre of jazz, where the musicians sonically demonstrate they've achieved an admirable level of virtuosity and produce actual musical notes. Now what can we get you?"

"Protein bar?"

"Come now," I say. "Let's buy the prophet an adult beverage. You do drink, don't you? I can't imagine how someone like you could live with yourself if you didn't drink. You remind me of my wife in that sense."

"What are *you* drinking, Bartleby?" Moses asks.

"Oh, just a beer, old sport."

"*Moi aussi*, Charles Bovary."

Bertie Applebaum walks over to our table and says, "I'd love a Hibiki."

"Ah, those Tokyo blues," Moses says, as he introduces Bertie to the couple. "You off the

Soylent Green I take it."

"I was drinking Soylent for a while," Bertie says, "as a meal replacement shake. But then I started dumping ice cream into it, for my dessert replacement."

"Have you traveled extensively in Japan?" Ellory asks

Bertie.

"I was just there, for work. My job job, I mean. And I played a gig, too."

"Three beers and a whiskey, then," I announce. I return with the drinks, place two beers in front of Ellory and Moses, and put down Bertie's whiskey. I try to get Bertie's attention, but she's back onstage playing some actual chords on the piano. The room darkens except for a spotlight on her. I take a deep breath. I feel at peace.

"I'm glad you dug our performance," Moses says, ruining my reverie. "We should all get out of here soon."

"No, we don't do that," Ellory says. "We're not poly."

"Why do you Chicago people keep saying *poly*," Moses exhales, flipping the napkin I gave him. "Poly, poly, pants on fire. We're just having a threesome."

"I don't want a threesome. I want an affair."

"Affairs are expensive. I think we've got two choices. Either we all have sex together now, or we all have sex together later, but separately. What'll it be?"

"I thought you wanted me to leave my husband for you."

"Sure, I want that." Moses flips his napkin.

"Then take me to Tokyo."

"I can't even buy you bodega sushi, honey."

"God I hate poly," Ellory returns. "Sounds like the word for people who never got laid in high school."

"I never got laid in high school," Moses says.

"If I were around, you would have."

"Believe me, honey, you were around."

"Polys are such phonies," my wife says. "They think they're bored with their husbands when they're just bored with their apps."

"I told the bartender," I say, "that I wanted a napkin for *my* beer, and he said, 'Here's a napkin for all three of them.' That's how you know the Den is a classy place. You know why, my friends?"

I wait for one of them to say something.

"No, why?" Moses bites.

"I'm glad you asked that, Kepesh. Because we must be *consistent*. That's what we always say at work."

"My husband works very hard."

"I don't care what we choose, one space after a period or two, Oxford comma, Oral Roberts comma, bullets with periods, bullets without, who or whom, further or farther. As long as things are *consistent*. Numbers don't care about words, you dig, numbers care about *numbers*. Numbers would never say, I don't care if you use a *nine* instead of a *three* in that formula, as long as you're consistent. No, numbers would never say anything so silly."

"We made it to Forks today," Ellory says. "I didn't get the text about your birthplace in time, or we would've paid respects. Would you call yourself a white ethnic? A dark Caucasian?"

"I wouldn't call myself a white ethnic," Moses says, blowing a note into his beer bottle.

"Oh, I love the way you do that, Don Q. That's the first note you've played tonight." I blow a note from my own bottle. "We blew very similar notes, you see, we are *consistent*."

"Would you call yourself a *native* ethnic, then? Or would that just make you an Indigenous person?"

"My god we're so consumed with our new religion of identity," I say, "when there are real things we should be thinking about. How can we be living in this bourgeois novel when the ice caps are melting?"

"What did you expect the ice caps to do—freeze? Have you ever heard of this little thing called *spring*?"

I point to Bertie's whiskey, wave her over. I suspect that because she's a bigger girl, she's likely a woman socially conditioned to follow the erratic mumblings of dense, intelligent men. That's probably how she ended up humiliating herself by 'playing piano' in the Moses Murray Quartet.

Moses spreads his hands out over the table, which has a map of the Pacific Northwest. "In a few years, the New Yorkers think a tsunami destroys this. All of this. Including Seattle. Even Bill Gates must die."

"Don't you think he'll get out in time?"

Moses holds his finger on Seattle, Ellory places her hand over his, and he doesn't move her away.

"The tsunami matters more than who we are as men. The future tsunami matters more than any tsunami happening right now."

"Why can't both things matter?" Ellory says. "You can be a man with drawing room opinions, and there can also be a tsunami with tsunami room opinions."

"My mother's Indigenous," Moses regroups. "From here. My father's a typical New York Jew who moved out west to supervise the loggers and steal their women."

"AKA a dark Caucasian."

"I guess so, man. I told you today. No matter who I am, I just keep getting poorer and poorer."

"You're an *American*, Moses," I say. "Because you have the freedom to make yourself up. You wouldn't have that freedom if you were a n-word. But you get that freedom because you're a person-of-color."

"But you're not truly a person-of-color, and you're not truly Jewish," Ellory says, "if your mother isn't Jewish."

"No, Daisy Buchanan. I really am Jewish."

"I like that. Call me Daisy Buchanan again."

"Daisy Buchanan."

This time Bertie sees my wave. She stands up from the piano and makes her way over to the table.

"Hello there again," Ellory says to Bertie, like she's a bumblebee. "So, we're going to Tokyo tonight, and I'd love to know if you have any recommendations."

"Sweet. Yeah, maybe."

"Bertie's driving back to Seattle tonight," Moses says.

"How far is that?" I ask.

"Like three hours. But I can do it in 2 ½."

"Maybe you could give me a ride," I say. "I'm going to Seattle tonight as well. Moses, your bandleader, is stealing my wife, so he and my wife are going to stay at our cabin. Which is right here in Beaver."

"What do you mean?" Bertie says.

"What I mean, Bertie, is that you've walked in on more than you bargained for. Moses is stealing my wife and I'm asking if I can leave with you."

"Okay," Bertie says slowly.

"So that's a yes?" Ellory asks. "Ty can go with you?"

"Great town, Seattle," Moses adds. "Used to just be a sleepy port city, blue-collar. Now it has the most cranes in the world."

"Tick-tock," Ellory says, asking Bertie if she can try on her chauffeur cap. "Oh, but this wouldn't fit me."

"It's one-size-fits-all."

"Most of your things wouldn't fit me," Ellory says, leaning into Moses.

They start kissing, slow and soft at first, then harder, faster, hotter. Bertie and I hold our tongues in disbelief.

***

We leave the Den, and drive in separate cars to the

200

cabin, Moses and Bertie in the piano player's Civic, my wife and I in our Blubaru.

"This is tawdry," I say, driving down the 101 in the straightest line I've managed the whole trip. My toenail hurts every time I press the gas. "And it's sordid. It's motherfucking tawdry, motherfucking sordid."

Ellory pulls a cigarette out of her bag.

"You can't smoke in a rental car, the fine will be like $10,000."

"Oh, who cares?"

She tries pushing the window down just a little bit, but it goes all the way down. She pushes it back up, almost all the way back up.

"What amusing words in your mouth, Ty." She blows smoke out the window. "Tawdry. Sordid. They're hard words for you, with your Queens accent."

"This is tawdry, sordid, despicable, hideous, and horrible. Even for you."

"Did you notice I didn't even drink tonight?"

"You had four beers."

"That's what I mean, babe. I feel really clear about this."

"Why don't you just drop a hot water bottle on my head, place a seesaw in front of my foot, lay a banana peel down in the bathroom? I had so many golden opportunities to kill us on this mountain. I could've driven off so many cliffs. I thought about it every time, the countless times I saved your life today. I should've pushed you off the mountain when Moses knocked you in the mouth. I was more depressed to lose the chillum than I would've been to lose you. I saved your life so many times today. And this is how you repay me."

"This is what we have to do right now."

"Well, if this is what *we* have to do right now, what should *I* do?"

"Get a hotel in the city. Buy a sex worker. Bang Bertie. She obviously likes you. I know you have a thing for fatties."

"I'm glad you were able to create this episode for yourself tonight. This shmuck will validate you for a weekend, at the most, and then you'll come crawling back to me."

"We've both needed a change for a long time, Ty."

"We've known each other for a day."

"Don't get mad at me for being the one who goes through with it."

She blows smoke out the side of her mouth and into my face. I swerve.

"How many beers did *you* have?"

"You think this journeyman barista is taking you to Tokyo? You think you'll fly first- class with that hipster douchebag? He can't even afford to play his saxophones."

Ellory rubs her eyes.

"Don't cry. Criers sit in coach."

"I'm not crying for you, sweetie. It's the smoke. You know what Moses said about you? He said *you're* the hipster douchebag."

"Okay, whatever. Let's cancel ourselves out as hipster douchebags. He is a very nice guy, you're right, I don't want to argue about this."

"You're such a freakin' coward, Ty. If you'd been man enough to get me pregnant on our wedding night…"

"…you couldn't even *walk* on our wedding night. *You* were the one who needed diapers. If I would've propositioned you on our wedding night, I'd be in jail."

"Maybe not. Maybe I would have forgiven you publicly and said publicly you are a good family man. This is a good man, this father of my children…"

"…we have no children, thank God, you'd be a miserable mother, you heartless bitch…"

"…and I made a terrible mistake accusing this spineless coward of whipping me with his genuine leather belt. He didn't punch me in the face in our driveway, officer. He didn't rape me after his botched knee surgery. He didn't stick a finger in my ass in the Nordstrom dressing room. Everything's just fine. I retract the statements I made during my sworn deposition that you threw me off the roof on our wedding night. That you incinerated my wedding dress, that you stripped me of my purity for your hideous, male-dominating rites."

"Hilarious."

"Hilarious—you sound like the Nanny."

"And what would *you* have done with your feces dress?"

"I'll never know. Stuff it in the top of my closet forever? Like every other basic bitch with permission to get fat? But at least I'd know where it was."

"Why are you doing this to me?"

"Maybe I will tell the press on the courtroom steps that I forgive my husband."

"Why are you doing this?"

"My husband is a good Jewish man, and he would never raise his hand to me. I retract my earlier statements, officer. My husband didn't throw me down, smash my head against the credenza. My husband didn't break a vase across the small of my back, I'm just being silly."

"Why did you pick me," I cry, "if you were going to do this?"

"You don't get to have it both ways, Ty. You don't get to be funny and sad at the same time."

"You sound like Jenny."

"I am Jenny. Or I'm nobody. I'm nobody to you."

"WHY DID YOU DO THIS TO ME!" But I'm not asking Ellory. I'm reaching my head out the window and looking up.

"You did this to *yourself*. To prove to yourself you aren't middle class. And to get away from that raggedy zero wife you pretend to hate. That's what you should do, though, Ty. Find Jenny. Find her at Rhonda's apartment and apologize."

"How do you know about Rhonda?"

"You talk about her *all the time*. You should go there."

"I will," I say.

"Go there, Ty. I give you permission."

"No, I got it, I understand."

"Get out," Ellory says. "I mean that in a good way."

We arrive at the cabin and park at the door. Bertie's Civic pulls up behind us.

"Okay, let's start over," I say while we're still in the car. "I understand that this is the right move for us."

"It is, Ty, isn't it? I'm *so* glad you see that. We could still be poly, I guess, whatever. I mean, he suggested it."

"No, no, now. You want to have an affair. Poly is for folks who think having hardwood floors is charming."

"It's for twentysomethings who think they don't want central AC. And I'm tired."

"Well, you've come at least three times today, and you only had four beers."

"I'm just in no mood to explore progressive forms of kinship tonight."

"Me neither. I just want to be alone. Alone with a nice hotel."

"I want you to get a nice hotel, Ty. You need a good night's sleep. And if there's anything I can do to help you with that, let me know. Okay, baby?"

We exit the Blubaru, stand in front of the trunk. Moses leaves the Civic and sits against the hood, his saxophones around his chest. When I see Bertie Applebaum sitting in the car, I wave her out. She reluctantly emerges, and stands next to Moses, bracing herself for a role as possible moderator of whatever happens. But what will happen? No blood will be shed. All we will do is discuss the *Quixote*. The real meaning of some Pearl Jam song.

"Should we three take a walk in the woods, maybe? Or up the mountain?"

I ignore Moses's questions and ask Bertie if she can give me that ride back to the city.

"I said I could," she says. "I will, yes."

"She can do it in 2½," Ellory reminds me.

I say to Moses, "You know, she married me after a day, too. You're never going to feel like she's yours."

"Did you know," Moses says, addressing Bertie, "that they came out here to have a baby? A procreation vacation."

"That's so nice," Bertie smiles.

"But the two of them," Moses says, "I mean, look at them. These two? They should not procreate."

I step to the prick.

"Oh, come now. Who cares if Ty and Ellory can have a baby? Think about that. Think of *the children*."

"Wait, Ty, before you beat him up..."

"…I'm not beating anyone up…"

"…give me the Amex."

"Don't you want Ty's Freedom?"

"No, you should hang on to that one. Just the Amex."

"The Amex."

"Yes, please. I'm happy to give you points for anything related to your upgrade on your flight home. But maybe you can expense some of our Tokyo trip."

"Expense it. Yes. No, here, wait." I reach for my wallet and hand my wife the Amex. "And let me give you something," I say to Moses. "Some pocket money."

"No, please."

"Come on. Let me give you some car fare. As my father used to say."

"So many protein bars."

"On second thought," I say to my wife, "give me that Amex back. Take this one. The Delta one."

"The Delta one," Ellory says carefully.

"And here. Here's a $100, American, for you, Moses. A dollar for each of your vegetarian tubas."

"Thanks, man. I appreciate that."

"No, of course. Don't mention it. Our marriage was ending so I didn't have time to check out your merch."

**

I walk back into the cabin for my bag, Ellory

trailing behind me. The TV shows the DVD menu for *Independence Day*. Ellory starts making the short queen bed.

"Those sheets have our fluids on them," I say. "You could be pregnant right now, you know."

"I'm sorry. I've never been good at endings."

"Yet you cause so many of them. I understand now what all those men before me meant when they said nobody loves you."

"Marcus loves me. Mr. Lim loved me. Moses loves me."

"Moses won't love you for long."

"*You* love me."

"I did love you, once."

"And you'll never forget it. I'm so glad we danced together. The best things happen while you're dancing."

"I just can't figure you out."

"Of course you're never going to figure me out, Ty. Because we were never really being truthful with each other. You were cheating on Jenny, I was leaving Shelly, we both felt young for a night, okay, and I loved that, dancing to our college music. That was *it*. We both felt so free. *Let's get married! In a big cathedral by a priest!* I loved that. We did something important for each other, okay, and we may never even figure out what that was. And I'm okay, okay, with the mystery in all of that. I'm okay with the people we become when we go our separate ways. No matter what, I'll never forget you. No matter what, you will always be one of my great loves."

"I love you too, babe," I say with tears in my eyes.

"I know you do, lover. I know."

We kiss. I pull myself away. We go back outside. Bertie Applebaum sits behind the wheel of her Civic, but Moses is nowhere to be found. He's probably hiding in the woods, I think, just as he was when we found him. I remember the warning, on Moses's missing sign, that if you found him, you might want to let him set the terms of his own rescue. Ellory Allen, it turns out, was one of those terms.

"Coward!" I yell into the sky. And then I settle into Bertie's car.

Ellory runs out of the cabin and taps on our window. I don't lower it at first, but then I do.

"Oh my god. It was Jennifer, Ty—*Jennifer*. My roommate in New York. Her name was *Jennifer*."

"It can't be that simple."

"It always is. You should go back to New York, Ty. Go get Jenny. Go get your girl."

PART THREE

"What must one do to educate a son before he's born?"
— Agnès Varda, *One Sings, The Other Doesn't*

7.

I'm in Seattle. I need a shower. I want it to be a rain shower. I search my phone for a Trump property but there are none out here. I google: *single-origin coffee near hotel very fast wi-fi* and receive millions of results. I reserve a suite at a Renaissance property. That will have to do.

After checking in, I call down to room service and ask them to send up a veggie burger, an ice pack for my injured toe, and a pack of cigarettes. They refuse. I go downstairs, and at the nearest drugstore purchase a Capone blue bathing suit, a bottle of Wild Turkey, a pack of Camel filters, and a Space Needle lighter. I go back to the room, drink some whiskey, rip the filters off a few cigarettes and smoke them in the room. I burn holes into the bedspread, the towels, and throw the rest of the cigarettes in the toilet. Then I wash my hands, brush my teeth, floss, run my fingers through my hair, and rub my tearful eyes, before taking a long, hot shower. After that, I ride the elevator down to the indoor swimming pool. I soak my bum toe in the whirlpool. I swim some laps before treading water in the deep end, where I watch a parent place their child in the handicap seat. The child screams, and the parent removes the child from the seat.

At a record store, I purchase *Inaction!!!!* by the Moses Murray Quartet. A photo of the band includes Warren

Buffet and Carl Icahn, wine stoned and barefoot on lawn chairs. Moses Murray sits in a tree, his back to the camera. At the time the photo was taken, he still had that "full head of hair" suggested on his missing poster. And a dog, probably Bowie dog, is captured shaking kiddie pool water off his fur.

During the ride back, Bertie told me the story. *Epic*, she called Bowie, whose death the month before had caused Bertie to remain in her dark bedroom for a week. Epic dog. She found him on Craigslist for free. She couldn't imagine anyone parting, until death, with a dog like Bowie. She knew he was meant to be hers. Bowie walked up, when Bertie approached the house to meet him, and nuzzled into her leg. She looked up and said, Can I take him home today? And they said, Yes. And then she thought, something must be wrong with him. Because she couldn't believe they were giving him away. They assured her nothing was wrong. The most incredible, Bertie said, moment of my life. She put him in the back seat, took him home, cleaned him up, got him a new collar. The rest was history. The kind of history where she now thinks to herself, even more now, that he's gone: what could life have even been, before Bowie? When he was dying, she kept thinking she did something wrong. They told her, You did nothing wrong. They were wrong, Bertie said. I must have done something wrong. She wants to write a book about Bowie, but she's scared to explore her feelings in writing, in that systematic way writing portends.

Outside of the record store, I see a man begging for change. I hand him Moses's LP, and a one-hundred-dollar bill, American.

"I saw these guys in Beaver last night."

"Beaver," the man says, pocketing the bill without saying thanks, or god bless you.

My wife wouldn't leave him five stars, I think. Because what's the point of five stars, if every bum gets them.

I return to the classic vinyl and CDs record store and buy another copy of *Inaction!!!!*, which I take back with me to Renaissance. After masturbating, which is unpleasurable, I wonder what I could possibly do next. Fly back to Chicago. Fly back to New York. I will take a cab to Jimi Hendrix's grave at the airport, and then fly back to Chicago. I want to be near a cemetery, and I can easily do that with Hendrix, but I can also fly back to New York, which is just a short flight across the country. There are graves in New York of contemporaries I knew intimately, but then again, I also intimately know Jimi Hendrix, and he is more important to me than some of the dead people I'm close to.

I go downstairs wearing the Renaissance bath robe, and walk into a different drugstore. My plan is to rest my aching toe against a 5lb bag of ice cubes, and treat myself to an Energy Drink, something I've never had before.

In the checkout line, I observe a single man, a divorced man, perhaps, buying three candy bars, a quart of milk in a plastic bottle, a quart of orange juice in a plastic bottle, a loaf of country-sliced bread, a dozen white eggs in a white container, a package of salami with, I'm thinking, extra antibiotics, extra salami growth hormone, and a pack of cigarettes, American Spirit.

I love this man. I know I have the potential to become him, this single man, this divorced man, who understands exactly what groceries a single man needs. Being divorced, I reason, will be a lot like being in your 20s, only older. I will have different thoughts than I did when I was in my 20s, but it's not like I didn't have just as many thoughts back then.

I linger in the drug store, sipping my energy drink. I can't leave, because now they're playing a song my father used to sing to me. My father, crossing his hands over his chest, when the opening bars of a song moved him. I begin to cry, or maybe it's more accurate to say I have a *tearful reaction*, infantile in its mysterious intensity, right there in front of a drug store rack, here in downtown Seattle, of east coast magazines. It occurs to me that because I'm a white man, nobody questions why I'm crying hysterically in a hotel robe in front of the magazines. Even in my emotions, especially so there, I am imprisoned by my race.

To calm myself, I pick up the *Atlantic Monthly*,

wondering if it has different content, out here, on the Pacific Ocean. The cover story says: *Everyone's getting divorced again. What gives?* Maybe I should move to Los Angeles. I would buy an Audi convertible, because only suckers lease cars, and sponsor a naturally dirty blonde. Los Angeles could be my fountain of youth. But I return the *Atlantic Monthly* to its slot, dismiss Los Angeles from my chakras, and steal a three-day-old *Wall Street Journal.*

Back in the hotel room, I read in the *Journal* that progress had been made on the Dakota Access Pipeline. Just like the Plains Indians used every part of the buffalo, the men and women of Wall Street have excelled at creating strategies with fees that can be harvested from every component. The comparison makes me hungry. It's the first realistic impulse I've had in I don't know how long. I need to get back to work. I pick up my phone, and see a new email, flagged high importance, from my former boss in New York, Tweed Spreckman.

Before I have the chance to read the email, Tweed is calling me.

I pick up on the fourth ring.

"You've been taking a lot of PTO this year, boss," Tweed says, in his profitably nasal voice.

"I'm in Seattle," I tell him. Tweed has traveled the globe for business, and always carried on the New York state of mind. "So Seattle is this old port city on the west coast of the country. It's now a technology hub. Most cranes in the world outside of somewhere like Bahrain."

"You eat any tossed salads and scrambled eggs?"
"No. And I'm hungry. They have confederate flags here."

"I can appreciate that."

Tweed's in a rush. He asks if I have a pen nearby. I pick up the Renaissance notepad, but I've burned too many holes through it with the cigarettes. I take notes on the not burnt parts of the bedsheet. Tweed tells me about the project. I take down its unique bullet points on the bedsheet. They seem to be the same unique bullet points from the last project we worked on together. He tells me he wants me in New York tomorrow for the meeting.

"That sounds great," I say. "But why *me*? Isn't Kaplan around?"

"She's not, no. She's on something else. We want you for this because you're good, Ty."

"You want me because Kaplan's busy."

"We want you because you're nice to look at."

I move to the bathroom and run my toe under the ice-cold bathwater. I want to suck on Ellory's ankles. I'm remembering a time Tweed told me that when you get married you don't want to have sex with other women, not really, you just want to suck their ankles. But the only ankles I want to suck right now are my wife's. Then again, my wife has left me, so she is now, too, an *other woman*.

"You're right," I say, wishing I could suck my own toe. "This is getting ridiculous. I'm coming back to Egypt."

"Project Egypt? We won that last year."

"New York, I mean. I've had enough of this denying, jet setting behavior. I need to work."

"I'll send you the briefing books nobody's read. Be sure to not read them on the plane."

"Good idea. I'll catch up on my flight."

After we hang up, I hear a knock on the door. It's room service, with a very rare steak and a bottle of MaCallan, courtesy of Tweed.

"You send me up a steak and a bottle of whiskey," I say to the attendant, "but you wouldn't send me a veggie burger and a pack of cigarettes?"

"Sir, is something in here burning?"

"Yes," I say. "Me."

I eat the steak. I pour the rest of the Wild Turkey over the painting of Hurricane Ridge above the bed, and drink a lot of the MaCallan. I think about leaving a bad review for the hotel, because they refused to send me the veggie burger. But my wife has left enough bad reviews for all of mankind, and I still feel as one with Ellory, I know she'll come back to me. I leave a one-hundred-dollar bill, American, on the table for the maid. And the Moses Murray Quartet LP.

***

The plane is three by three. I have an aisle. I always get an aisle. In the aisle across sits the woman in the bright red beret. She's got an infant at her chest. I sit straight back, giving her space, because she's talking to the man in the middle seat next to me.

"Is this your husband?" I ask, pointing at them both. "That your wife?"

They nod.

"I mean, we can switch, you know? So you guys can be together?"

"We can do that?" the woman asks, in a foreign accent I can't place.

"Yeah, sure. I mean, you can always switch aisle for aisle. It's aisle for window that gets dicey. And aisle or window for middle, well, that's a no-no. At least in this country."

We make the switch. It's the nicest thing I've done in weeks. I fasten my seat belt tight, not half-assed like some punk, and I listen to the safety instructions. The pilot calls herself Jennifer Jones. It was a beautiful day in Seattle, and it will be a beautiful evening in New York. The flight attendants pass out information on how to join the frequent flyer club. I've been a member since 2001, but I accept the weighty card stock and scan the benefits I already enjoy. When we reach cruising altitude

I wipe tears from my cheeks, put in my noise-cancelling headphones, and listen to the Bible on shuffle, Paul's Letter to the Corinthians.

Corinth. A large, unholy mess of a city, home to false prophets and screaming divisions, a cesspool of sexual immorality and—this is pretty hot—Jewish-Christians sleeping with their stepmothers. Thunder cracks. Lions roar. I am calmed by the sound of sandalled feet on oasis grass in this well-produced mp3.

Saint Paul teaches us the True Christian is no better than garbage. Not garbage for the landfill, the compost, or the recycling, but that true stench of Christianity: *not sure where it goes garbage*. Saint Paul tells the Christians of Corinth that they need to buckle up. If they're only working through this life for a first-class seat on the airline to heaven, they'd better be ready to spend their earth-bound layover eating pretzels in coach.

Saint Paul asks me to imagine I have the aisle. And the man in the middle seat next to me is married to the woman in the middle seat beside us. Suppose what just happened to me in real life was something way more radical? Suppose this man asked me, during boarding, if I could give up my aisle for his *middle*, so that he and his wife could sit together? It's an unfathomable question to imagine an American asking. But if I'm a Christian I give up my aisle. If I'm a Christian I know humanity is in the asking. If I believe in something as zany as the resurrection I say yes to the man, I put myself in that squeeze. If I'm searching for the wounds on the body of Christ like I'm searching for my keys in the dark, I'm at the extremes on the daily. I tell this man I will take his middle. But I am not some meek man. I will fight for both armrests the whole way through.

I'm not a true Christian, though. I'm in the aisle. It's the other guy's fault I'm not a saint. I'm feeling blue. Nobody's ever asked me to give up anything, I think, and then just as quickly think, Am I being honest with myself about that? I take stock of my reading materials. Along with the latest Men's Magazine, picked up at the airport newsstand, I have a novel with me, *The Maternal Man*, picked up at the anarchist bookshop near Pike Place Market.

This is the book Jenny tore up back in Chicago. Since then, *The Maternal Man* has won all sorts of literary business awards. Boardroom critics have called it the definitive story of Masculinity during the Trump Era. Kind of pompous, if you ask me. The Trump Era won't end until the next World War, but that's another story.

Masculinity in the Trump era is something I know quite a bit about, so I begin the book with a cloudy mind. Do I really want to read fiction about what I'm living through? I learn that *The Maternal Man* tells the story of a culturally Jewish professor who moved from Kansas to New York City. The professor loved the Kansas

City Royals baseball team in 1985, I loved the New York Mets in 1986—we have something in common. I know this professor. He's a character type that's long appealed to me. The only character type I love more than the culturally Jewish professor is the culturally Catholic sex worker with a bitchy spirit. Sometimes, if I'm lucky, the young Jewish professor and the Catholic sex worker team up on the same existential quest. That's one of my favorite books to sleep on.

I try to keep an open mind. I read the first few chapters of *The Maternal Man*. The prose is beautiful. Very intelligent. I relate to that, because I'm intelligent, too. I'm waiting for the young professor, also a young novelist, to get going with being a rakish asshole. When will he tell us he has a thing for Mexican teenagers in sandy thongs on all-inclusive beaches? When will he snort rails of Bolivian Marching Powder? Eat ham off the bone. When will the squiggles of saxophone trip up his gait on a predawn walk under the elevated tracks? When will he start sleeping around with all the beauties New York City has to offer the man from Kansas? When will he make lights-on love with unreliable hostesses, low-performing schoolteachers who keep it all inside, editorial assistants who can somehow afford big city apartments flooded with clarifying, man-hating pools of light? When will he applaud female authors like Jenny Marks, whose minor work he deeply respects, as long as it isn't about him?

My toe is killing me. On my phone, I read the first slide of the briefing book for the new project. I shake off the flight attendant's offer of free pretzels, I am twisted enough, and I buy two clickers of whiskey with a Coke chaser, no need for the full can. I pay with my airline credit card which returns a quarter of the cost of inflight purchases and earns me double miles. I put *The Maternal Man* down. I fear it is another of those 224-page novels billed as a novel that changes the idea of the novel itself. I sip the minibar whiskey and hum the andantino moderato from *Rhapsody in Blue*. On a walk to the first-class bathroom, I see a woman eating a snack pack. She's reading a book called *Never Eat Snack Packs Alone: The Proven 8-Step Process to Getting Nothing You Want*. I want to ask her if she'd like to trade my book for hers.

Back at my seat, I cry at the in-flight movie, relating more to Fix-it-Felix than Wreck-it-Ralph. I puke both bottles of whiskey into a paper bag. The woman in the bright red beret asks if I need help. I tell her I don't know how to answer that question.

"It's his fault," I say, looking at the top of the plane.

"Whose fault?"

"My creator," I say, hand over my mouth to hide my pukey breath. "God himself. The coat-check man upstairs."

My stomach settles down. I take a long nap. We're in our initial descent. I pick up *The Maternal Man* again. When will this prissy sanctimonious near-sighted jerk who has such a way with words meet some withdrawn yet recalcitrant females? I want spiraling reddish hair springing from female scalps, tangling as it widens up and out, cut paperboy fashion in the back, that's what, and I want hair scrawled out high above a busty woman's ears. If I didn't want female hair, I would've picked up *The Paternal Woman* at the anarchist bookstore, another 224-page novel which has changed the way we think of the novel itself, which tells the story of a Jewish woman who is never called 'Jewish' who looks at the shadows that are never called 'shadows' and sees them as they move for a Jewish woman who has the free time to watch the shadows move as they are and for what they are while she earns a modest stipend from a local university and sells her *Sesame Street* diaries to the *New York Times*. But I don't really have anything at all to say about female authors. The author of *The Maternal Man*, on the other hand, I should be able to understand. But he is depriving me. Where is my hair? I want heavy ropes of knotty black hair in this story. I want quivering bottom lips. I want elegant hands and glossy knuckles, heavy and maybe pendulous breasts that at some point during that final solution heave, and why won't this soy boy, he would say mollycoddler because he's too good for the internet, give me some dark soft eyes set off by kohl, where are my slow-blinking lashes, ample white backsides, sloping shoulders, and where the fuck are my folds, dawg, of fleshy voluptuous skin, folds of silken hotel robes— inviting necks, pensive foreheads, stick the big toe of a high-arched Egyptian foot into my panting mouth, give me an ardent, breathy throat to choke unironically. But all that gets edited out. Or never written in the first place. The young novelist doesn't permit garbage in his text—for that he has his Simple Human trashcan from the Atlantic Terminal Target. The professor is a good, nice, young man from middle America with memories and beliefs who sees the world as it is for a good, nice, young man from middle America with memories and beliefs who can afford to play with genre. Now his story fiction, then autobiography, memoir, soon enough childhood fantasy, a seedless florilegium fusion of the new French novel and old German poem winning the great white whale Masters of American Prose Contest.

I put down the novel and pick up the inflight mag. I get really into an article by an award-winning chef on the mysterious decline in white America's sperm counts, and then an article by a retired neurologist on the twelve best food trucks in Cairo. In my Men's Magazine, the actor Harrison Ford's still got it, and the Canadian rapper Drake has given up on making American women great again. Next, I read a saved article on my phone that ruins my shit. It went viral some months ago and I'd been meaning to get through it. The adviser is one of those Ivy League downtown New York types Jenny wants to live closer to, who would post her pretty feet on Instagram because they're the prettiest thing about her, but I can't front I'm not overcome by her advice. The column hits so deep that I get nostalgic for my therapy sessions with Scarlett, and I remember standing on the bascule bridge with Jenny before this nightmare took off, and I feel her here, right now, I'm reliving the mistakes I made that night, and I'm certain that when Jennifer Jones lands us in New York, and I get uptown, I will beg Jenny's forgiveness, and she'll take me back. Jenny was right. I am weak. But together, we'll make it.

I return my attention to *The Maternal Man*. I enjoy the experience of reading any novel. Even though I know it won't be followed by the experience of remembering, or even comprehending, what the novel said, what the novel was in for, and how the novel got out of it. Maybe, if the novel reader is lucky, they remember one idea, one fact, one problem solved, and on the last pages of *The Maternal Man* the young professor tells the woman he never describes the Latin term for humans who can wiggle their earlobes without touching them. I will never forget that Latin term. One day I'm going to use it at a cocktail party. Page for page, image for image, proprioception to proprioception, I must concede *The*

Maternal Man lived up to its hype. It is the defining novel of Masculinity in the Trump Era. And the textbook example of how the Jewish novel changed its stance on the war against Christmas.

No, fuck that. I go to the first-class bathroom, walking right by the weeping *Never Eat Snack Packs* alone woman, and, just like Jenny did, I rip *The Maternal Man* to pieces. Then, I make a mental note I need to buy some Scotch tape to put it back together. Of all the things I hate about the professor's triumph, what pisses me off the most is that the professor thinks he's out of Egypt. He thinks he's free. He thinks he's marched. He thinks he gets to be the still small voice at the protest. Maybe he does. He has a different creator than I do, and good for him. No, fuck that. You're a profiteer, professor, not a prophet. Stop pretending you can interpret the master's dreams. No, actually...

***

I ask the Uber driver if he'll accept a cash tip in addition to the tip I plan to leave in the app.

"I'm not an Uber cop," I say. "I know I might look like one. Don't think you're on camera. I'm giving away my wife's money. I'm the husband version of MacKenzie Bezos."

"Please have a flag," the driver says. It's the flag with

thirteen stars in a circle, on a toothpick, like a drink umbrella, and makes me feel like I'm back in the lobby of Trump International at the Fourth of July pre-game party. I wave the toothpick, whistle colonial piccolo, and hand the driver a hundred-dollar-bill, American.

"God bless this country," he says. I exit the Uber XL and put the flag in my back pocket. I am only one man, I like to think, but I deserved that big black car, yeah I'm one of those poor little rich boys from TV, I deserve my Yukon XL that could seat the Supreme Court comfortably.

My knees shake when I hit the uptown pavement. I weigh more in New York and the pressure's killing my toe. It's the Fourth of July. The streets are popping. I hear fight songs up and down Second Avenue. The dive bars don't close for an hour, and when they do, the real spots open.

I climb the warped, curry-scented stairs to Jenny's door. I knock. She doesn't answer. I knock again. She doesn't answer. I scream. The apartment smells of an even older curry than the stairwell. The blackout curtains are lowered. There are dead plants everywhere, ashtrays overflowing.

Jenny looks different. Anyone who only knew her from her author photo would be shocked or confused. Her breakthrough author bangs are gone, her old hair hangs down, unhealthy and a lot of it. She's lost weight in her cheeks, gained it in her shoulders. She wears something like her old uniform: black jeans, a gray sweatshirt. There's a red stain by the neck, dried pasta sauce or dried blood.

"I've been thinking about you a lot, Ty, because I went to the cemetery the other day."

"What other day?"

"The day before Thanksgiving."

"So, the Fourth of July."

"Around then, yeah. And I saw your dad, there. I went with *my* dad, to see my grandparents. And I remembered it was the same place. One of the largest cemeteries in Queens, on one of those drab stretches of Woodhaven."

"I think I've heard of that one."

"I wanted to pay my respects to your father. What does that even mean? Why are we always *paying* for it in this country? Anyway, I wanted to tell your dad I was sorry I couldn't make it. The day he was buried."

"He forgives you."

"It's always forgiveness with you, Ty."

"I just don't know what else there is."

"Maybe he hasn't forgiven me. Maybe your dad's burning in hell, screaming, Jennifer! I'll never forgive you!! And I really think you're on to something. Because I've been thinking a lot about your dad. I've been thinking a lot about the dead, you know, because I've been thinking only about myself. And Aurora."

"Me too."

"Every woman I told and every woman my mom told, they all said, Honey, I had a miscarriage, too. But nobody talks about it. My mom told me I was almost a miscarriage. I asked what she would've done if I were, and she said she would've tried to have another me."

"Maybe miscarriages aren't a big deal for society. But it was a big deal for us. We were going to change. We were going to make commitments. We were finally going to do it. We would've stopped with all our shit, because we would've had something else, something helpless, to take care of. We would've helped her. We would've educated her, and I wanted that so much."

"Your dad called me Jennifer. Nobody ever does."

"In college he used to warn me: Jennifer only calls when it's convenient for her."

"In college, that was true. And I'm sorry. People don't even call me *Jenny* anymore. Nobody calls. I never fully realized, until you abandoned me, that you were my only real friend."

"You're mine, too."

"Even though I'm always having a conversation now. I get these long emails, from the literary men, the men I don't know. They address me, Dear Ms. Marks. They're nice letters, literary men know so much about literature, but if you knew so much about literature wouldn't you read the ancients instead of me? I never

231

reply. Or maybe I write, *Thanks!* But *they* reply to their own emails, and then they reply to their replies, and by the third paragraph they're calling me a dumb bitch for not writing them back. Remember that day you were sick? And I brought over *Vertigo.* Your Dad said, Jennifer brought a movie over. It's by the Godfather of Suspense."

"That was a big day for him. It was like his first movie that wasn't *Rocky* or *Superman* in decades."

"What if your dad is looking down on me and saying, I'll never forgive you, Jennifer, for not correcting me that day I called Hitchcock the Godfather of Suspense. It makes me dizzy, Ty, when I think about how he called me *Jennifer.* I was thinking about it at the cemetery. It was such a moment of kindness, your dad was so kind. Like you. Sometimes. So *my* dad and I, we saw these young parents nearby. The parents you see only in cemeteries, crying at a grave with an American flag, because their kid got their heart blown out in Afghanistan or wherever. When I saw that, I started crying on my dad's shoulder. It's not something that would affect me unless I were in the cemetery. It's like when you hear the words *Marcel Proust* and you think you should read Marcel Proust, even though you weren't thinking about him before. I cried for that parent and their child soldier. And then I went over to *your* dad. We had to drive over, actually, it was far. I liked putting 'Rossberg' into the find-your-dead computer. Five dead Rossbergs showed up."

"We represent in that place."

"I cried more tears for your dad than I'd cried for my own grandparents, or the dead soldier. I loved that cemetery, more than most of them. I never wanted to leave."

"Did you guys eat at Abbracheminto's right after? You love their veal parm."

"No, my dad said it went downhill and closed, so we got croissants at Dunkin'."

I take a step back, knocking over an iced coffee container. "Shit, I'm sorry, do you have any paper towels?"

"Sorry not sorry, by the way, for the mess."

I step over more fast-food wrappers, and more than a few used condoms, and into the kitchen, a few feet away from the bed. There's nothing resembling a paper towel, or even takeout napkins. Down in the sink my gaze freezes on three large roaches. They're on the smaller side of the big ones you'd see crawling over a Second Avenue sewer grate. They don't move, they march, with that rummy New Orleans stride. On the stove I see deformed pasta and mice droppings, and more mice droppings and smaller, fuccboi roaches when I open the utensil drawer, which I immediately slam shut. On top of the refrigerator there's a row of poetry volumes, bookended by an action figure of Han Solo encased in carbonite. In the pantry space there are more books, armies of stop motion ants ollieing on the rims of Jenny's serving bowls. Palpitating, disgusted, I take one groaning step out of the kitchen and reach the bed, where nothing else seems to live, only dried-out makeup tubes, spray bottles missing spouts.

For every creeping animal I've seen on this expedition around my apartment, I've jumped a little, like I'm on fire. But Jenny hasn't moved.

"I wish you would've called me," I say.

"I did. You didn't answer. I wrote you at your office. You never wrote me back."

"I never got those."

"There was something about the way you didn't answer me, when we were in Chicago, that made me realize you were gone forever. More gone, more forever, than ever before. I think I underestimated how broken we'd become. I even started to think it must be hard for a white guy right now, but I quickly took that thought back. It's always easy for the mean white guys and unfortunately for you, you're not one of those. When I got back to the city I realized that I'd had enough of all that. I knew I was right. You'd get married to someone else in an instant."

"I wasn't married that night. What's going on here, Jenny? What have you been doing with yourself? Other than breaking down in cemeteries. Don't you know you're a promising young author?"

"I've been a promising young author for twenty-five years."

"It's different, now. You're bigtime. Call one of your famous friends, and get the name of their cleaning lady."

"Do you remember 'Something by Tolstoy?'"

"I remember a few things by Tolstoy."

"No, a short story. Professor Gross gave it to us." Jenny points to the side of the bed. "I found it the other day."

I see the pages near the condoms. "I can't believe you still have all this stuff from college."

"I've devoted my life to literature, so what else would I have?"

I flick the condom and some ants off the mimeographed sheets. I don't smell the pages, only hand them to this woman who has devoted herself to literature. She says, "I wanted to stare at the essential landscape. Like Professor Gross told us to do. I wanted only to write what was there. My light would be the sudden beam on a cloudy day. I wanted to stare, but I didn't stare hard enough. I cried so much my tears were blinking. My work amounts to nothing more than that kid from third grade who appears in your dream. What is she doing there? No matter what I saw, that's all I saw."

"My God, Jenny. Don't be so hard on yourself."

"Lighten up, kiddo, my dad told me in the Dunkin'."

"Yeah, he's right. Who can say what anyone sees, or

whether it's right or wrong? The point of life is that we try to see. The point of life is that we look. And you look. You look good. And that's what I love about you. Who cares if you can't stare yet? Maybe staring comes later. Maybe staring never comes at all."

"Are you staying at Trump tower? Because you're not staying here."

"The Millennium Hilton."

"The most depressing hotel in New York. Remember when they built that shit and we were like, wow, the 2000s are going to suck even more than the 90s."

"Give me the too-long-didn't-read on 'Something by Tolstoy.'"

"It's only two pages. This old man owns a dusty bookshop. He works there alone and lives in the backroom alone. His wife left him, like, decades earlier, and she's been gone so long he's completely forgotten her. But then one afternoon, she returns and pretends she's looking for this book, this beautiful love story. He asks her what the book is about. She tells him the story, and it's the story of their love, the story of their life. But the bookseller doesn't remember his own story. It sounds too beautiful, and he assumes it must be something by Tolstoy. He turns away from his one true love and resumes reading his book."

"That's nice," I say. "Sounds like something by Tennessee Williams."

"I didn't want that to happen with us. I never wanted to come to you and say, 'This is the story of our life,' and you look at me, like you did that night on the bridge, like you had no idea what I was talking about."

"We should get out of here," I say, because Jenny's apartment is getting grosser by the minute, the kitchen crawlers are clomping toward the condoms, and now an insectarium number of creatures are pouring through the walls. "We need some fresh air. Tolstoy will still be here when we return."

***

We push up Second Avenue and into a sloppy crowd. At the bar we tell everyone we're getting married. Shots arrive, shots arrive again, and then we leave that bar, stumbling and laughing. At the next bar we tell everyone we're getting divorced. Shots arrive and there's no turning back, so we don't turn back.

Jenny's out of cigarettes. She bums one from a white Cuban carrying a souvenir bag from the Met. She goes on and on about a cocktail she learned from her Cuban mother before the revolution.

I talk with the white Cuban husband. This guy and I are great friends. He wears a red Make America Great Again cap but he seems so nervous wearing the rival team's colors on his blue state vacation.

"I finally got my wife pregnant," I tell the white Cuban. "During *Independence Day*. When I came I was looking at the Fresh Prince dressed like Tom Cruise from *Top Gun*. But my wife doesn't want me anymore. She's sailed to Tokyo with the postmodern Glenn Miller. She will probably abort our child, and there's nothing I can do to stop her."

"You can kill her," the husband says.

"I *knew* you were married," Jenny says.

A Ukrainian chemist comes over and asks the Cuban for a cigarette. With a pencil behind his ear, he is one of the brightest men in America and he will soon be deported.

"How do you say in English, I am supreme clientele, I am valedictorian? But this nation doesn't want me."

"I think you just said it in English."

"I would never kill my wife. But instead of coparenting our kid, I might switch to dogs."

"Why not sire children and raise dogs?" suggests the Ukrainian. "Many lives are possible."

We don't know where to go so for a moment we don't go anywhere. Jenny's walking ahead of me, and I pull on her shirt when I catch up.

"So, listen. You're right. I did meet this woman. And I was in a deep relationship with her. A relationship similar to a marriage, okay, and okay, we're married, prenup'd to the gills. We married in the Trump

International Paradise room. It wasn't the greatest night of my life. And I'll get nothing. She basically did to me what Mackenzie Scott did to Jeff Bezos. But this happened *after* you left me on the bridge, Jenny. Even though I feel like I'm still standing on that bridge with you, wishing I'd done the gallant thing. And I hate her now. My wife. She has perfect teeth. She never asked about my dad's death. She never asked me one question about myself, but we told each other everything. What I mean is, I know everything about her, but she knows almost nothing about me. She called you my zero wife. She loves your writing."

"Shut up."

"Or the reviews, anyway. I don't think she's ever read a book, like the words inside. She read 200 pages of *The Idiot* in Junior High and thought it made her anti-death-penalty, even though she's caused the death of millions of people, you know, in a white supremacy sense."

"Where is she?"

"Japan. Or on her way. With a fake jazz musician. Although Roberta said he has chops."

"I hope you feel better now," Jenny says, looking down at her iPhone.

"Who are you texting?"

"No one you know."

The Blue Nile is packed. The bar stretches across the front wall, behind it a large mirror that makes the cramped space look bigger. For the larger singing parties there are red leather trimmed booths, and before the stage, two-drink minimum tables, faded flowers, black chairs you can spin around and mug Cole Porter tunes. Up on the stage, a worn upright piano, toned like a tooth smarting from too much ice cream. All night long at the Blue Nile piano players like Tommy "the Wizard" Visconti knuckle out piano rolls and sing campfire songs about the sinking American lollipop. When we walk in, Tommy's playing Meat Loaf's 'Paradise by the Dashboard Light.' He embodies Meat Loaf's weighted swagger, a young man sure of his 10-minute duet for two adults remembering being kids, barely 17, kids who needed to do it right now, because all would be lacking if sex were lacking. The boy in the song says he has a 'big surprise to make the girl's motor run.' But more than reliable organs, the couple has time, no matter how much time passes, because there's no point looking back at missed chances, the song teaches—there's no backward and forward in paradise.

"Welcome back," the bartender addresses Jenny. They're always cordial at The Blue Nile but they don't coordinate your indiscretions—if they saw you the night before, they welcome you back. I start wondering if the condoms on Jenny's floor came from any of these wrinkled old men posting up around us, any of the younger men on the hunt for the older women who hang around piano bars, women who self-identify as fag hags with closeted husbands. I used to be one of those younger men, and now I'm one of those older men. Before I screwed it up, we were trying to make a baby.

"I've been here again," Jenny says.

"No problem with that. Best bar in the city."

"Maybe too much, I don't know. This place reminds me of coke, you know. But I'm mostly turning it down."

"No, I get it. You're on this writer's block bender thing, I get it. Sleep is overrated. And morning may never come. Two house gin shots..."

"...no, wait. Will you buy me a proper martini? Remember martinis?"

"Two Grey Goose martinis."

"This," Jenny says, taking a big sip, "is as far as we go."

"My martini tastes like a Manhattan," I say. "That can't be good."

I go to call the bartender back, but a girl holds her hand to mine. She says hello in an always-be-interviewing voice. Natasha is younger, wasted again, and has never been drunk. She has short hair with styled bangs, a sharp nose that bends in the opposite direction of the thicker bangs.

I order house gin shots to chase the martinis, three bucks, three shots.

"Do you remember when we first started texting?" I ask Jenny, my lips smarting. "Like, right when texting became a thing."

"You guys have known each other," Natasha burps, "since before texting became a thing."

"And instead of talking on the phone we were like type type type. Type type type. I'd be walking back uptown in winter, in and out of drugstores to stay warm, and we'd be furiously texting about what exactly? When we talked on the phone, we had to break speech for an ambulance. I would say, Hold on, ambulance. And while we were holding, the ambulance raced the failing heart up First Avenue. I would think to myself, That better not be Jenny in there, and then I'd be like, Duh, Jenny's on the phone, she can't be in there. But what if she's calling from the ambulance? That better not be Dad in there. Or Professor Gross. I'm glad it's not me. But then when we started texting. When we starting texting, the sirens get out of our way. Typing meant we got to complain about the emergency. Talking on the phone meant the emergency won. The emergency, I think, should win."

"I'm all for emergencies," Natasha says.

"One night I asked you to meet me here. You were at a party, like five blocks away, and you wrote back, No way, fuck off, too far."

"I was doing too much blow then, Ty."

"And I texted back, it's only five blocks, babe, it's the Blue Nile, not Betelgeuse! But on the phone, if we were talking, I never would have said that, you know. I would've said, It's the Blue Nile, babe, it's not Brooklyn! But in text I chose Betelgeuse. I wanted to see Orion and say nothing, like you were always asking me to. And I don't know how to spell Betelgeuse. And I bet you I'm not saying it right. But I know how to text it out of my stargazing."

"Don't be so hard on yourself, Ty."

"Isn't it just like how you're saying it right now," Natasha says. "Like, Beetlejuice? Beetlejuice!"

"Beetlejuice!"

"If you leave with her tonight," Jenny says, "I'm never speaking to you again."

A boy, even younger than Natasha, gets Jenny's attention. He has a pharaonic pate, steady eyes. He wears a paisley gaiter around his neck, and peeking out of his white shirt pocket is a bright red notebook, a mini fountain pen.

"*There* you are, Jennifer. Why did you stop answering me?"

"Do we know each other?" Natasha asks.

"I actually can't tonight, Luigi. No."

"Luigi," I say. "Any relation to Mario?"

"You think you're the first person to ask me that? Then why did you text, Jennifer? I was in Brooklyn."

"Oh yeah," I say. "Were you at a protest, lending your still small voice?"

"Do you know this creep?"

"I ran out of cigarettes," Jenny says, "and this creep was telling a fascist about leaving his wife, so I needed something to do with my hands."

"She left *me*, babe."

"Last night," Luigi says, "or wasn't it early this morning, my sweet, we told each other everything we know. I told you I loved you. Now, in this moonlight, I love you even more."

"This isn't moonlight," Jenny says. "We're wasted at a bar."

The condoms on Jenny's floor likely came from this young Italian poet. I apologize to Luigi, tell him it's been a long day. Just a few hours ago I was in the swimming pool in Seattle, listening to the screaming child. Luigi accepts my apology and offers to buy everyone another round, but when the drinks arrive, he lets me pay.

"Thank you for saying you love me. It's very sweet. But I can't take your size. When a normal penis is in me, I have some of my deepest thoughts. Like yours, Ty. With you inside me, I can think. But Luigi's leaves me speechless."

"Thank you," I say.

Jenny drops her head onto my shoulder. "I just want to meet you for the first time. And hear the story of your life."

"No!" Luigi cries. "*We* tell each other everything, not you and this guy. I told you things I've never told a soul before. I left nothing out."

"Then I hate to tell you, buddy," I say. "But your relationship's doomed."

"You're my dream girl, Jennifer," Luigi says.

"If this is your dream girl, wake up."

"Oh, fuck off, Ty," Jenny says. "What are you even doing here, anyway?"

"I love you, Jennifer," Luigi says. "I love you because you're a poet who understands men."

"You're messy, Marks," I say. "You're raw."

"You were born after the invention of texting, Luigi. Don't you want Natasha?"

"It's true," I say. "Luigi, ravish Natasha. She's not a poet."

Natasha says, "I've got a room at the Marriott in Times Square."

"The Marriott in Times Square," Jenny and I sing in unison. "I want you to know," I tell Jenny, "that if you choose me tonight, I will be there for you. Always."

"No!"

"I told you, Ty—the martinis are as far as we go."

"That's not what I mean. I will be there for you at the

end, the way I've been here since the beginning."

"Unlike your wife."

"She and I, we had no secrets. But you and I have secrets. And that's why our love survives. One day we will lose our memories, Jenny. Maybe we lose all the memories. When we've forgotten it all, what we remember can be our little secret. Nobody else needs to know."

"Just beautiful, Beetlejuice," Natasha says. "But I thought nobody needed to know."

***

The four of us leave the Blue Nile and walk toward the apartment, Jenny and I straight ahead, Natasha and Luigi encroaching from both sides. Everyone does their own sure-footed swerving: Luigi under awnings, Natasha bouncing off the curb like a schoolteacher in a technicolor musical, Jenny and I in the carefree romantic middle, but me also blocking and tackling Luigi's path to Jenny.

I fake a punch. Luigi punches back. I duck, then stiff-arm him as we turn onto York Avenue. I reach into Luigi's shirt pocket and threaten to stab the boy with his own fountain pen.

Luigi shrieks when two drugged rats follow each other out of a garbage can.

"Fucking tourist. You've never seen two rats jump out of a garbage can before?"

"I live in Bed-Stuy, asshole."

"Oh, rats don't eat garbage there?"

"Maybe they eat Beyond Mice," Natasha says.

"What the fuck did you say?" I ask Natasha, tightening my grip on Luigi.

"Let me go, let me go!"

I release the young Italian from the headlock. We stop in front of Jenny's apartment. The moon serves as our spotlight.

"There!" I say. "*There's* a pool of light. No, now it's there."

I mock myself up with a Mosaic staff, spread my arms to make a cross. "Dear Lord. Oh Lord. I am parting your pool of light."

"What are you talking about?" Natasha asks.

"I'm a slave," I say. "I'm a slave for your Egyptian love."

"I hate to inform you, sir," Luigi says, wiping blood and fountainpen ink from his nose, "but you're not in chains. For you, the revolution is just another story. But some of us still burn for freedom."

"Oh, I simply adore a summer rain," Natasha swoons. "Who has an umbrella?"

Luigi takes a deep breath, produces an umbrella from his back pocket. "I don't think it's time, yet."

"Well, it's snowing," Natasha says in a plantation saga accent, "so now would be the perfect time to proffer an umbrella if a gentleman had one."

"You are that dude," I snarl at Luigi, "who thinks just because you carry an umbrella, any girl will sleep with you."

"What will you do for Luigi," Jenny says to Natasha, "if he shares his umbrella with you?"

"The Marriott in Times Square."

"Oh boy," Jenny says. "I need to sit down."

She sits next to me on the stoop. Then she says, "I need to stand up." She pushes Natasha out of the way and sits in my lap.

"Ow!" I say. I reach back and pull the American flag from the Uber driver out of my back pocket.

"Looks like the stars and stripes," Jenny says, "came back to stab you in the ass."

"But isn't that," Natasha says, "supposed to be a bright blue chillum?"

"Would you shut the fuck up?"

I take out my phone and run away from the group. I see dozens of text messages from Ellory.

Ty, are you there? I don't know what I did. How could I? I'm disgusting, I'm heartless, I'm a 21st century fox, I'm a walking nightmare, I'm sick. I want to feel like I'm so regretful. I want to sail home. Tokyo is so boring without you. It has a big mountain like Seattle but it's just not the same.

You're there already? I write back.

There you are! Oh baby, we got here last week. But it feels like we've been here a year. Do you remember, how we danced, the night we met?

I do remember, I write back. I remember so well.

I miss you, baby. And I love you. The best things happen while you're dancing. Did I ever tell you that? Marcus needs to talk to you about the Oakland property.

You mean, I write back, holding the American flag like it's a cigarette, because of the tsunami?

What tsunami? No, not a tsunami. It's about the professors, dear. They want a new microwave and they're threatening to start a blog if Daddy doesn't install one.

Thanks for letting me know, I write back. I send a message to the anarchist professors, warning them I have abandoned the plantation owner's daughter, or rather she has left me for a racially ambiguous, postmodern jazz musician—the poets will understand this—but don't fear, she's coming back, moreover, I will take her back, and we're going to have a beautiful baby boy, and the professors should pay up.

"Who are you texting?" Jenny asks.

"No one I know."

The toothpick flag falls to the ground. Once it's there, I stomp on it. Then I get down on my knees and bang into it.

"Ty, stop! That's your bad knee."

"I wanted this flag to save me. Like it always had before. But no, this flag has always hated me. And people like me."

"That flag *loves* people like you, dude," Luigi says.

"Shut up, Bed-Stuy. This flag destroyed my life. I wanted to believe in this flag. Like I always had. I helped my father put it in front of our house. He told me he couldn't do it by himself. That the flag had to be raised by two people, lowered by multitudes more, and I always believed that. I wanted to keep on believing in this flag, believing in him. And I didn't want to sell my father's house, but I sold my father's house, and I didn't want to bury my father in a Catholic cemetery, but I buried my father in a Catholic cemetery. And I didn't want to treat you bad, Jenny, on the bridge."

"It's okay, Ty—calm down. You left me a hundred times before. Watch your knees."

"Finally, I am on them. I'm sorry I didn't write you back that night. I'm sorry I got the Trump hotel. I'm sorry I insulted the donkey rabbi. And I should've treated the jeweler off Via Condotti with respect. And I never should've threatened the delightful Greek boy. And I never should've worn Shelly Fink's tux. And I never should've gotten married, it was only to learn more about the Oakland property. I am sorry I couldn't build us a tender house. I wanted to burn myself. When what I should've done, what I should do, is burn this flag."

"Does anybody have a match," Luigi says. "So this trickster can set himself on fire? Don't listen to him, Jennifer. He doesn't love you. He will say anything to hear himself talk."

"I agree," Natasha says. "You know yourself so well, Beetlejuice. But I don't care for men who know themselves." Natasha wishes Jenny good luck and walks to the curb, turns her back on us.

"Let's go up," I tell Jenny.

"No, no!"

"Or come downtown. I've got the hotel, and I need to get to work in like an hour."

"No, Ty, I'm sorry. I don't go downtown anymore. I don't even go below Fifty-ninth Street anymore."

"That's great. So, I'll buy us a bigger apartment. Here in Yorkville. Even West Lex, whatever."

"Where is West Lex?" Luigi asks.

"West of Lexington, you moron."

"Right, right. Why don't you just say Park Avenue, you creep? You ancient New Yorkers still think anyone in the world gives a shit about your fake neighborhoods. I cannot believe this."

"Why don't you go make yourself believable with Natasha?"

"Goodnight!" Natasha yells back.

"Get thee to the Marriott in Times Square."

"No! You have to choose, Jennifer. This guy, he doesn't care about you. He's just scared of being alone."

"You think your love is limitless," I snarl at Luigi. "You think you're never going to leave this stoop. You think you'll mewl till the end of time because you think you've got it, and you know how to use it. But you don't. Unless I kill you tonight, you're not going to die before you turn 29. And you're going to find that cosmic betrayal makes it impossible for you to love anything. And you will live a long, heart healthy life, wondering what happened to your soul."

"Yeah, thanks, you talking head. What about you, asshole? You're still on this stoop, too."

"Why," Natasha yells back, "don't you both go away? Why does Jennifer have to choose either of you? She can just choose herself." Natasha gets into her taxi. Seconds later, the same taxi arrives on the other side of the street. And the same Natasha exits that taxi and walks back to us, bathed in a pool of light. "Oh, Betelgeuse," she swoons. "Can we brown our toes in the moonlight? Because I love feeling the heat of the moon on my toes. Not everyone knows this, but the light of the moon is just as hot as the light of the sun."

She sits down next to me, kicks off her heels.

"Have you ever tried to stare into the moon? You can't. You'll go blind."

"Wait," I say. "I thought you were wearing Chacos."

"Ewww, I'm not a hippie."

I pull off my shoes, my socks, and point my feet up.

"What happened to your toe, baby?" Natasha asks.

"Oh, we forgot to pack the right clipper, sugar, and I cut too close to Ben Stiller's nail."

"Tan it for me, stud. It makes me wet to watch you brown. Nothing's sexier on a man than tanned feet."

"Funny thing," I say. "My feet feel like they're on fire."

"Oh my God," Luigi jumps. "They are!"

I jump too and put my foot in one of the puddles of snow. I succeed in putting the fire out but then a rush of numbness snaps my head down. A shard of street glass, buried in the snow, has split open the side of my foot, revealing novel layers of skin.

I'm gushing.

Everyone moves away from me.

"Will somebody help me? Please? I'm bleeding out."

Nobody moves, nobody helps.

"Okay. I promise you I will no longer be the center of my own story. But please help. Please? I really am bleeding out over here. Jenny, will you help me staunch this bleed? Ellory, will you help me staunch this bleed? What about the park ranger, who gave us the map up Deer Creek Road, will she help me staunch this bleed? My dad was looking for a National Parks passport stamp and everyone was ignoring him!"

"What are you talking about?"

"He's going delirious from loss of blood," Natasha says. "But it'll do him good to lose some of the blood he's been hoarding from everyone else."

"No, come on," Jenny says. "We should help him."

"Oh Marilyn, Marilyn. I believe your name was Marilyn, and if you can't give me the alternate wi-fi password, will you at least help me staunch this bleed?"

"Let him die," Luigi says.

"No, please, Mario, you have to help me. Don't you want to help a brother?"

Luigi turns away, lights a cigarette.

"Can I bum one, dude?"

"You really think this is a good time for you to be smoking?"

"That's what the soldiers always do in World War II movies before they die."

"You need to clot."

"Oh, Natasha. Will you help me? Don't you *have* to help me, aren't you a nurse?"

"I thought you worked in retail?" Jenny says.

"Regrets, Beetlejuice. I'm scared of blood."

"Maybe you're right. Maybe we'd all be happier if I bleed out."

"Is there no limit to your self-hatred, Ty? Wake up, Mr. Rossberg!"

8.

I wake up. I smell coconuts. And hear what I think are raindrops. I'm trying to remember her name. She turned her back. Hailed a taxi. It was the strangest dream. Where did it begin? The sheets are warm. She appeared in the same taxi. Going the opposite direction. And I'm in New York. I must be. It was raining and snowing at the same time. How did she know about Beyond Mice? Why did Natasha, that's her name, call the bright red chillum *blue*? And was she a nurse, or a buyer for J. Crew?

I'm patting myself for the American flag. And Jenny's daisy from the bookstore. I'm looking on the nightstand for my powerhouse club.

Ellory.

I type *E-l-l* into my contacts.

Nothing shows.

I pull my feet out from under the covers, turn them to the floor. They're white, undamaged. I see my pants and pull them on. They fit. I flex my toe. No pain. I walk to the window and open the blackout curtain. A busker plays on the bridge. I can see the trumpet, but not hear it. I see the tender house. I'm in Chicago. In Trump International.

There's a TV remote on the nightstand.

And now for more on the stories nobody's talking about.

I mute the TV. I hear, again, raindrops. They're coming from the bathroom. I see light through the bottom of the closed door. I knock. And hear Ellory's voice. She stands at the vanity, applying eye makeup. There's a wireless speaker, playing Beethoven's "Pastoral" Piano Sonata.

"No," I say.

"No what, baby?"

"Baby?" I point to Ellory's stomach. She's very pregnant. She wears a white yoga outfit, shiny black penny loafers. She raises a can of coconut water to her lips.

"No!"

"What, baby, what?"

"Don't drink it."

"Why? I'm addicted. You know that."

"I had this dream. So vivid."

"You've had so many vivid dreams, babe, since you stopped smoking pot."

"When did I stop smoking pot?"

"Ty. We said we weren't going to talk about Tokyo anymore."

"No, I know. I just had the strangest dream."

"Research shows your spouse doesn't care about your dreams."

"Jenny Marks was in it."

"Especially dreams about your ex-wife…"

"...she wasn't my wife..."

"...today, Ty, don't mention her. Of all days."

"My toe. It was aflame. My foot was on fire."

"Oh, baby. You have to have that MRI."

Ellory drinks the coconut water. I must restrain myself from knocking it away. I'm positive it's mixed with the ashes from her wedding dress, the bits of charred battery from the Athenian camera.

"I'm sorry for asking you this. But did you see my powerhouse on the table?"

"I'm not talking about your powerhouse. I have no idea what it means, and honestly, you're starting to frighten me. Sometimes, you get so weird."

"No, I know," I say, patting my jean pocket. "Sometimes, I'm so me." I take out a pack of cigarettes. Odd, I quit smoking. But then again, it makes sense. All of this stress. I go to the bathroom speaker, turn the Beethoven up.

"You can't smoke in here, baby."

"This feeling. You know this feeling I mean. When you just want to listen to classic Beethoven. There should be a German word for it. When you just want to forget that anything has happened, since you were six. When you just want to be six. When you just want to close your eyes and hear raindrops."

"Put the cigarette out, Ty."

"But life forces us to listen to something new. Life

says, you can't have Beethoven. But Beethoven is all you want."

"Oh, baby, that's so sweet. But the fine will be like $5,000."

"I remember telling *you* that. In this very room."

"You said you'd stop when the baby came."

"When is the baby due?" I ask, handing her the cigarette. She turns on the faucet and runs it under the water. "Right," I say. "We're headed to the hospital."

"I'm being induced."

"You're being induced. I think it's because we're here, you know. I'm thinking about the night we met. But today, you're being induced. That's right."

"We have one stop before the hospital."

"Where?"

"Come on. Finish getting dressed. We don't have much time."

***

It's the Art Institute's late night, free to Illinois residents. We run up the lion-flared steps, warmed by the rushing heat inside the main hall. An attendant summons us forward. We hand over our licenses.

"These," the guard say, "are accepted starting at five."

"What time is it?" I ask.

"It's not five."

"Can't you see she's pregnant?" I say to the guard. But I also feel like I'm saying it to myself.

Ellory hands over another card.

"Do you have an ATM card to verify?"

Without looking up, Ellory flashes an ATM card.

"What's your zip code?"

"I don't know," Ellory says.

"60602," I say. "That's right," I smile. "Our zip code is six-oh-six-oh-two."

"That one," Ellory says. "60602."

We enter the coat check line. An attendant summons us forward. Ellory says she needs a second. She removes items from her shoulder bag. A pair of flannel pajamas, a copy of *The Paternal Woman*, a makeup case, her wallet, keys, a dryer ball, and a microwavable heating pad. She hands me her placard, on a string. I put it in my back pocket. She hands me a star of David pendant.

"Help me with this," she says.

"This is different. Where'd you get it?"

"I lost my old one, babe. In Rome. You *know* this."

"But where is this one from?"

"From Moses. For our pact."

"No, I know. Right."

I stand behind her in the mirror and do the clasp. Then, we check our coats and bag. At the entrance, the next attendant asks for our tickets.

"Ty, show him the tickets."

"No, I don't seem to," I say, patting myself, "have them. You had them. Did you leave them in the bag?"

"Do you have the coat check ticket?"

"No, you do."

"No, I just handed it to you."

"Wait. I have it."

Ellory walks back to the coat check line and gets her bag. She finds the admission tickets and rechecks the bag. The attendant scans our tickets and hands them back intact.

"Isn't it too bad we don't rip tickets anymore," I say.

The attendant doesn't answer. We walk through. I rip my own ticket. And put my arm around my wife. I think about us starting out on a hike, how much we loved each other, in the mountains.

"Ready?"

"Ready," I say. "Lead the way."

We ride the elevator up to the modern wing.

"I need to shit," Ellory says.

"We'll find the bathroom."

"I'm shitting right now."

"Are you sure?"

"I'm disgustipated."

"Well, let's find the bathroom, then." I look at her white bottom and see a brown spot.

"No, it's fine. It's just a little shit."

We enter the New Contemporary galleries. We stand

260

close to an Andy Warhol. The Andy Warhol beeps.

"Step back from the artwork," the guard says.

I step closer. It beeps again.

"Please, step back from the artwork."

A foreign-looking couple, wearing matching Michael Jordan jerseys, stand too close to the Warhol. It beeps again. Teenagers giggle, move forward, making the artwork beep on purpose, to impress each other. The beats become erratic, but steady, like the final pulses from a heart monitor, calling the artwork's time of death.

"Ma'am," the guard says to Ellory, "would you like to sit down?" The guard sniffs. "Can I help you find a bathroom?"

We leave the gallery and find a family restroom. Ellory sits on the toilet, holds her breath, pushes. When she stands up, we see a bloodflower in the toilet water.

"That wasn't me."

"Are you sure?"

"I can't remember. Was it there before I sat down?"

"Is your, water breaking?"

"Water only breaks on *Grey's Anatomy*. I want a wine at Caffè Moderno."

"What would Mrs. Prowler have to say about that."

"You called her, right?"

"No, of course. Take that necklace off. I don't like it."

"We talked about this."

"I remember. I remember. Take it off, though, for me."

I stand behind her in the mirror and take off the necklace, put it in my shirt pocket. I type *Moses Murray* into my phone. Nothing comes up. I type *Indie Sleaze Dance Party*, and Ellory Allen's number appears.

We stand on the Caffè Moderno line. The man in front of us says, "Please, you go, I'm in no rush."

Ellory orders a glass of red.

"Are you a member of the museum?"

"Why do you want to know?"

"Members get a 20% discount."

"What about this ATM card?"

"That means 10%."

"Thanks so much," we say, bringing the discounted wine to the tables.

We live in a luxury townhome, north of the Chicago River. In a neighborhood emptied of all its pockets. Our townhome started in the low $800s, but we paid more, much more, with an assist from Ellory's father. We sacrificed good public schools for a high walkability score because we would never think of sending our child to a public school. We have a magnolia tree, outside of our bay window. The leaves turn sooner in the fall, come back at the first blush of spring. We have a Japanese maple. We have a flower garden, beebalms and spider lilies. We have a Black Lives Matter sign. The snows cover up the word *Matter*, when it snows more it covers up the word *Lives*, when there's a blizzard you can't even see our sign.

I work for my New York firm, here in Chicago, partnering with Nathan Wilde. Ellory doesn't work. She doesn't volunteer. In the evenings, we read books on parenting, we read articles on our phones, we watch TV, there's this show *Jewish Drama*, our fav. We read in one of our books that "pregnancy is the war that stays home," so we stay home.

Ellory kept her condo, bought out Shelly Fink. She goes there to be at peace. She goes there to make love to Moses and other men. These men come, these men go. It's not that my wife cheats on me, I give her the green light colored red. She relaxes on a fainting couch, reading about trans desire and having cishet affairs on the pink-sheeted bed. The men visit Chicago, meet my wife at the Art Institute, make love to her, and leave the city. I don't know if the child in Ellory's belly is mine. I assume so. After Seattle, with an assist from Abe Allen, we paid Moses's relocation expenses. He lives on the other side of town. I always think about this one thing I said to him up Deer Creek road: the great thing about capitalism is that people who can't afford to live in beautiful neighborhoods at least get to the work in them. Moses works close to our townhome. He's a barista at the Bank Café. I don't know if our child is mine.

In the evenings, we read books and phones, and we listen to Gustav Mahler's *Kindertotenlieder*, songs on the death of children. Our child isn't dead, but not yet alive. It's good to be prepared. There are two events in the life of a pregnant woman. One event is when the baby comes, the other event is everything else. We are two. Soon we'll be three. If you include Moses, we are four.

Ellory sips her wine. "We must have hope," she says. "Hope that we will not have to sing songs on the death of children."

"Has he answered you?" I ask. I buy her another glass of wine. She opens a draft message to Moses, shows me the words. The note is, she's come to realize, the first love letter she's ever written. She reads her words over and over again until she comes to believe Moses had read them, too. Reading her beautiful words makes her weep. She weeps. I hold her hand. I buy her another glass of wine. These are some of the most vulnerable things she's almost sent to another person. She could have hit send weeks ago, but something has held her back. She isn't sure if it was the fear that he wouldn't respond or her inability to seize control if he did. She wanted him to be a part of our labor. She wanted him to see all we'd become. The baby she carried, our baby, also belonged to him.

"I don't have the courage," Ellory says.

"You have courage," I say. "And Mrs. Prowler will be here soon."

We'd visited a fertility doctor. I found one in the

medical portal. Her office was a maternal space. Lamps, not overheads, lit the room. A desk photo of the doctor's triplets dressed in bumblebee costumes. She took notes on a Nexplanon notepad with a NuvaRing pen. In her office, we argued like couple's therapy. The doctor suggested we fall back in love. We are in love, I said. Then take a trip. I suggested Bhutan. Ellory said, I'm never going to Bhutan. The doctor got tired of us. She told us, There's nothing wrong with you.

We travelled. We tried. We were white American Jews in our early 40s. We were lonely together, lonely apart, failed intellectuals, narcissists jazz and classical. We tried as much as Ellory could stand it, as much as I could stand up. We tried twice in one night, like newlyweds, cuddled, kissed, fluttered, flicked—no results. We tried in Paris, Stockholm, Lisbon, and Miami in the rain. We tried before second sleep on Sunday mornings, on midweek sick day afternoons, on the steps of Buckingham Fountain, on a dive breakfast of High Life chasers and soggy pretzel rods we tried like master and slave, barebacked runaways, we tried like returning champions. We tried during intermission and brought licorice back to our seats. We tried at the investment opportunity in the Smokies, the Breck ski-in, ski-out, on the heated floors of an Appalachian glamper, in the candlelit cabanas of a private Mexican beach. We tried near home, driving through the nature preserves across the western suburbs. We skated the snowy bogs, sought sexual cover in the savannah, brushed our sore genitals against the prickly prairie grass. We overnighted in the hick villas beyond the border towns that once carted slaves from Kentucky to work the salt mines near Equality, Illinois. We tried on a meandering road trip through the driftless area of Wisconsin, an area of deep green hills minutes from the side hustles of the Mississippi. We tried in the airport lounge, we tried on the plane. We tried like husband and wife. We tried like wild animals.

We tried mostly in our townhome, on the great green sectional, with one eye on our phones, one eye on our books, half our bookish eye on the flatscreen streaming. We tried on the chaise and standard cushions, on the floor, backs against the frame, Ellory propped up on pillows. We tried in the primary bedroom suite. We called it the master. In our community, fertility troubles were an open secret. Open secrets are the only ones left. We reached out to others. Responses poured in. Ellory had asked consultative questions, that is, questions that lead to more questions. Describe your fertility journey? When did you realize it was a journey? When did you start trying to conceive? How should we approach fertility struggles in our community? How does your judgement of our privilege factor into our desire to sire an eldest? How should I feel, as the woman? How should he feel, as the man? How should we feel, as one? And how does global warming figure into this? Is that a dimension you can speak to? Let's face it: we're trying to conceive, so we're thinking about these things all of the time? But what about you? What do you think of us?

One of Ellory's ex-friends wrote, You two sound like you deserve each other. Another ex-friend tried to sell her an amazing juice fast. Not that she would have any problems, once she did get pregnant, returning to her pre-baby weight. Another ex-friend said, Babies aren't cool, or didn't they teach you that at aging hipster school? Ellory's ex-boyfriend Ron wrote that he still dreamed about her. Ron lived in Florida now. Ellory should hit him up if she needed any help. He would, "fuck her ass so hard she'd shit out twins."

"What are you learning?" I asked from my section of the sectional.

"Ronnie moved to Florida."

"Disgusting," I said. "I could never live in Florida."

I took sperm tests. I passed. I tried acupuncture and drank Chinese herbs, shot B-12. With Ellory's green light, I paid prostitutes. Gwen was a former catalogue model, a two-or-more-races personal shopper who called herself an emotional consultant. She was like someone who only exists on the internet, which is where I met her. Severe bob. We dined at NoMi Kitchen and Shanghai Terrace. She used contemporary slang, I wrote it down. Some afternoons we slummed it, beer and wings in an empty Jake Melnick's, the fish fry at Nico inside the Thompson Hotel, Daley Manhattans at the Dearborn. After a session of slim fittings, we took a breather at the Nordstrom cocktail bar. I sipped my Italian Gentleman, Gwen her Italian Shandy. A man walked by wearing one of the priceless casual button-downs shirts I'd just purchased. It's jarring to know you can buy one of the most beautiful shirts in the world, but a copy of that shirt exists for someone else, too. I meditated on that depressing fact while staring at a life-sized poster of Michelle Williams in campaign for Louis Vuitton.

"You can just see it in Michelle's eyes," I said. "She misses Heath."

"Which one was Heath?" Gwen asked. Her skin was the color of the sky during World War III.

"Heath was the husband."

"I thought it was Casey Affleck."

"Heath was the Joker. He died."

"You should buy the women in your life Louie," Gwen said. She claimed to be a socialist, but that was just one of her stories.

"My life partner isn't into brands."

"Everyone's into brands," Gwen said, her voice a kill order for more bombs. "Everyone's into everything."

"You're too young to remember this, but in my day

268

we called that 'selling out.'"

"I don't know what that means. Like a distribution problem?"

Gwen had a body in the 0.01% of bodies, youth inextinguishable, salamander in flames. When I kissed her sexy brown feet, I stopped believing in science. When we made love, I stopped believing in causes, effects, cause and effect, affect theory, the near future, the recent past, particles, atoms, kill or be killed, climate change, experts, the phrase, "at the end of the day," political economy, four-dimensional chess, late capitalism, and the public square, supply and demand, and the phrase, "at any rate."

"I believe in climate change at the beach," Gwen said. "When my phone asks to cool down."

Even though I didn't have to, I would've done anything to impress Gwen. I even got down to my army weight, and regretted never joining the army. I was now an extra slim fit man by any measure, even the French president. She helped me buy all these suits, and I wore them, because there's no reason to keep your suits in the closet, if you've got them. Ellory noticed, but Gwen commented. We started seeing each other every afternoon, when I was supposedly very busy at work, and even though I was a millionaire many times over, I was going broke. Gwen probably didn't have time for her other friends. She noticed my stubble immediately. She noticed when I shaved. I paid extra to snag us barstools at a west side restaurant with no name, no website, no phone. Four different waiters refilled our waters. We guessed the principal on their student loans, if their interest rate was fixed or variable. We softly handled deckled menu pages, ate oysters topped with caviar-flecked condiments, shared lobster spaghetti and paid extra for shaved truffles. The nonbinary sommelier, whom Gwen called the som, wore a prep school blazer and announced they were only recommending wine from women-owned vineyards this season. The som asked me if I'd ever done the year of drinking wine from women-owned vineyards and I said, Yes, of course I did that. We smoked homegrown dope from Gwen's Barneys New York chillum, which led to Wendy's Frosties and fries, which led to dirtier, high school sex. I came so hard with Gwen it arced from the river to the sea.

During pillow talk, Gwen told me she was moving to Berlin to start a line of men's essentials. I told her I would buy her balms and creams, her removers, serums, her acids. I told her I would never forget her. As a going away present, I left a set of Louis Vuitton luggage with her doorman, and a Blu-ray of Heath Ledger's *The Dark Knight*.

"Can you make sure the young woman in 4709 gets this?"

The doorman didn't immediately look up from his

phone.

"Sir?"

"What is this?" the doorman asked.

"It's a Blu-ray disc."

"What does it do?"

"It holds one Hollywood feature and its extras."

"Got you," he said.

I never received a note of thanks from Gwen. She afforded me a richer, more pleasurable life. And she left me a poorer man.

Ellory asked me if I wanted to see another prostitute. I told her, No. I think that did the trick.

In our townhome, she performed ceremonies. She had this custom amphora made that said, You can't kill the mother without killing the son. We staycationed at Trump International. We laid out photos of Noah Baumbach, Jeff Goldblum, Lawrence Fink, Ben Stiller. We never burned 'The Last Jew in Vinnitsa' because we didn't want to burn ourselves. We burned the Stiller with the Fink, the Goldblum with the burning Stiller, the Baumbach with the still burning Fink, and then we made love in the good Jewish flames.

Maybe that did the trick. The thing is, you never know.

***

Mrs. Prowler looks exactly the way she did to me, in my mind, when Ellory told me the story of the sick fox. She carries a leather notebook, a small but heavy looking pen, a creased museum map.

"It's just a whole different world," Mrs. Prowler says, of the Art Institute. "It's heaven. *It is art.* Imagine the artist who lives in Chicago, who might want inspiration from the masters. They would just come here, to study. They would just come right over here."

We both give Mrs. Prowler a big hug. She declines my offer of a drink. We talk about the lectures being given right now, the chamber music performances. We talk about the Prado, the Reina Sofia, we talk about Ingres. We talk about how strict they are with the Illinois ID shit, when it's, "not yet five o'clock." We talk about how you don't need to believe in breastfeeding. A woman can choose rebirth instead of birth, the way men have done for centuries—*Abraham begot Isaac.*

"Do you remember the day of the sick fox?" Mrs. Prowler asks.

"Tell us," I say.

"It had been a very humid day near the end of the school year when the class went on a field trip to the forest preserve. In the adopted animal area, there was a skulking fox. He was an arctic fox, the sign said, so what was it doing in Illinois? He looked tired, sick, deathly ill, lots of fur missing from the abuses he'd suffered as a pup. He was barely recognizable as what we would think of as a fox, his fox-ness foxed right out of him. The sign said that one of the trustees of the forest preserve had rescued the animal, and brought him to this place, where he would live out the rest of his subarctic life peacefully, in a prairieland habitat. And we all said hello to the fox. The rest of the class moved on, to the other rescued animals nature had left behind: the alligator who wouldn't snap at a fly, the squirrel who no longer had a taste for acorns, the owl who forgot how to hoot. But you, my dear, stayed behind with the fox, putting pressure on yourself. I came back to check on you, because I was always worried about all of my children, but I was worried about children like you most of all. I worried that you were too sensitive to become a person in this world, that you would never be strong enough to fight for the justice you strained to understand. I worried that you had the knowledge, but you didn't have the wherewithal, to fight for what you believed in."

"I was lonely," Ellory says.

"That was only part of it."

"I was *solissima*."

"You were?"

"*Solissima*. Very lonely in Italian."

"It sounds very lonely in Italian. You were always concerned, dear, with the worst. You had one eye in the slaughterhouse, one eye in the solitary confinement,

273

your nose in the genocide. But you were never looking at what was in front of you. Because you took 'love thy neighbor' too abstractly, too hard. You never understood that loving your neighbor should be the easiest thing a person can do. You never understood that it was none of your business, saving the sick fox."

"Why not?" Ellory asks.

"Because the sick fox," I interject, "had already been saved. Won't you come with us, Mrs. Prowler, to New Contemporary? Ellory's spirits always brighten when she sees Joan Snyder's *Summer*."

"I'd love to. But I'm headed to Gauguin. I'm glad you gained some weight, dear, since the last time I saw you."

"This is baby weight," Ellory says.

Mrs. Prowler frowns at the wine glasses on the table.

"Baby weight," Ellory says again, "is not something you hold."

***

We muddle past the Twombly paintings and enter the room on the edge of the gallery. There are only a few works here, lots of walking space. One is Jeff Koons's porcelain sculpture, *Woman in Tub*. It depicts a shocked woman in a backwater bathtub, red fingernails protecting her large breasts.

"This is how I see myself, Ty. A woman with a mouth,

no eyes, and half a head."

"You like the headless men best."

"They don't have the cerebral heaviness of the headless, or the mindlessness of those with heads intact."

"I'm so happy we're here."

Woman in Tub surprises museumgoers. They raise their phones. They take selfies with Koons's bust, or, in pairs, one person stands headless-level while the other takes a your-head-here hole photo. The sculpture beeps and the guards yell, "stand back from the artwork, stand back from the artwork."

Ellory turns toward Damien Hirst's *Still*, the medical cabinet that fills the wall opposite. She asks me to help her to the floor. Even with my assistance, she plops. The Koons sculpture beeps, so my wife waddles, inch by inch, until the half-headed woman stops beeping.

Because it can't be photographed, few tourists bother with *Still*. But they do start to pay attention when they see the pregnant beauty, in white yoga pants and shiny black penny loafers, weeping on the cold ground in front of it. Since the photo would now include Ellory Allen, *Still* is no longer unphotographable.

"*Solissima*," she says.

I take the placard out of my back pocket and place it around my wife's neck. It reads: 1977, Humboldt Park/Winnetka/Highland Park, 5 foot 7, oval face, shocking blue eyes, perfect teeth, that ass, those tits, tan lines, those lips, big Israeli hair, and water. To that concise description, we've added the info of our hospital, the name of our OB, and our PPO group number.

"*Solissima*," Ellory says.

"*Solissima*," I answer.

Still responds: "You think you know yourself. But you know nothing until I know you, until my knives know you, you ungrateful hateful bitch. You selfish, heartbreaking, heartbroken wench, you white culture bitch who has caused so many people of color you've never met so much pain. You will know my black clamps, you will know my cold knives, you will know my scalpels, saws and hammers, my fasteners, spreaders, and probes, my scrub-blue saucers will overflow with your pre-code blood. You think you're lonely now, but your loneliness will be extended. Your loneliness is the disease, not the cure."

The night Bertie drove me back to Seattle I argued with her about staying at her place or getting a hotel. She convinced me to stay at her place. I slept on her eggplant-colored couch. We joked about how calling an aubergine-colored couch an eggplant-colored couch doesn't make a purple couch more comfortable. In the morning, I flew back to Chicago. I waited for Ellory to return from Tokyo. I watched our Japanese maple bloom. The day I lost hope, she came back to me.

The museumgoers are photographing Ellory, and now they're taking videos. Ellory says the word for "very lonely" in Italian so many times that it becomes an untranslatable moan, until the moaning changes to an even more primitive hissing. The tourists are hip to the fact a real-time event, an actual moment in history, possibly even feminist history, is occurring on their museum phone watch. They raise their phones to film my wife's increasingly ancient ceremony.

Nausea forces her up. She knows she's standing up too quickly, but this only makes her stand up faster. I try to contain her rise. Her film crew steadies their cameras. I also want to raise my phone. Even the guard, and guards from nearby galleries, have stepped forward to add themselves to the picture. With an actual event taking place, everyone seems to have forgotten about the art.

Ellory does stand, in a sense. But then she falls backward, very hard, toppling the Koons bust. The museumgoers howl with delight. The beeping of the artwork flatlines.

"*Solissima*," Ellory screams at the guard now kneeling above her, who screams at the tourists to give my wife space.

"Is that your doctor's name? What's Dr. Solissima's number?"

Ellory doesn't respond.

"Is anyone here a doctor," I say. And then I pass out, too.

***

In the ambulance, I google: *pregnant woman Art...* and Google completes my query with *Institute of Chicago*. The number of hits startle me. My wife is a viral sensation. Most recordings shake on Ellory's collapse, but not BEST ANGLE, captured by a tourist who is also a YouTube sensation. That vid is used for the FOX/CNN segments. FOX has *Liberal Bust* as its headline, CNN *Art Fall*. There's a Twitter moment. About sixty-two-thousand people, including young adults whose everyday thoughts on late capitalism are observations I cherish, are tweeting about the birth of my healthy baby boy. Later tonight, on the local news, before even the first preview of weather, or the second preview of sports, there will be a full segment on parking dibs in northwest side neighborhoods, and then a short segment on my wife's *Special Delivery*.

I check my email. Reporters have reached out. Am I available for a quote? No, I'm not. I return to YouTube because when I left that browser window, the video stopped playing. I watch the special delivery again. I cheer, even raise my fist in the air, as my wife collapses, as the Koons breaks. In one of the vids I see myself falling down. I look good, wearing one of the suits I bought with Gwen. I want to leave a comment on the post, something to the effect of, *that's my girl*, but I would have to log in to comment, and I can't remember my YouTube password.

The top says, *What happened to our norms? I'm genuinely curious.*

"Can I hold my child?" I ask the nurse. Even here, in the maternity ward, the hospital scent of death.

"Soon," the nurse smiles. "Your son is in good health."

I need a moment. I am your father. And the dead rise around me, like taking all the drugs at once. I'm with my grandfather, neutral through the car wash. I'm with my father, jumping the waves. I'm with my uncle the night he pretended to fit in the children's bathtub.

What if I am a bad father. What if my child grows up to be no good. What if I'm worse than the father of Dylann Roof, whose boy killed nine and injured one in an African American church. Or the father of Elliot Rodger, whose boy killed six and injured fourteen on a college campus in Santa Barbara. Seddique Mateen, the father of Omar Mateen. In many ways he seemed like a #1 Dad. His son Omar murdered 49 and injured 53 at a Florida nightclub. The father of Stephen Paddock, whose boy murdered 58 and injured 851 in Las Vegas.

I could stop, but I could also go on, and I would never catch up. Men killed because they hated being. I shared the same chromosomes as these fathers and sons. There was no reason to ask the question *why* because the chromosome is called Y.

The father of Timothy McVeigh, whose boy murdered 168 and injured 680 in Oklahoma City. I thought about Mr. McVeigh's healing process. How he was now friends with some of the victim's families. But McVeigh's father couldn't be friends with all his son's victims. There weren't enough hours in the day.

The father of Adam Lanza, whose boy killed 20 between six and seven years old, as well as six adult staff members of an elementary school in Connecticut—and his mother. Adam Lanza's father's has been quoted as saying, "I wish my boy had never been born."

Ellory sleeps. I pull over a hardbacked chair and wait for her to sense my presence. All the drugs at once have peaked. My ancestors are gone, even my grandmother blowing on the wind chimes, my aunt scrubbing the chicken.

"Sweet potato," Ellory whispers. She's once again wearing Moses's star of David necklace, and she's still wearing her placard.

"Cashew au gratin," I whisper back.

"My lips are very dry. Like I just got off the plane. Can we go home?"

"Not yet. But you're strong. The nurses say they've

never seen a woman like you before."

I tell her the story. A female doctor, an OB, happened to be in the New Contemporary galleries. She delivered our son, breaking the glass of *Still* and using some of its medical devices. I wonder, will we be responsible for the cost of replacing *Woman in Tub*? And the doctor responsible for the cost of repairing *Still*? In my head, I put the cost of replacing *Woman in Tub* at ten or twenty million dollars, maybe thirty million dollars.

"And you're famous online. Even the teenagers care."

Ellory remembered none of this. For her, there seemed to be no transition between the beeping artworks in the museum and the beeping monitors in the hospital. When she regained consciousness, she feared her body had undergone the worst excavation. She thought because of her devotion to *Still*, her son had been stilled. She could never have imagined that her favorite work of art would literally save her life, that a work of art could sacrifice itself for others.

"You're a viral sensation," I add.

"That makes me sick. I thought something bad was going to happen to us."

"No. Remember what that fertility doctor said to us?"

"Don't mention her."

"Nothing bad every happens to people like you and me. From here on out, the three of us will be on a winning streak."

"Moses," Ellory trails off.

"The four of us are going to make it."

I curl up next to her in the hospital bed. We stay in that position all night, or is it all morning? The first night, the new morning, of the rest of our lives.

9.

I pick a therapist who prescribes drugs. There's a white noise machine outside of his office door, the same one we use in the baby's room. Dr. Kordana sits in a drab chair with his notepad, and I sit on his sinking couch, clutching a pillow with who knows what kind of stains on it, revisiting what could have been, what never was, and trying to calm my fears.

"So, Tyrone," he says.

For a long time I can't say anything. Then I say, "Ty's fine."

"Why are you here, Ty?"

"Is that important? I'm an orphan."

"Is that important?"

"I must tell you about my ex, Jenny."

"Why?"

"You know, I don't know. You're right. That's an amazing question. Maybe that's not really why I'm here."

Right off the bat, Dr. Orlando Kordana is the wisest person I've ever met.

"Maybe it is, though," he says.

"Maybe she's not. Maybe she's just this story I think I need to keep telling myself. One thing's for sure, though, I keep seeing Jenny in my dreams. That is, when I can sleep. As the father of a newborn, you only get an hour or so, if you're disciplined enough to *sleep when the baby sleeps*, which is a cliché, just like everything about parenthood is a cliché, which is nobody's fault, parenthood is the oldest profession so it's got the most clichés."

"Congratulations. Maybe you want to talk about becoming a parent."

"No, that's boring."

"Why is that boring?"

"No, you're right, it completely defines my life."

"Do you think that's true?"

"I've got to tell you about this dream. I send Jenny a refrigerator in the mail, begging her forgiveness."

"What do you want to be forgiven for?"

"Booking the wrong hotel. I've stocked this fridge, this fridge of forgiveness, as my dream-namer is calling it, with readymade meals, probiotic beverages. I've stuffed the condiment shelves with relishes, marmalades. I see them all, you know. Like all those varieties of Heinz you wonder about, the other fifty-two or so, they're all in my fridge. And the front of the fridge displays these magnets, of all the places Jenny and I ever went. Although Jenny and I never went anywhere. We were born in Queens and we moved to Manhattan. The end. But somewhere in those years, we went to Yankee Stadium, Brooklyn, the Jersey Shore, rode the Staten Island ferry, and this hotel outside of Albany with a ginormous coffee maker."

"Was that the wrong hotel?"

"No. The wrong hotel was Trump International."

"Tell me more about the refrigerator."

"There's this to-do pad with a smiling pickle on it. You know like the pickle is in a lounge chair, wearing sunglasses, the pickle knows something you don't. And I write on this pad. I can see the words, in the dream, so clearly: *please forgive me for browning my toes with Natasha in the moonlight.* Natasha was either this nurse, or a buyer for J. Crew. She had a room at the Marriott in Times Square."

"A lot of hotels."

"'Every man has a hotel beating in his heart.' Don DeLillo said that."

"Is Don DeLillo a friend?"

"'Hotels hold me. So many hearts beating in one place.' Jeff Tweedy said that."

"Is Jeff Tweedy a friend?"

"Moses Murray is my only friend, and I never see him. He kidnapped my wife. But I miss him. I love him. He presented another way."

"Maybe we should talk about Moses."

"I can't," I say, eyeing the box of tissues on Orlando's table.

"That's fine. Is it the hotel you want Jenny's forgiveness for? Or is it something else?"

"In real life. Do you want to hear about real life? In real life, Jenny's moved on. Just like me. She's a famous

285

person, though, in a sense. She suffers from that mental illness, I'm not sure if you've come across with your patients, of having too many social media followers. So *we*, quote unquote, know more about Jenny's 'moving on' than anyone knows about yours or mine. She moved downtown. She got married. To a non-artist. An investment banker, of course. He got her pregnant. She wrote essays about this. I've read them. I'm not going to lie. They've inspired me in my own parenthood. Jenny and I were on the same fertility journey, we just transitioned to other carriers."

"So you still," Orlando says, "have a kind of relationship with her."

"A parasocial one, you mean. Sometimes I think that's the only relationship we ever had, even though we dated for twenty years. Is that bad?"

Orlando shakes his head.

"I still think we're standing there. On the bridge beneath the Trump International. I'm asking the busker to play Ornette Coleman's 'Lonely Woman,' and Jenny is walking toward me, holding the flowers from her reading. It makes me think of this Charles Ives song— also not a friend, by the way—called 'Two Little Flowers.' In the garden are the marigolds and violets, the orchids, the roses. But the two little girls in the garden, Edith and Susanna, are the rarest, fairest, flowers of them all. Very sentimental song. The loveliest one I've ever heard.

I keep thinking, there are only two flowers in this world, and one of them is always on the verge of disappearing. And that my life has failed that flower. That my life has only been a dream."

"Zhuangzi," Orlando says.

"A friend of yours?"

"The philosopher. He dreamed he was a cheerful butterfly. After he awoke, he pondered how he could be sure he was a philosopher who had just finished dreaming he was a butterfly or a butterfly who had just started dreaming he was a philosopher."

"Exactly. For me, his butterfly is the tender house on the northside of the Wabash Avenue bridge."

"You can go back."

"You can't go back."

"You can return to the Wabash Avenue bridge. Walk over there."

"It's about a ten-minute walk."

"And show yourself, things *have* changed."

"So the refrigerator. It suddenly turns into a set of martini stems. The martini stems of forgiveness. I'm trying to hold them up but they're heavier than the refrigerator. You know this weightless observation of Gogol's: 'On Nevsky Prospect, it is as easy to lift a woman in the air as it is to lift a glass of champagne to the lips.' Because I need Jenny to know I'm sorry."

"For booking the wrong hotel."

"For everything. But I'm trying to think of a more complicated word than "sorry" and that fills me with fear. *I finally get it now*, I write on the pickle pad. Again, in the dream I saw these sentences so clear: *I think we were doubly blessed to lose Aurora and to lose each other and to lose anything else we couldn't carry. I read in* Elle *that you stopped drinking. So use these stems to hold your pencils. Or use them for a relapse drink that will make you forget me slowly. You and I will be redeemed, my love, in the days of olives.* And it hurts, it really hurts my warming hand, to write all of those *eeeee*s in redeemed. My hands are hot, my toes crackling. I raise the box of martini stems over my head, but then they crash to the floor, shattering like flowers.

"Who is Aurora?" Orlando asks.

It takes me a long moment to get to a place where I can explain it to him, and then that moment passes without me saying anything. I say to myself, Little Flower, who walked unannounced into my life, and almost blossomed there. But to Dr. Orlando Kordana I say, "Aurora is such a porn star name, right. Every baby is just some porn star waiting to grow up. I hate myself for saying that. I'm so corrupted."

"Everyone," Orlando says, "gets corrupted."

"You're not supposed to," I laugh-cry, "say that anymore."

"I'm interested," Orlando resumes, "in something

you said. About being filled with fear, trying to think of a more complicated word than 'sorry.'"

"I think maybe I misspoke."

"I don't think you did. I have some homework for you."

"I'll do it," I say, and I mean it. I would've done anything for Orlando at that moment. He is my best friend.

"I want you to write down what you fear. It doesn't have to be perfect, it's just for you. Jot down for me, those first few fears that come to mind. And I'm going to write you something."

"Like a prescription."

"Yes. For your sadness. And congratulations on becoming a father!"

***

We always say, raising children isn't easy. We make this joke about how we're doing child labor. Tonight, we say it will get better. We say, Let's do that tomorrow. We say, we got through today and it could've been much worse. We say, God willing, and from your mouth to God's ears. We say, the days are long and the years are short. We are older, and look older, but feel younger. Life is one long process of feeling young again: when you graduate, fall in love, marry, have children, when the decades turn over and 71 feels younger than 68, at the beginning of your disease, right before the last moment, and once again, at death, when we are born again.

"That being said," I often now say. "I don't mean that in a bad way," is another thing that enters my voice, and I don't mean that in a bad way.

One weekday afternoon our family of three spends three hours in an Old Navy. We never thought we would find ourselves in such a cheap store, but it's a good destination to pick up American flag t-shirts made in China.

"My God, the paradoxes of the supply chain are so obvious," Ellory says, "but they can't be said enough."

"You're not allowed to say that," I say, "no matter how many times it gets said. And yet, coming to an Old Navy really opens your eyes."

We see more adults in this big box retailer on the other side of the highway than we've seen in a month of sitting at home and keeping Hope alive. A female shopper notes our son's cuteness. A mother herself, she calls Hope one of the cutest little ones, and tells me the baby looks just like me.

"You both look so tired," the woman says.

"We're trying to sleep," I say, "when the baby sleeps."

"You," she says, pointing to Ellory with a knowing grin, "look more tired than him. Don't worry. These are the ninety-nine days of hell. It gets better."

"God willing," I say, "because right now parenthood feels like robbing Peter to pay Paul."

"You said the ninety-nine days of hell," Ellory says. "That's so beautiful."

In the late hours, now the only hours, I sit at the dining room table and push my laptop away. The world inside my computer leaves me with few feelings, since my feelings, indeed my entire being, are now contained in Hope, and now exist outside of my body, exist even outside the failing body of my laptop.

I take my pen to an elegant four-quadrant notebook. This notebook, which Moses bought me in Japan, will serve as my diary for the remaining ninety-nine days of hell. In each quadrant, I'll record what the son did that day, what the father did that day, what the mother did that day, what the world did that day.

Hope doesn't do much. Not anything I can engineer into a description. The world also does very little. In the quadrant 'what the world did that day,' I write: *The world outside our home is not our world. The world did nothing today. Tomorrow, there may be a different world.*

Ellory does even less. She sits with one eye on laptop content, her under eye on the next episode, her longer eye rereading her favorite rote epic of India, and her nipple's eye on the special bond she has with Hope, an uncircumcised insect for whom she pumps milk like a

Smithfield pig.

She tells me she doesn't want to breastfeed anymore. It's so boring. She wants her old life back of having all the time in the world to be disappointed by it. And she wants to start drinking again for good this time, and for real, not just wine and beer, and, after pumping and dumping, has already started in on it. Motherhood feels like the beginning of a never-ending hangover. My wife misses the real ones.

In 'what the mother did that day,' I write: *This is our 31st day of hell. We're switching to formula. Breastfeeding is matriarchal bullshit. The busy work women create for other women. Neoliberal, I fear, because the privately-owned son grows, and the publicly-owned wife decays.*

We research hundreds of options, even consider the flyers from American formula companies which have suddenly appeared in our postal mail. Maybe the world outside our home *does* exist. But American formula is engineered from a feed denied the grass-fed cows. German-made formula sounds best. The Germans have a stricter definition of 'organic' than the U.S., like their stricter definition of 'luxury' as it relates to automobiles. The German powder arrives in tightly wrapped boxes, like kilos of movie cocaine. It isn't cheap, and we need more. Shipping never becomes free. There is no rewards program. We wonder, when considered from a certain point of view, if Germany's cows are fed on soil enriched

by slaughtered Jews. In a way, that could be beautiful—
to nourish Hope from the soil of the hopeless.

***

We sleep when Hope sleeps or we don't sleep when
Hope sleeps, which means we don't sleep at all. We laze
on our sectional, watching the next episode of *Jewish
Drama*, a prestige television show that elevates American
Jewish voices. It's our favorite show. It's so good. We
resisted it for a long time but now we're so hooked.
There are so many interesting stories, and you really
feel like you know the characters. We love shows like
that. Shows where you care more what happens to the
characters than you care what happens to yourself, or
other people in real life. *Jewish Drama* is totally like that,
and that's no small accomplishment. It was first a book. It
went into treatment. It survived, and was reborn as this
TV show. We love shows. We love shows so much. We
love those shows where the people remind us of us, only
they're slightly funnier, and much better looking. With
nicer furniture. Especially the lamps. We love shows
and *Jewish Drama* is like that for us and everyone we
know or think we could know if we knew them. *Jewish
Drama* is just one of those shows you need a second to
get into and then you're hooked. The first ten seasons
are not that good, but then, you know? Then it gets so,

so good. We rewatch our favorite installments. Shows are so, so good. We don't sleep when the baby sleeps, we rewatch every season of *Jewish Drama*, forgetting major subplots, even though those subplots are good stuff, expertly constructed, not forgettable at all. *Jewish Drama* is so well written. It's not for everybody, but it's for us and everybody we might know. What a wild ride.

America's favorite assimilated Jews have driven in separate Audis to those near-city recreational areas that are such a draw for Americans who can afford a West Coast lifestyle. And now they stand atop a stunning Sierra peak, applying SPF50 to their olive-skinned faces.

"I bet you Nate uses under eye serum," I say to my wife. "For that tender part of his gaze."

"Quiet," Ellory says. "We've been waiting for this."

"I know. It's so good. Can you finish me off while we watch it?"

"No."

"These really are the ninety-nine days of hell."

"There are a million teens in your phone. Ask three of them to finish you off."

"Remind me what happened last episode."

"Nate explained to Josh M. how his numbers were directionally correct. Later that night, Josh C. and Nate had dinner at a WeHo bistro that Josh C. got to pick."

"Oh yeah. Yeah. And they wrestled over whether Nate should reimburse Josh B. via Cash App or with cash. 'I think that's right,' Josh M. had said. 'Nobody uses cash anymore.' And Nate wondered if that was true. He was going to put a poll in the field. Now I remember."

The American Jews climb the Indian mountain. Our Ashkenazi recreators, except for Josh E., who looks kind of Sephardic, wear base layers designed in California, sewn in Vietnam, they wear Italian-made polarized sunglasses framed in China. Just a few minutes before the ascent, they'd gotten stoned on legal Gorilla Glue, purchased from a lean-to dope pharmacy in the foothills named after Joan Didion's dead daughter.

Gabi tells everyone to hush and take in the no-filter scenery.

Jess, who has just gone through her fourth round of IVF, asks a rando white Christian man to take a leaping photo of the whole gang.

The Christian man says, "I'd love to. But when I take photos for Jews, I charge by the person."

Isaac M. says, "What is your per-Jew fee? Maybe we can work out something that benefits all parties."

The white Christian says, "I'm only kidding, dude, I'm not going to charge you to take a photograph with your camera. I'll snap a few, and then you guys let me know how they came out, okay? And if you need me to, I can always take a few more."

Rebecca, who is waiting to hear back if she got the Chief Giving Officer position at Amazon, says, "Great, that sounds good, but we would've been happy to negotiate with you if you did, indeed, charge a fee."

Bashful Aaron gave the white Christian his camera.

America's favorite Jews leap for the photo. And while in mid-air, the finale happens: the white Christian man with Aaron's camera is actually the white Christian Terrorist with Emotional Problems who has been following the gang since season four.

Instead of taking the picture—BOOM!

"This is what I'm always waiting for," Ellory shudders. "We'll be strolling by the river, our beautiful river, and we'll get shot."

The credits roll up the mountain, with a familiar enough sounding indie rock tune that we can't place.

"That was so good," Ellory says. "I can't believe Josh C., Josh M., and Josh B. are gone."

"They can't be gone," I say, looking at porn on my phone because my wife told me I could. "Josh C. and Josh M. and Josh B. are the whole show. Nate can die, but not the Joshes. The writers have their work cut out for them, but the writers will figure it out because the writers have nothing better to do than make up bullshit like this."

"Refill, please," Ellory says, swinging her glass.

"But ultimately," I say, looking at a CD like it once did something useful, or unwrapping the 30th anniversary edition DVD and thinking, *this is going to be so great*, or slathering a pita with hummus, or Earth Balancing my toast, or undertipping my pedicurist, or telling Ellory at Home Depot I'm uncomfortable buying automatic rifles, or toasting an Up & Up waffle, "the cause of living in the Jewish past is dying right in front of us. Who cares if Rebecca and Aaron can have a baby? I want to puke spending just five minutes with Becca and Aaron. Try as they might to stay hip, the contemporary references flowing out of their mouths already sound like ancient history. Do they think our mud-eating descendants are going to understand what Rebecca P. meant when she said, Christians who did the ice bucket challenge are going to hell? And that's not even because of the mighty collective text being written on the Internet, the capital-I Internet, I mean, even without the contenterati these people would still blow."

"Don't say 'contenterati' ever again."

"Who cares if they find American history inconceivable. The inconceivability of American history is its leading feature. Maybe they'll have their baby, maybe they won't. We'll still root for their divorce. Can you imagine how nauseating it will be in season fourteen to see them petting little Ben? We'll have to suffer the episode where they agree circumcision is cruel. And then we'll have to suffer the episode where they join the insanely liberal temple so they can perform a metaphorical bris before having an afterparty at an average Italian-Chinese fusion restaurant. And Samuel will be back from Brown University. Where he took an entire 300-level course about how American Chinese food is racist. And he'll tell everybody about it. And Nana will say, Oh quiet Samuel eat your snow peas. Remember? Remember when you were a nice little boy with no opinions? You didn't used to like snow peas, our tastes can change. I have only one question for Caitlyn, Nate, Andrea, Becca, Gabi, and Jess…"

"…Gabi and Jess will surely adopt now…"

"…Aaron and little Ben. What does it feel like to be yet another impairment upon the timeline of supremacy and oppression?"

"Would it bother you," Ellory responds, "if I answered your question with a question?"

"No, of course not," I say. "Our people expect nothing less."

"Is season fourteen out yet?"

***

We fall asleep in front of the TV. We wake up. We bring Hope to the synagogue. It's a beautiful morning. It's always lovely on a Jewish holiday. We will leave Hope's penis intact but still want to throw a small party. We invite Moses Murray in separate messages, but the prophet responds with apologies only to me. I text back,

Want to get a drink sometime? He doesn't answer.

It's official. We have given our boy the name Hope. A boy, like a book, must give hope. A boy must embody hope. A boy must have a bright spirit. Without hope, a boy is not a boy, a book not a book. The work of hope is giving hope to other men. Hope, the unraveling of form; form, the acknowledgment of hope's delay. Hope, the leaping feat, spring.

Randall Bowers, the father of Robert Bowers, whose son killed 11 and wounded six at a Pittsburgh synagogue, who killed himself years before when faced with a rape allegation. Our synagogue keeps a retired African American police sergeant posted up at the entrance. He is here to fend off white men bored enough with their home-grown video games that they will bring automatic weapons to this house of worship and kill Jews.

"Where's your gun?" the temple coordinator asks the sergeant. "Keep it where we can see it."

The cop has to go back to the South Side to get his gun.

While he's gone, we're scared for our lives.

When the retired cop returns, armed, we feel safe again.

After the ceremony, we celebrate alone, as a family of three, at an average Italian-Chinese fusion restaurant. We have little to talk about, so we talk about *Jewish*

Drama.

That night at home, Ellory asks, "Do you feel differently about Israel now? It doesn't seem as exotic to me as it used to. We should go."

"I get scared thinking about that part of the world," I say.

"Free Palestine is its own brand of nationalism. Politics is the denial that history has losers."

"I think that's right. Or, wait, isn't politics is the struggle for existence? Of course, I believe in freedom for everyone."

"Of course you do, honey."

"Do you hear something?"

"Yes, I do. The baby's crying."

"He wants his mother."

"No, I think that's the dada cry."

"And non-Jews don't understand what the word *Jew* means. Although they should. What's the line from that movie? *Jew Jew Jew. Jew Jew Jew.* It's one of two words in the language that means exactly the same thing any time you say it."

"What's the other one?"

American riots flood our phones, and we even sometimes hear the rioting on our own streets, just steps beyond our golden mezuzah. The mayor, a black woman, takes good care to protect the borderless international property of Trump International from U.S. rioters.

In a panic, Ellory calls her father. Abe Allen settles her down by explaining that the black yokels have bussed themselves up from the South Side to steal our luxury goods, egged on by their white abolitionist teachers, readers of the Berkeley poet-professors who can't reheat their own burritos. In the afternoons, these teachers are out with the oppressed marching in the streets. But at night, the white professors go home to their John Coltrane and their *Jewish Drama*, and the true blacks, the real animals, the marauding crews, drive up to our beautiful downtown and strip our gridded streets.

That was a mistake. Ellory hates her father. She has no desire to forgive Hope's grandfather, he is the devil, just look at what he told her just now, and she doesn't want him anywhere near her son. She is a little bit like him, she fears, but she is trying to get better. She wakes up and thinks, I hate Bill Clinton. And I hated Bill Clinton before everyone else. She quotes Prince Myshkin in the comments section of Chelsea Clinton's Instagram. Like Jonathan Franzen, Abe Allen is the kind of right-wing maniac who saw Timothy McVeigh's actions as a 'news story' that was messing up the press cycle for one of his celebrated social novels.

In the quadrant, 'what the father did that day,' I write: *conferred with Marcus on the Oakland property. He transferred me to Abe. Told Abe there would be no* bris. I used empathetic, or is it emphatic, reasoning, and acknowledged Abe's position that his beautiful daughter is being unreasonable. I agreed with his position, even though it made me uncomfortable, that I didn't know why my wife had so much on her mind, why a woman as beautiful as her couldn't just 'cheer up.' Told Abe he could still send gifts. Set up a trust, etc., or cash right now is likely best. Children are expensive, we destroyed two 'priceless' works of artworks to produce his grandson, German formula is meeting with supply chain issues, and I spent a million dollars on a prostitute who failed to become a retailer of Men's Essentials and is now in Bali, on a yoga retreat, considering a career in psychotherapy, etc., etc., etc. By setting up a trust, Abe could ensure Hope would never have to spring for anything.

***

I fear hope. I fear for Hope. I fear the marketplace, misdirected anger, I fear bowers balustrades porches decks and lanais. I fear the internet, people who don't fear the internet, people who text 'kk!' as a response to anything and everything, meditating because it is neoliberal praxis, I fear forgetting what praxis means and drills that would improve my memory. I fear cocks in my ass, tongues in my cunts, illegals in my breakfast cereal, trans persons in my Old Navy, and not knowing if Louis C.K. is a woman or a man. I fear being faithful, cheating, being ignored, recognized, rejection and acceptance, nice dreams, and snakes living in cake boxes inside refrigerators under floorboards in unfinished basements. I fear a scrambling free safety and a percussive tight end, b-sides and fire drills, yeoman's work and snooty cicerones. I fear lightning in the prairie distance, inhaling deleterious vapors, baking cakes for fags, how date pits resemble roaches. I fear choking on a chicken bone, reusing a Ziploc that fell to the floor, and children sucking on chairbacks in an airport food court. I fear guidelines and useful tips, balls smell, balls too small, scrubbing the clitoris too hard, trusting my process, generous portions, magnificent obsessions, blurry male face rotisserie porn thigh, and one day launching a podcast where I gather my thoughts. I fear thinking that's right. I fear tonight's special guest. I fear an 18-wheeler driving 100 MPH into the H&M in the lobby of One World Trade, Bob Dylan wearing a non-iron button down, asserting one's individuality through an unbelief in the individual, and killing myself with a frying pan in our post-Bourdain climate of eternal suicide. I fear losing my wallet, my passport, my keys, my noise-cancelling earbuds. I fear the farts of another. I fear a pussy that expands like taking all the drugs at once. I fear my uncle the night he pretended to fit in the children's bathtub, going through the car wash with my grandfather, learning from my father how to jump the waves, learning from my mother how to use the protractor. I fear forgetting my mommy's loops. At the base of her cursive Q. How she could close her Q and write capital Q and even capital Z and E in cursive. Her B in Brooklyn, her S in Staten Island, her T in Tyrone, her X in Xylophone. Who else could do that, but my mother? Someone I fear.

***

In the early hours, and they are all early hours now, we dance with Hope. These are moments of indescribable happiness. Every morning when you see your child's face is like starting out on a hike. We never realized we could smile this wide. We hold each other, hold our son, we dance as three to 'Build Me Up Buttercup' by The Foundations.

Late at night, a time now hourly, I read Hope important works of economic literature, chanting into my son's ears the overwrought underwritten never-read language of businesspersons.

Language should be dry, like wine, flattening the tongue.

It's a college mistake to introduce an infant to lyricism.

Myriad stakeholders, he's hungry for German powder.

Based on our experiences, he's feverish.

Off-balance sheet commitments, he's teething.

Knowing how much she adores books, distant family send Ellory mass market poetry, the kind of book her undergraduate self would've cruelly mocked after raising her nose from a line of cocaine before being told by an art school prick who wanted to get into her pants that her observation about mass market poetry was quite the devastating *précis*. But now she relates to the mass-market's graceful, everyday profundity. She reads the successful poet's words with one hand over her open mouth to muffle her own.

Ellory knows she is changing. She would often hear children cry and think, That's how I feel on the inside. Now, when her son cries, she knows Hope isn't the only child in the world. She realizes, as the mass market poets know, that she is just one of these women who had to wait to be a mother to understand this. And she will not apologize for this joining.

Hope cries himself to sleep, wakes with tears, he can't self-soothe, Ellory reads, but I can soothe him. With her breasts returning in homage to their original shape, and me making sure her elbow never sees the inside of a saucepan, all of my wife's love pours easily into our little boy. She puts down her phone, her laptop, her rote epic of India, she turns off her *Jewish Drama*. Her entire soul, her blood, her energy, pour easily into Hope without wanting anything in return, without knowing what that would even be. She will be his first kiss but not his last, his first love but not his last, she is the body of his beginning, and she prays she will be there only in spirit at his end. The knife lodged in her must never be the knife lodged in him.

This successful millionaire poet inspires Ellory to write poetry of her own. In the depths of the afternoon, and it is always the depths of the afternoon now, she puts pen to paper and her thin Japanese paper rips! Ellory Allen is no writer. She's too literal to be literary. She's too smart to be just dumb enough. She doesn't have a mechanistic process for the distribution of her metered feelings. But then one morning, she awakes to something other than her son crying. The ninety-nine days of hell are ending. She hears birds singing. She is so happy. She will call her father today. She will even take a shower. Remaindered winter words echo out of her dreams, bare ruined choirs where late the sweet birds sang. Look at her. Sweet poet of the baby. She writes those words down, feeling at first they are her own, but then she knows they are mere scraps of Shakespeare, permanent sticks and stones in the alleys in her mind. She presses the words down anyway. For once, feeling has preceded them.

***

"My mother died when I was 12. Breast cancer, cardiac arrest on the dotted line, at a rundown hospital in Queens. If she'd had better care, she'd still be alive. Like I wrote down, I remember her cursive loops. And I fear that one day I won't. On my first day of kindergarten, she packed me a protractor. Even on my first day of kindergarten, I was thinking, How can I work my protractor into this? That's what I remember about my mother, and the day my pastina had a worm in it. As for my father, he died only a few years ago, right when everything started to go wrong with Jenny. He died typing an internet comment, *and what did Barack Hussein Obama do for this country? Nothing!* It wasn't healthcare that killed my dad, it was politics. This was around the time *Twice Shy* was coming out with all its glossy reviews, and I couldn't believe some of the things Jenny was saying about us. I should've just married Meg. I met Meg right around that time. Meg seemed so good for me..."

"...before we get to Meg, Ty, or anyone else, I don't think you're being entirely honest about what you fear."

"You don't think I fear inhaling deleterious vapors?"

"I'd like you to be serious right now," Orlando says.

"You want a cure for humor. Put my subtitles on. You'll see the jokes coming."

"I want you to understand humor is only a part of you, interacting with your other parts."

"Which part of me went to sleep at Trump International and woke up a zillionaire?"

"You should tape yourself listening to yourself talk."

"I can't do that. My biggest fear is taping myself. What I need, what I want, is a fuller relationship with Moses. Or any relationship with him. He's my only friend."

"We haven't talked about Moses that much."

"We text a lot. But I never see him."

"Texting is friendship."

"We text constantly."

"So, you're friends."

"In a sense. But we never text about the thing that matters. We keep meaning to have him over for dinner."

"Why do you want to have him over for dinner?"

"He's possibly the father of my son."

"Tell me more about this dinner."

"He'd be like, You think this is the first time some chick has flown me across the country and paid my relocation expenses, just to have me close to her, just to have me there to say things like, Let these mountains mar the limit of my desire?"

"Tell me about these mountains."

"I've been thinking a lot about what you said. That it's Jenny I fear…"

"…stay with Moses…"

"…or, really, I fear I will forget her. And then what? They'll be no more desire in my life. And I'm glad. I'm glad desire's over. I want you to speak to me off the record. Can you do that? This is my question: was it all in my head?"

"I don't know," Orlando says. "I've never been in your head."

"It just doesn't seem fair. It doesn't seem fair to the imaginary people."

"The imaginary are a resilient bunch. If I could offer something, Ty, something I don't think you fear. That I might almost say, I know you don't fear. You don't fear experience. You reach beyond an arm's length into life. And there is a conceptual connection in our human condition between experience and hope. In order to have one, you must have the other. Do you fear experiences?"

"No, doc. I want more."

"Then you don't fear hope."

"I can accept that," I say.

Orlando must reserve a minute at the close for logistics. He says his office isn't renewing their lease. He's decided to work on his own. He's moving to an online-only model for seeing patients, and while I'm permitted to stay with the service, I could also come out with him.

"You can make an exception, of course, for me, right. To see me in person?"

"I'm afraid I can't, Ty, no."

"Well, I don't want to do that. You're the only man I see face to face."

Therapy is OK, just like it is in the movies, but what they don't show you in the movies is the procedure of getting to the office. The talking cure, I've learned, is really a commuting one. I look forward to seeing the buskers around Orlando's gentrifying neighborhood. How frail my body feels in the medical building elevator. When I open the door, the office smells like the bleached arcades of my childhood. I can't recreate that smell at home. The single servings of herbal tea, and next to the tea machine, the cork board, the laminated labor laws. The Starlight peppermints in the dish shaped like an autumn leaf. I help myself to a mint because I'm always five-to-seven minutes early to my appointment. I hear the white noise machine, the plastic unwrapping. These are the sensations of therapy that guide me the most, not the work itself but the expectation of work, the needle puncturing the tea pod, the pocketing, upon my exit from Orlando's room, of a Starlight mint for the road. Seeing Orlando in person is like being at Disneyworld. Seeing Orlando on a computer would be like going to Florida.

"I want you to continue the great work we've begun."

"But the mints."

"What about you buy yourself a bag of mints and put them in a bowl at home?"

With Orlando's help, I've learned the same things I'd learned from my New York therapist, Scarlett. My father forgives me. My mother's guilt is not my own. In order to change my life, well, I must simply change my life. It isn't going to be easy. And I've learned, once again, that I am made up of *parts*. I have the *hippie* part, and the *husband* part. And these parts shatter, play dress up, wink in and out, recombine. I now have the *father* part, too, and my *father* part introduces what I fear the most, that main product of experience and hope: acceptance.

"We should continue. You're making progress."

"Thanks. But I should free up one of your spots. So you can concentrate on the people who really need help."

"You," Orlando says, "are one of the people who really need help."

10.

Imeet Moses Murray at the Bank Café. The bilevel business sits on a slim corner in a yoga corridor downtown. It is bright, the music droningly unremarkable and pretty chill. Knowledge workers visit this bank to engage in deep work. There are picnic tables, standing desks with and without treadmills, library cubbies, and sanitizing wipes. Toward the back, near the gendered restrooms, early arriving workers scoop up the two life-sized meeting rooms and spend their entire day soundproof, operating conference call empires from stained ottomans. Phones ring. Nobody steps away. Nobody lowers their voice. Everything is public for those who can afford to go home at night. Freelancing oncologists field telemedicine calls, viewing x-rays on wide open laptops and explaining to their weeping patients the tumors were more serious than they'd hoped. One underemployed resource, his laptop almost closed, yawns while turning the pages of the bestselling book, *Bullshitting About the End of Work is My Job*. The book is from the library. It will be due in five days because thirty-five patrons are waiting for it. *Bullshitting About the End of Work is My Job* can't be renewed.

The Bank Café is the most bustling environment I've been in since the excursion to Old Navy. The air smells of roasted beans, liquidity events, and burnt veggie sausage. My eyes flash across prism boards, which offer proven tips on achieving financial wellness and a recap of the season's Oscar winners. I have never heard of the winners or the losers—it's an honor just to be ignorant.

iPad in hand, Moses Murray greets me. The prophet wears a faded suit, dark brown, his wide tie crooked. His shoes are comfort-forward, round-toed, in need of a shine. His beard needs a trim and oiling, his hairless head a gentle shampoo. It is odd for me to see my mountain prophet in the journeyman polo of the coffee shop manager who has passed a bank teller test. The day we met, Moses was somehow starving and filled with energy, lost in the forest and bursting with unclean ideas. Now, he's just another bum on the clock.

I'm nervous. We've developed this epic texting relationship. In text, we can be our perfected selves. In text, we cycle through Don Quixote, Hendrix, Euripides, Vedder, Mozart, Thomas Pynchon via Paul Thomas Anderson via Fiona Apple, the impertinence of the suffering Christ, how social media is the true 'body without organs,' and back round again to *Don Quixote*. Ours is not a friendship that makes life easy for autocorrect.

In text, we discuss how to sequence our self-immolations.

You self-immolate first, I write him, punctuated with

flame emojis, and I promise to light up right behind you.

"Are there any banking questions I can help you answer today?" Moses asks.

"If you have any time to chat, I'd like to sit in a booth."

"I'd love to buy you a coffee and talk, Ty, but I've got a situation here."

"Why are you suddenly dressed like an Indian from a Western?"

"It came down from corporate. Today is Indigenous People's Day."

"No, today is the Fourth of July."

"I don't think they're grasping that this is not Halloween. What I don't get is, well, I don't get a lot of things. But what I don't get is how many well-educated external communications people we employ at corporate. Didn't any of the multilayers of generational review catch this gaffe? Did they let it go for the laughs at our expense? Are they all on a companywide paid family medical leave that is not available to permanent contractors like me? We all took the required sensitivity training. I just don't understand."

"Where is Bank Café corporate?"

"We're headquartered in South Brooklyn."

"DC suburbs, you mean."

"I think that's right. Just outside of downtown Alexandria. You'd think one of them would read the news and realize Indigenous People's Day is not a day we're handing out M&Ms."

"One thing I don't get, my friend, is why it can't be *both* days. Aren't 24 hours enough hours for two holidays? Twelve hours for Columbus, twelve hours for Indigenous?"

"That's a very colonial conception of time. All morning I had to tell my people that the wilderness masters the colonist. It finds him a European in dress, industries, tools, modes of travel, banking preferences, and thought. It takes him from the railroad car and puts him in a pre-paid birch canoe. It strips off the garments of civilization and arrays him in introductory interest rates, hunting shirts, and moccasins. Before long, he has gone to planting Indian corn and plowing with a sharp stick; he shouts the war cry, gives up calling-us-anytime and switches to chat only, taking the scalp in orthodox Indian fashion. Little by little, he transforms the bank, but the outcome is not like the Parthenon. At first, the frontier was the Atlantic coast. It was the frontier of Europe in a very real sense. Moving westward, the ATM vestibule became more and more American..."

"...no, I totally understand," I say. "And I can see you're in a rush. Ellory and I have really been meaning to have you over for dinner. Conversation with us should always be elevated, as we say, because we met at a high elevation. Never again in the history of America will there be a prophet like you."

"Something horrible happened. A customer found a hair on their hash brown. I can tell from the look on your face, Ignatius J. Reilly, that you're picturing more diced potatoes, a hair in a haystack situation, but not at all, quite the opposite. More like the McDonald's patty. As the customer was squeezing the ketchup into the center of the hash brown, the user saw they were reddening someone's hair. A single, long, curly hair."

"That's disgusting. That small man by the register, wearing the kippah and screaming?"

"Yes, that's the individual. He comes in here all the time and there's always some kind of dubious emergency. But this time I can understand where he's coming from. A hair on a hash brown is no laughing matter. He's accusing one of my African American employees, whom he believes out to get him, because she wears a Free Palestine pin on her shirt."

"You allow her to rep Palestine while she's on the colonial clock?"

"It's unsettling. But I've conferred with my supervisors, and they've pushed it up the chain. We aren't really a bank that serves coffee, we're more of a tech company. Right now, given Indigenous, we're content to leave well enough as it is. Our employees are encouraged to express whatever will energize the American People to avoid the polls on Election Day."

"My god. It's like she's radioactive. I thought the

whole point of honest work was political suppression."

"We don't need NBC in here, we don't need Fox. If Dan Rather tweets anything autumnally eloquent about this, it'll show up in my performance review."

"What about that woman wearing the hijab, filming the man wearing the kippah?"

"I know," Moses says. "I'm so stressed. Honestly, man, I don't even know what I'm doing here. I'm going to grab my kayak and paddle home."

"Do you think it's possible to travel by water from Chicago to Seattle?"

"I can't stop her from filming it, can I?"

"I love how she can hold the phone like that. Gen-Xers like you and me, we can't hold the phone like that. You know like the prostitutes on Instagram..."

"...the sex workers..."

"...holding it in front of their face, looking in a mirror, showing us their hulking glutes. I love that. Selfie art. So modern. So good! Well, aren't you the manager?"

"Yes, but what does that really mean? We want this bank to be an inviting café. Since the emergence of Starbucks, the banking community has felt that coffee is stealing our sugar. This environment is a step in the right direction to spark a constructive discussion that will repair that. We've got no checking minimums, higher saving rates than the boomer branch across the street, we've got FDIC flavored creamers. I understand why the customer's upset. But this could've been worse. If the ketchup didn't come out watery bright after that first squeeze, I don't think the gentleman wearing the kippah would've realized there was a hair beneath it, and then the hair might've gotten stuck between his teeth."

"That sounds worse. You shouldn't have to remind people they have to tap the bottom of the ketchup away from the food item so that it doesn't come out watery and cause a viral sensation. Speaking of, did you hear how Ellory gave birth?"

"How's fatherhood treating you? I'm sorry I couldn't make the Christening."

"It wasn't a Christening. We're Jews."

"Oh, I didn't know that."

"Is that a joke? No worries either way, bud. It's been somewhat of a letdown since the actual birth. You saw the vid, right? My wife sunk *Woman in Tub.*"

"One of her favorites."

"God it was crazy. A nearby tourist happened to be an OB. She broke open this glass case of medical supplies by Damien Hirst and brought forth my son. It was even on Letterman or whatever those dipshits are called now. You know how much money we made from it? The *special delivery* as the news punned it? Zero dollars."

"You should've hired a publicist."

"We had no time. We had to keep Hope alive. That's our kid's name. Hope."

"Cute."

"We thought so."

"Hirst giving life," Moses says contemplatively.

"Although there are all these great conspiracy theories on the internet that *Woman in Tub* would've been nailed down by the museum, and therefore couldn't have been knocked over. Many people are saying Hope's birth is a lie. I mean, you should see the way these guys comment about it. I can't believe how *smart* people on the internet are."

"Hirst has said, on many occasions, that death is an unacceptable idea."

"That's good."

"But there could be suicide by Hirst, too. His pharmacological series."

"Overdosing, you mean. Not death by fire, as you and I always dream about."

"That's right."

"My God, I've missed you."

"I disconnected my internet."

"That's troubling."

"Is Hope sleeping well? I feel as though I should ask about naps."

"It's a fine subject to broach with new parents, and he does nap, thank you for asking. But it seems so weird to talk about children, right? Between us, conversation is always elevated. Why do we even exchange pleasantries?

Because we feel the need to pace ourselves? Why do human beings even do that? We know why we love each other. Let's just dig in and discuss Euripides. Do you think you can tell by the shape of the hair on the hash brown if it was the African American's or the Jew's? Isn't that the question we're all trying to answer most of the time?"

"That's a road I'd prefer to leave less travelled."

"Why am I dreaming," I say, "about such stupid things? Why are there armies of silverfish massing beneath my armoire? My father died typing, *And what did Barack Hussein Obama do for this country? Nothing!*"

"Didn't you tell your therapist this?" Moses asks.

"I wanted to tell you. You are one of the people who really need help, and we failed you. I found him. My father. Slumped in his chair."

"Conceiving was difficult for you and Ellory, wasn't it."

"Oh, it was like our sexual organs were trapped in alternate 1985. *And what did Barack Hussein Obama do for this country? Nothing!* My father stopped breathing as he typed one of America's many received opinions that the far left and far right can agree on. He only got as far as *And what did Barack Husse* and in honor of my father I changed 'Barack' to 'Barry' and finished the comment and posted it to the comments section below the *Wall Street Journal* editorial. Then I erased my dad's browsing history. Why Twitter is never more a buy than it is now, four ways they will monetize their essentiality. An article about the possibility of life on Europa, found and replaced from an article about the possibility of life on Enceladus. Never again will my dad say, Space is just out of this world. And never again will he have his preferences aggregated, receive pleas from gym trials requesting he *rejoin the challenge.* All of the Facebook messages, too, his politely punctuated replies to vanished Ukrainian teens, for in death, to recharge, my father will be taking a short break from the winds of social media. Northrup Grumman has never been more of a buy than it is now, four countries we can bomb to maximize the stalwart's profits. And Dad's ultimate conformation code, renewing a subscription to my favorite magazine: GQBXGQW-GQ97FBTWTRAMZNBPGQMGHZGQMGQ. But before deleting that message, out of respect for my old man, I printed the confirmation off the laser printer. And I have it with me, Moses, this scrap of paper, GQBXGQW-GQ97FBTWTRAMZNBPGQMGHZGQMGQ. I carried it with me all the way from the desert sands of Egypt. Because, when you really think about it, the German settlers who arrived in Wisconsin after Black Hawk's defeat brought their cows with them, rebranding Wisconsin America's Dairy Land. And Wisconsin kept on innovating, embracing more and more pitiful sides of its natural wealth. For example, in this decade, the state rebranded for fracking. There's no oil in Wisconsin, not even close, but white Wisconsin sand gets freighted to Texas to be used in fracking operations in the fiercely independent Lone Star state. And that is the insanity of the American desert, carting sand for the making of oil to a place that already has its own sand, to bury your strikes over there, as you, my friend, buried the Egyptian before fleeing to Midian to find your hot wife. And I want to give you the confirmation code because I know you're the kind of guy who likes to receive the print issues in the mail."

"What do you mean?" Moses asks.

"I guess I'm trying to say, a man wants two things in life. A container that says FLOUR and a container that says SUGAR. You want to believe in those countertops. But, as life goes on, you amass rubber bands in your FLOUR, and soy sauce packets in your SUGAR. That is the cost of living a human life. But, really, the one thing I wanted to talk about with you, was, well—do you think we can be best friends? That day we met in the mountains, I didn't want our friendship to end. Ellory and I didn't want that *day* to end. When you meet someone like the way we met each other, you never want the meeting to be over."

"But the meeting did end, Ty. You drove back down Deer Creek Road with your protein bars, almost killing us all because of how jealous you were of my freedom, and I headed back to camp. With nothing in my stomach."

"That's not what happened. We drove you back to the Beaver Den and you stole my wife. By the way, we're broke."

"I see it on our 4K displays—the market's terrible right now."

"I wouldn't exactly blame my downfall on the market."

"But doesn't blaming it on 'the market' always work for your kind of people?"

"Ellory's birth had many complications. We're like one of those families in the newspaper that goes broke from medical debt. I also spent a million dollars on a hooker..."

"...a sex worker. How much do you need? 5K? 6K?"

"$85,000 should get me back on my feet."

"I wish I had eight *dollars*, amigo. But download our update."

"I'd been seeing this prostitute..."

"...this sex worker..."

"...the whole time Ellory was pregnant. To remain at my pre-baby weight. And I don't even know her real name."

"Check your account. I just opened you a checking that will deposit a taxable $75 reward after you make petroleum purchases totaling $15,000 at BP, that stands for British Petroleum, in the first month of use. That's the best I can do right now."

"Thanks for that," I whimper. "Ellory and I want you to be a part of Hope's life. He is your child, after all."

"I had a vasectomy long ago, *mijo*."

"That's no excuse. What else is there to do but raise a child?"

"I don't want to raise my children," Moses says. "I want to to die."

"If you die, we would mourn your death. I've been writing in this four-quadrant notebook. Trying to trick my pen into revealing the things I care most about. This notebook with little squares, for right-brains, for engineers. I write the most distant things."

"It's hard to judge distance in a quadrant."

"You judge us, negatively, because we had a child."

"Not at all. I think you did the right thing, for you, and it sounds like, for you, you know why you did. A man like me, who makes up his mind that he cannot afford children, financially, biologically, or spiritually, has lost some of what it means to be a good man. A public man. My politics are pessimistic. Your politics are brighter."

"That's true. I do feel brighter now. The game exists now, it is in progress, and there is only one rule: don't die before your child."

"How much oil it takes to have a child. Did you know the standard oil majors hire ex-educators to write curriculums promoting child-bearing? The thinking goes, more children, more oil. We have too much time to think about this, because we're not busy making babies. And if we're not busy making babies, we're busy telling the world why we're not making babies, instead of carrying out the courageous, honorable, productive act: setting ourselves on fire. Today there is a great literature, which barely existed before, on a question that barely existed before: should we have children? Once we thought we had to procreate to advance the species. Nutrition for the conservation of the individual, procreation for the conservation of the species. We no longer think that. We eat like shit and we don't want kids. For how obvious this is, we still feel the need to explain why we will eat well tomorrow, why we eat poorly today, why we will have children, and why we won't. Future generations will interpret our body of work as the final human bodies, asking the only human question left before our upload into the cloud."

"But what about having no children. Lots of good topics there. Without children you can still have books, sex, music, wine, dogs, coffee—restaurants. Ellory says she misses only one thing: restaurants after twilight. Of course, I can't self-immolate now. My child needs me. Someone must protect my son from his mother."

"Parents know death," Moses says. "From watching a child being born, they know what it means to watch someone die, what's at risk, what death means. For the childless, death can only be vanity."

"That would be wonderful."

"I don't want to murder you."

"You're not a burden at all. I would never think of you in that way. I am a man with nothing. You have everything. You have your life, your wife, your Hope. Life moves differently for you than life does for me."

"Tonight is the last time I will see you, and you are my only friend."

"You don't want me for a friend. I'm surrounded by sweet muffins and savory certificates of deposit, and I'm starving."

"Only prophets survive on the hunch that starving themselves means they will not die."

"We must stop telling jokes. The world isn't as funny as it used to be. Humor saved men like us all these years, but what if we aren't men worth saving?"

"For Jews, the frontier will never be the mountain. For us, the frontier is in our hearts, our ghetto, the chambered town we can't reach. The real Jew builds a wall around his heart, never lets the still, small voice in. The Jew is lonely because the Jew doesn't have Christ, and without Christ the Jew has no way to heal the suffering world. The more the Jew longs for Christ, the lonelier he becomes, the lonelier he is, the closer to Christ he gets, the less he finds humorous."

"I think that's right," Moses says like a podcaster. "The loneliest hearts of all find nothing funny."

"The loneliest people of all," I say, "are those who say, as you are killing them—wait, is this a joke?"

"I think that's right. But there's something else I really want to tell you."

We hear the door of the Bank Café open. Ellory appears. She wears a shirt with a spray of stars, a gibbous moon above them, and the words, I NEED MY SPACE.

She asks, "Do you boys know 'Something by Tolstoy'?"

"Wait, that's Jenny's story, babe, not yours."

"We know a few things by Tolstoy, sugar."

"A short story, child. By Williams."

"William Carlos?"

"No, Tennessee. The way I remember it, a lonely old man owns a bookshop. His wife left decades earlier. She has been gone for so long, he was able to forget her. Then one afternoon she returns to the shop and tells him the old story of their young love. But the old man doesn't remember it. Too much time has passed: what was real in his life and what was real in his suffering had blended. He listens to his wife's story, which is his life story, but he doesn't believe her. He says, That sounds like something by Tolstoy."

"Sounds like something by Tennessee Williams, Daisy Buchanan."

"We wanted you, Moses," Ellory says. "We wanted

you to be our other person."

"No," Moses says, "you didn't want another person. You didn't want a friend. You didn't want those 'new forms of kinship' you routinely mock, because you're scared to feel. All you wanted was a copy, who would stare up at you with scattered devotion, who would smile back at you with your own smile. You never wanted the smile of another. You never wanted my foul breath on your face. You wanted a reproduction, so you reproduced. Congratulations on your beautiful baby boy."

"Stop!" I scream. "What I really wanted to tell you. What I really wanted to tell you is this. I have to tell you this, what I really wanted to tell you."

"What is it, Ty?" Ellory and Moses say. "What do you want to tell us? Tell us!"

"I wanted to tell you something so important."

"Spit it out!"

"I wanted to tell you, GQBXGQW-GQ97FBTWTRAMZNBPGQMGHZGQMGQ."

***

In the morning, I tell Ellory about my dream. We were starving. In the desert. Moses Murray was there. He was playing 'The Bright Redness of the Bright Red Chillum,' but we couldn't hear it.

"Isn't that the right way to play it?" Ellory asks.

"He was starving, too."

"Did you give him a protein bar?"

"I'm serious, babe."

"Are you, Ty? It's all so shallow."

"You're calling *me* shallow?"

"No, baby, of course not."

"And we ended up at that café that's also a bank."

"The Bank Café?"

"Yeah. Across the street from Breathworkers. Moses worked there."

"Oh, I know why," Ellory brightens. "Remember when you told him the cool thing about capitalism is that people who can't afford to live in nice neighborhoods, at least get to work in them?"

"And they were making elbows of the hash browns. Or the hash browns were my elbows. Or the tomatoes were hash browns of yesterday's... never mind."

"When are you seeing your therapist again?"

"I'm not."

"He said you were cured?"

"He said something like that."

"Let's forget about dreams, then, baby. And, please, let's forget about Moses. You're a father now."

"I know. I just feel like I'm living in someone else's story."

"That's what I meant. You are. That's what fathers do."

"I was trying to see my good ancestors again, but all

I kept seeing was the bad."

"It was just a dream."

"I was seeing how my grandmother smacked my father for kissing the colored girl. How my mother cheered on the cops when they beat up protestors on TV. How my uncle tried to fit himself in the children's bathtub, which was a good memory, and a bad."

"Ty, I don't like it when you talk this way."

"You don't like it when I say something real. Instead of our stupid shit. He was asking me about naps. Moses. He was disgusted. Constipated. Disgustipated, like you. I told him we should crucify each other and he said crucifixion sounded expensive. I told him we could cut off our heads. If he cut off his head first, I would be right behind him. But I can't get a head of myself in that way."

"Not if you want to come out on top."

"What do you think it means, that the woman frying the hash browns looked like the woman who wouldn't give us the wi-fi password?"

"Ugh," Ellory says, "I hated that bitch."

"She called herself Marilyn. You'd be surprised," I say, mocking Marilyn's accent. "What people know and don't know around here."

"Oh, I love our private jokes. John Muir this and John Muir that. I want you to go back to therapy, baby."

"No, babe, I think that was it. Last night was the end. I think from here on out, everything will make perfect sense. Maybe we should go visit him."

"Who, babe, your therapist?"

"No, Moses. It's crazy we haven't had him over for dinner."

"We will," Ellory says.

"Let's do it. My calendar is up to date."

"Don't be a coward, Ty."

***

Ellory wears Hope on her chest. We leave our house, kiss our golden mezuzah, and decide to walk to the river instead of the lake. We stand at the center of the bascule bridge. There are more people out than usual. A time for noticing. But we aren't quite sure how to process the noticing. This is the first time, other than trips to the doctor, the synagogue, and the Old Navy, that we've been out of the house together since we brought Hope home from the hospital.

On the bridge, a busking trumpeter plays Ornette Coleman's 'Lonely Woman.' Ellory takes out a fifty-dollar-bill and places it in his hat.

"We really shouldn't," I say, squirming down to replace her fifty with a five from my pocket. "We must think about the future," I add, glancing down at the lost five.

"We never thought about the future before."

"We can't kick the future. Hardest habit to break. It didn't exist before. It does now."

I look up at the steely sky, but the skyscrapers haven't yet arrived. There are only a few settlements, the stench of garlic, the river is running in the old direction, shelter from the rushing waters of the lake. No ax throwing gluten free steakhouses, only a dense forest. I am not the first person to dream here. The continent's original peoples crossed the Bering Strait. Much later, there were the Potawatomi. And the French. The English. The Jews and Germans, the Poles, the Italians.

"Sometimes the river looks so awfully sad," Ellory says, imitating the accent of a dame from an old film. "At least that's how I sometimes think. But I don't get lines to think. Honey, get my cigarettes from the gold box on the end table."

"For the river," I say, "it's not a question of your thinking. Or my thinking. There's no doubt, for the river, that the Chicago River is one of the saddest rivers in the world. Sadder than any common Indian creek. Sadder than the Ohio and the Missouri, which goes, like, all the way to Montana. Sadder even than the Amazon, the Neva, the Nile, the dried-out Euphrates, even the Mississippi. I hope we can keep Hope ignorant about the spelling of Mississippi. That's one thing I wish I could forget. After I learned to spell Mississippi, I didn't learn much more."

Our eyes are drawn down into the water. Sunlight has won its war against the clouds, and centuries of living history have tinted the Capone blue with menthol triple action. One kayak appears, a safety orange color, a curved piece of moving ice. The boat seems to catch on the teeth of the water like the breaking zipper on an old winter coat.

"Hello!" I wave. "Hey, he's waving back. His oars are saxophones. Do we know him?"

"Of course we do," Ellory says. "It's Moses!"

The rowing figure waves up at us. He wears a fisherman green cap, an orange life vest. He paddles on, with more confidence now than when I first saw him, chording himself through the waves.

"He comes from the water," Ellory says. "Look, boo-boos, down in the little boat. Look, Hope, that's your Uncle Moses. Your other Daddy."

We wave until the figure is behind us, rowing under the steelwork of the bridge and down into the locks of Lake Michigan.

He yells the word *peace* at us.

He yells the word *peace*.

Ellory hears *fox*.

I hear *rabbit*.

Hope hears *hope*.

He yells the word *peace*.

Ellory sneezes, which pushes Hope forward, almost

over the railing.

"I'm always blown away when you sneeze."

"I fart, too, you know."

"If you sneeze that hard again, Hope might fall into the river. Or should we just throw him in the river?"

If we threw our child in the river, he would surely die. The son would fall, the wife would fall in after the husband fell in, and we would all fall toward the dying son and die ourselves. But that cute little face kept us from killing our child. Hope counted on that mystery. If only, when it went this way, it could have. Hope would come to know everything we thought before we thought it, and Hope would understand whatever his parents could never say. Hope had our time. Hope was in no hurry. Hope had the rest of our nights.

STUART MICHAEL ROSS came via caesarian April 17, 1977, 10:54 A.M at Brooklyn Hospital. *The Hotel Egypt* is his second novel.